GUTS & GLORY: HUNTER

In the Shadows Security, Book 3

JEANNE ST. JAMES

D1419958

Copyright © 2019 by Jeanne St. James, Double-J Romance, Inc.

All rights reserved.

No part of this book may be reproduced in any form or by any electronic or mechanical means, including information storage and retrieval systems, without written permission from the author, except for the use of brief quotations in a book review.

———

Acknowledgements:

Photographer: FuriousFotog

Cover Artist: Golden Czermak at FuriousFotog

Cover Model: Matt Zumwalt

Editor: Proofreading by the Page

Beta readers: Whitley Cox, Andi Babcock, Sharon Abrams & Krisztina Hollo

Warning: This book contains explicit scenes, some possible triggers and adult language which may be considered offensive to some readers. This book is for sale to adults ONLY, as defined by the laws of the country in which you made your purchase. Please store your files wisely, where they cannot be accessed by under-aged readers.

This is a work of fiction. Any similarity to actual persons, living or dead, or actual events, is purely coincidental.

———

Dirty Angels MC, Blue Avengers MC & Blood Fury MC are registered trademarks of Jeanne St James, Double-J Romance, Inc.

———

Keep an eye on her website at http://www.jeannestjames.com/or sign up for her newsletter to learn about her upcoming releases: http://www.jeannestjames.com/newslettersignup

Author Links: Instagram * Facebook * Goodreads Author Page * Newsletter * Jeanne's Review & Book Crew * BookBub * TikTok * YouTube

A Special Thanks

To Alexandra Swab for assisting me with Hunter's blurb when I was once again buried with all the author things. Your help, as always, was invaluable!

Also, thank you to ALL my readers who belong to my readers' group:
https://www.facebook.com/groups/JeannesReviewCrew/
You all encourage me to keep writing! Love to you all!

Chapter One

HUNTER STARED at the older man on the other side of the thick, shatter-proof glass.

Orange wasn't his color.

He had deep lines on his face, especially around his grayish-blue eyes, and the bottom half was covered in a long salt-and-pepper beard that matched his shaggy hair.

Rocky.

Jewel, Diamond and Jag's father. Diesel and Slade's "father-in-law."

Doing life without parole in SCI Greene for a couple counts of murder. One of those "victims" being Slade's father, Buzz.

And Buzz was the reason Hunter was here, sitting on the other side of that fucking glass. Because Slade asked Hunter's boss, Diesel, to track down a possible sibling. One no one knew about, but Rocky might have info on.

Maybe.

But maybe not.

The man giving him the eyeball might not know shit. All this could've been a play to see his grandchildren. Because that had been the "payment" to get Rocky to talk. He wanted Diamond and Slade to bring their son, Hudson, and Diesel and a currently pregnant Jewel to bring their girls, Violet and Indigo, to a max security prison to meet their granddaddy.

They all agreed to it, though reluctantly, since a state correctional institution wasn't any place young children should be.

Now, Rocky sat back in his bolted down metal chair, his heavily tattooed arms crossed over his chest, looking like the cat who ate the goddamn canary.

And still, Hunter had shit to go on.

Good thing a thick glass partition and a cinder block wall separated them. Because, at this very moment, Hunter felt like gutting Rocky from dick to throat just like the man did to Buzz.

Not that Buzz hadn't deserved it. He most certainly fucking had.

But Hunter was weary of this wild goose chase that began because of a few words Rocky had uttered to Crow many months ago. And then Crow had mentioned it to his Dirty Angels MC brother, Slade.

Who let that info fester.

Now the DAMC member wanted to see if what Buzz had uttered in his last few moments of life was true. That Slade had another brother out there somewhere, another product from Buzz's sperm.

And if he existed, Slade wanted to find him.

Why? Hunter couldn't care less. He was getting paid to find this long-lost brother, so that was what he would do.

If it didn't kill him first.

He was good at what he did, which was finding people. But this case, this job, was enough for him to throw in the towel and go get a fucking job cleaning toilets.

And he hated cleaning toilets.

That's why he hired a cleaning lady to come in twice a month to do just that.

But here he sat—*again*—in a small, enclosed room trying to get Rocky to shake some memory loose that might help him with this "case."

Because what he had to go on was basically bullshit.

No fucking name.

No fucking birthdate.

Fucking nothing.

All Rocky said to Crow was Buzz mentioned a son during his last moments of breathing and he didn't think that son was Slade. Why Rocky thought that, Hunter didn't fucking know.

But one thing Hunter wasn't, was a quitter.

He was going to do his fucking best to find this possible second offspring Buzz put on this Earth.

Unfortunately, the only thing Hunter had was Buzz's real name and the fact that Buzz knew he had a son. Buzz didn't know Slade existed. At least, Slade didn't think so.

Hunter scrubbed a hand over his hair, surprised he had any left to do so. Which really pissed him off, because he wanted to keep it. Especially since there was nothing better than a woman pulling on his hair when he was eating her pussy and making her come.

Something Rocky hadn't gotten to do in decades.

Poor bastard.

That was one good reason Hunter needed to stay on this side of the glass instead of being on Rocky's side. The other was, he hated tight spaces. And prison was full of them.

"Let me just say, I'm fucking glad I'm on this side instead of that one," Hunter muttered.

"An' lemme just say, with the shit you probably done in your life, you should be sittin' on this fuckin' side. You probably done more than I ever fuckin' did. Just got fuckin' lucky, boy."

True fucking that.

But that's where he and Rocky were different. While, yes, he would have fucking trussed Buzz up like a freshly killed deer and gutted him, Hunter would've gotten rid of all the evidence and not gotten caught.

Rocky and Doc had been out of their fucking minds when they wreaked havoc on the rival MC, the Shadow Warriors, so they weren't careful when they did it.

"You talk to Doc?" Hunter asked him.

"Yep."

Hunter sighed when Rocky didn't continue. "And?"

"Doc's got old timer's. Doesn't remember shit."

Hunter knew about the diagnosis. Diesel had visited his grandfather hoping to get some details about Buzz from him. Unfortunately, D had no luck and said Doc had no memory of even what he ate for breakfast. Even so, Hunter was hoping the old man would have an occasional sliver of clarity. Apparently not.

"Got nothing to go on," Hunter grumbled.

"An' why the fuck should I care?" Rocky asked, frowning. "Why the fuck do you want to dig up a spawn of a fuckin' animal, who not only raped Crow's momma but slit her throat an' her ol' man's, too?"

"'Cause Slade wants to find this *spawn.*"

"Bad enough that my baby's fuckin' the other one an' havin' his babies."

Hunter fought the roll of his eyes. "Your *baby* is happy."

"Yeah?"

"Yeah. And you ever think if you'd been smarter about what you did, you never would've been in here and you could've protected your *baby* from what that motherfucker Pierce did to her?"

Hunter's jaw flexed. *Fuck.* He hadn't meant for that last part to slip out. But his patience with this whole thing was down to nil. He needed to get his temper in check. And it wasn't helping that the walls were closing in within the room he was sitting.

"What the fuck you talkin' 'bout?"

Damn. Rocky didn't know. That made his mistake even worse.

Now the man was leaning forward in his chair, both palms pressed to the glass, his jaw hard, and his gray-blue eyes intense. "What'd Pierce do to Diamond?"

Hunter pressed his lips flat. It wasn't his story to tell. And, fuck him, his slip of the tongue was pulling them off track.

"You would know if your ass wasn't in the joint."

Rocky slammed his hands against the glass and growled, "So, you're gonna tell me, asshole."

"I'll think about it if you answer some of my questions you've been avoiding."

"Shit I've been avoidin' 'cause there are fuckin' ears in here." His eyes flipped to the speaker and back.

"Yeah, so? It's not like you're ever gonna see the light of fucking day again, Rocky. That ship has sailed. You won't even get that chance with good behavior because since you've been in here, you've been in the hole more often than not."

Rocky sat back and shrugged. "I can fuckin' meditate in the hole."

Hunter snorted. "Yeah, I bet."

Rocky studied him for a long moment. "You gonna tell me if I answer your fuckin' questions?"

"You were supposed to answer my questions because you got to see your fucking grandbabies."

Rocky shrugged again. "Payment terms have changed."

Fucking motherfucker.

"You don't answer my fucking questions, I will make sure you never see your fucking grandkids again. You got me? All I gotta do is tell Diesel how you're fucking over one of his club brothers by going back on your word. And don't forget, that brother you're fucking over is your *baby's* ol' man. Think Diamond's gonna be happy about that?"

Rocky scowled but Hunter could see his wheels turning. And turning.

Finally, the older man gave a single sharp nod.

Right. Time to get to business. "Where'd you kill Buzz?"

"In an abandoned building right outside of Shadow Valley."

"Where'd you find his ass?"

"Outside of Uniontown."

"That where he was living?"

"Yeah. Some dumpy trailer park."

"You know who he was living with?"

Rocky shrugged. "Nope."

"He mentioned a son, you sure he didn't say a name?"

"That shit was like thirty years ago. You expect me to remember somethin' like that?"

"Yes."

Rocky tilted his head and scratched at his beard. "Well, I fuckin' don't."

"You kill him because he butchered Coyote and his ol' lady?"

"Yeah."

"He didn't kill Bear, though, right?" Bear was one of the founders of the Dirty Angels MC, along with Doc. Bear had also been Rocky's pop.

"No. When those fuckin' Warriors killed Bear, that's when the war started."

"So, you went back and forth killing each other like the wild fucking west."

"Sounds 'bout right."

Hunter blew out a breath. "As you know, Diesel tasked me with finding this possible son. You ain't making it easy, Rocky."

Even with Rocky's thick mustache covering his upper lip, Hunter could see the fucker smirk. "Life ain't easy, boy."

"Betcha doing life ain't easy, either. Hope it was worth it."

"Would do it again."

"I'm sure your fucking wife and kids appreciate that."

"Was doin' it for them."

Sure he was.

"Tell Diesel I cooperated an' to bring his girls back for a visit. An' also Jag's little girl, too. Alexis didn't come last time."

That's because Rocky hadn't mentioned Jag or his baby girl, so Jag wasn't volunteering to bring Lexi to this hole.

"When's the last time you saw Jag?"

Something flashed across Rocky's face before he hid it. "When he was still livin' with Ruby."

So the man hadn't seen his only son since Jag was probably a teen. And once Rocky's kids got out on their own, they probably never visited. Or rarely.

But then, Hunter had never visited his father, either. And his mother never forced him to. She wanted nothing to do with Danny Delgado, Sr. once he plowed the tractor trailer he was driving full speed into a crowd of people while drunk. And in doing so, killed six children and two teachers on an elementary school field trip. Not to mention, the many others who were injured.

After a couple of years in the joint, his father fucking hung himself in his cell because he was too much of a pussy to do his time like a man.

Hunter ground his teeth.

So, yeah, he wasn't going to judge Jag, or even Diamond and Jewel, for not wanting to visit their old man in prison.

A loud buzz filled the small room Rocky was in and the metal door swung open.

"Let's go, Jamison. Time's up," a guard yelled into the room.

Rocky stood and leaned toward the speaker, saying, "You tell Diesel. Yeah?"

Hunter pushed to his feet, too, relieved at the thought of getting the hell out of there. "Yeah. I'll tell him."

"An' I wanna know the truth about Diamond."

"I'll tell him that, too."

With a last nod, Rocky turned and headed toward the door and the waiting guard. Hunter waited until the heavy door slammed shut behind them before spinning on his heels and heading toward freedom.

Today was a good reminder that he always needed to be careful and cover his tracks. He did not want to end up like Rocky or his own father.

It was time to head to Uniontown to do a little hunting.

Chapter Two

HUNTER DISCOVERED a few things when he went to Uniontown. One, he'd never want to live there and was glad Diesel's granddaddy settled in Shadow Valley instead. Two, a trailer park, when managed properly, could be nice. But the one Slade's brother had been supposedly born in was far from that. Unless it had seen its better days since Brandon Bussard emerged from his mother's baby baker over thirty years ago.

Frankly, Hunter doubted the park had ever been nice.

And three, while he now had a name for Slade's possible brother, he didn't have a body. Nor was anyone in that park very helpful. Most of the residents who lived there for any length of time slammed their trailer doors in his face. Which was quite fucking rude.

Most, except for one.

A lady who had to be a hundred years old and not a day younger. But, even though she had lost all her teeth decades ago, she was still as sharp as a tack.

Thank fuck.

Because if it wasn't for this elderly lady, who was

desperate for company and needed someone to ramble to, Hunter still would be spinning his dick in the wind.

His dick that was now tucked safely in his cargo pants and his ass back in Shadow Valley with some interesting info.

"From what Mabel told me——"

"Mabel your new bitch?" Steel interrupted with a smirk.

"Just tell us what you fucking know," Mercy growled, frowning at Steel.

They were gathered in "Badass Central," what their boss's ol' lady called the room where they kept their electronics. It even had a crude sign with that name nailed crookedly above the door.

Hunter had his ass planted in front of one computer with three oversized monitors, while Walker was tapping furiously at the keyboard of another. Steel had propped himself against a wall, working a toothpick around his yapper. Brick was leaning against another, but the former Navy SEAL sniper was busy on his smart phone. Probably on Tinder trying to get laid. Or, hell, maybe Grindr instead. Who knew with Brick.

Not that there was anything wrong with that.

Ryder was absent because he was finishing up a case he volunteered for in Chicago to get away from a certain someone who'd been fucking with his sanity. And Mercy filled up the remaining space with his bulk and grumpy expression.

"Here's what we..." Hunter lifted a hand, "*I* know. Gavin Bussard, aka Buzz, shot the load that created Slade, whose last name is Stone, which turns out to be his late mother's last name. Buzz also shot the load that pegged an egg in a woman who lived in East End Estates, two trailers down from Buzz's single-wide. While we assume Buzz didn't know anything about Slade, he did know about his son

Brandon since it's hard to ignore your offspring a couple trailer lots away."

"That what your girlfriend told you?" Steel asked.

Hunter ignored him, running a hand down his whiskers. "As we all know, Buzz was a Shadow Warrior. Little Brandon, though he had a shitty father who didn't contribute one fucking nickel to his upbringing, looked up to said sperm donor, even though Buzz constantly beat the fuck outta his mother right in front of him. Great role model, right?"

"Was Mabel's mouth as good on your cock as it was telling stories?" Steel asked.

Again, Hunter ignored him. "So what do you do when you think your pop is the shit? You follow in his fucking footsteps. Because nothing says success more than an outlaw biker who's a total fucking psychopath."

"Slade's brother was a Warrior?" Mercy asked, his brows furrowed, making the thick scar across his face wrinkle.

"That I'm not sure of yet. Mabel only knew so much. She only knew he ended up patching in with some MC, but she didn't know which one. My assumption is the Warriors, but if so—"

"If so, we would've taken the fucker out," Walker said next to him.

"Right. Does that mean I'm searching for a man we've already dispatched?" Hunter asked.

"Do we know his road name?" Mercy asked.

"Mabel couldn't remember, it could be Spaz, Kaz, Taz, or something like that. It was a name he started using when he rode his stolen Mongoose around the park at like eight years old."

"Okay, so Slade does have a brother, whose name we now know, who could be nicknamed Spaz and was raised in Uniontown. What else?" Brick asked.

"Got your Grindr date all lined up?" Hunter asked him, since the man was now paying attention.

Brick's brows knitted together. "I got my hook in a piece of pussy who would make all you fuckers haters."

"'Cept Mercy," Walker reminded him.

"Does this pussy have a dick?" Steel asked.

"If she did, you'd still be a hater 'cause I'd be getting double the action."

Steel laughed. "Anytime you want double penetration, Brick, just ask."

"For fuck's sake," Mercy barked. "I got shit to do, let's keep on track."

"You got Rissa to do," Brick murmured.

"Rissa's in Vegas," Mercy grumbled.

"No wonder why you're so fucking cranky," Walker exclaimed. "Fist ain't cutting it, huh?"

"Maybe I should use yours," Mercy responded, his eyebrow with the scar running through it raised.

"Mine's pretty tight and experienced."

"Figured that," Mercy said, shaking his head.

Hunter clapped his hands together sharply once to get everyone's undivided attention. "We need to figure out who he patched in with and what his road name was. His cut could've already been hanging on the wall in Mercy's little shop of horrors."

"He got rid of those," Steel said matter-of-factly.

"When?" Hunter asked, surprised.

"Once the Warriors were all gone," Mercy admitted. "Told Jazz I'd burn them and I did."

"But *are* they all gone?" Walker asked, typing even faster, if that was possible.

Hunter assumed he meant the Warriors and not their cuts, a biker's leather vest which displayed their club colors.

"Sure as fuck hope so. If not, we still got fucking work to do," Mercy said.

"We don't know if he patched in with the Warriors.

There are plenty of other MCs in the surrounding area, if he even stayed local. Or he could've ended up a nomad."

"If he did, it means we could've taken out Slade's brother. How's he going to react to that?" Walker asked.

"Well, now that we have a name, an approximate birth-date and place of birth, we can do some digital digging," Hunter said, ready to do just that. "He might have a bank account, a driver's license, a social security card, something I can dig up and begin to hunt him."

"If you need my help, I can trail him," Walker said, his eyes lighting up with a possible challenge.

"I thought you might be heading to Chicago to take over for Ryder?"

Walker shrugged. "He's wrapping that shit up and heading home soon, so I'm available."

"I'll let you know," Hunter mumbled, staring at the screen. He hacked into two law enforcement programs, J-Net and CLEAN, and had already begun running the name Brandon Bussard. Luckily, it wasn't too common of a last name. "Well, looks like ol' Spazzy boy has a long record and not just in Pennsylvania."

"That surprise you?" Mercy asked Hunter.

"Nope. Guess Slade's lucky he never met his pop. He clearly wasn't a good influence."

"A-fucking-men," Steel murmured.

"Got a couple mug shots here, a list of his tattoos... and surprise, surprise, he's got club colors inked onto his back."

"Does the description say who the rockers belong to?" Mercy asked.

"Yep. Spaz-Matazz's road name is actually Taz, short for Tasmanian Devil. And his colors belong to none other than," Hunter paused for dramatic effect, "the Warriors."

Steel whistled. "No shit."

Hunter stared between the slight gap of two monitors at

Mercy. "You remember any of those cuts with the name Taz?"

"No."

"I don't remember a Warrior named Taz, either," Brick mentioned, his head tipped down and he was back to typing on his phone.

"You sexting this chick with a dick?" Hunter asked.

Brick didn't bother to look up when he grumbled, "The only dick she's gonna have is mine."

Steel snorted.

"*Any-fucking-way*, he's done short stints for domestic violence, agg assault, burglary, armed robbery, distribution of multiple classes of narcotics, DUI, and on and on, ad nauseam, starting at the ripe ol' age of fourteen. Sounds like a productive member of society."

"Weren't they all?" Walker asked dryly.

"The million-dollar question is, if he's still breathing, why didn't we find him?" Mercy asked.

Mercy was in no way sloppy. None of them were, so how this asshole slipped through their fingers... Hunter shrugged and sat back in the chair, scratching at his beard, which always helped him think.

"'Cause he went underground," Walker murmured. "Had to have. Otherwise, we would've sniffed him out. Especially a dirty fucker like that."

Mercy stepped closer to where Walker and Hunter were sitting, jerking his chin up. "Who was the victim of his domestic assault?"

"I'll have to dig up the court dockets and check, but there's not just one charge, there's multiple," Hunter said. "Even so, that's a good starting point. Maybe go through each of his charges, even summaries and traffic citations, see when and where they occurred and track that fucker's ass from age fourteen until now." But curiously, the charges abruptly stopped about three years ago. The man could very well be incarcerated or dead.

"You ever think now we have that info, Slade won't give a fuck about finding his brother?" Steel asked.

"Even if he decides he now doesn't, it still means we failed by leaving one breathing. And we have to fix that fuck up," Mercy said, his silver eyes turning to ice.

"I'm up for a little target practice. Last melon I exploded was that douchebag who had snagged Rissa."

"We need to get a twenty on him first," Hunter said, reminding Brick they needed a location before they could do anything.

"And that's your specialty," Brick responded, lifting his head to look at Hunter. "Once you do that, I don't mind introducing a little metal to brain matter. Just say the word."

Walker slammed his hand on the table that held the computer he was working on. "For fuck's sake, I can imagine this conversation with one of our veteran brothers, 'Hey, Slade, found your long-lost brother, you want to have a touching reunion before we dispatch his ass?'"

Steel shrugged. "Or we don't tell him at all. Say it was a dead end and Rocky was talking out of his ass. Slade might believe that. He has no love for his ol' lady's pop."

"We can decide that once I locate him," Hunter said. "Yeah?"

"Yeah," was the resounding answer around the room.

"Or maybe let D decide, once we do," Brick suggested. "That takes the pressure off our backs."

"Not sure he needs something else on his shoulders with baby number three on the way," Hunter murmured. Hard to believe the man who never wanted children was cranking them out faster than anyone. But then, he and Jewel were always fucking. And that was usually required to make babies. Unfortunately, the Shadows had learned to listen carefully before entering any room that had a closed door, otherwise they got a view of their boss none of them wanted.

"The boss man's got the biggest fucking shoulders I've ever seen, I'm sure he can handle it," Walker said.

Hunter turned to him. "Wanna help me map all of this fucker's crimes and follow the path he's taken? Maybe we can get an approximate twenty on him. It'll be better than what I got now."

"You got it, brother. You know I eat that shit up."

Thank fuck for that. Brandon Bussard aka Taz had a conviction list longer than his arm and he wasn't looking forward to piecing it all together on his own.

He just knew by the time they were done, there wasn't going to be a happy reunion between two brothers.

Good thing the biker had Diamond and his son, because Slade deserved some happy in his life.

They all did.

It was just a matter of finding it.

Chapter Three

HUNTER EDGED his blacked-out Range Rover to the curb and shut the engine down as he stared at the unassuming house.

He could be in Anywhere, Any State, USA and see the same house. Lower middle class—*barely*—fixer-upper that needed a good paint job or vinyl siding to cover the peeling paint.

Who the fuck still had wood siding beside a house with cedar shakes in New England?

Why the fuck did he even care?

He didn't.

But he wasn't in Anywhere, USA. His vehicle—which was out of place in this neighborhood—and he were smack-fucking-dab in the center of a small town named Manning Grove, PA, about an hour north of Williamsport.

This town wasn't occupied by the Shadow Warriors but used to be by the Blood Fury MC, a now defunct motorcycle club that had died a tragic death. Because of that, he doubted that Taz aka Brandon Bussard was now wearing BFMC colors.

Manning Grove was a sleepy little town burrowed in a

valley surrounded by mountains occupied by, from what he found, some white supremacist "militia" that cooked meth to make ends meet and finance their plot against the government. They probably had as many teeth as the occupants of East End Estates.

Hunter sighed, the sound filling the silent cabin of his Rover.

He had visited every victim of Taz's domestic violence cases, trying to uncover the missing Warrior's ass.

Without luck.

And the long list of women he talked to weren't cooperative, either.

Taz had left his mark on a lot of fucking women in his thirty-five years. And none of them appreciated it. Which was to be expected.

Because of that, none of them were harboring his ass. Which meant Hunter had come up empty-handed.

There were two women left on his list he hadn't visited yet. And he would skip the one who was buried under a headstone in Ohio. That meant, in reality, he had one living, breathing victim left of Mr. Bussard who he hadn't talked to.

A Ms. Sucely Hernandez. A thirty-two-year-old single woman, from what little he could dig up.

She had been last on his list, because, unfortunately, Ms. Hernandez made herself difficult to find. Almost as tough as good ol' Taz. He and Walker had to spend way too much time digging around to find her.

Curiously, it was almost as if she didn't want to be found.

Which he couldn't blame her since she might have wanted to shrug off a loser named Taz. Especially since he did time in the joint after knocking her around and breaking a few of her bones. Not just any bones. Her right cheekbone, her left wrist and a few ribs. And that was only one ER admittance. He didn't bother to check if there had been more. That one had been more than enough for him.

After reading the medical records of that episode, he spent two hours at Shadow Valley Fitness with a heavy bag, while having Steel hurl insults at him so he'd hit harder.

He did.

And almost broke some bones in his own hand.

He stared out of his dark-tinted driver's side window. The small house across the street had a covered porch, also in need of a good painting, and a single car detached garage with no vehicle in the short driveway, which in itself needed a fresh coat of sealer. He had no idea if anyone was home.

He would shortly.

And by shortly, it turned out to be right then and there when the garage door lifted, and a woman rolled out a push mower.

The mower had seen better days and was old and ugly. The woman was not.

Fuck no.

She wore white denim shorts with the bottom hems frayed. A pair of pull-on white sneakers and a turquoise blue bikini top. That was it.

He pursed his lips and forgot to breathe when the woman, with long, very dark brown hair in some kind of messy knot at the top of her head, leaned over and gave Hunter a view he took a mental picture of and would use later.

This woman had hips and an ass that wouldn't quit. Her waist was tucked, though she was not what he would call skinny, but instead, curvy in all the right places. Hips, ass, tits. Something a man could hold onto. Her thighs were also thick enough to cushion a man's hips when he was pumping hard and fast into her.

He watched in total fascination as she grabbed the pull cord and yanked.

How her tits remained in that top while she did so, only the good Lord knew.

And, thank fuck, it didn't start the first time.

Or the second.

Or the third.

Hunter should be ashamed of himself for hoping the fucking mower never started. But if that happened, she might go back inside, and he wasn't done observing yet.

He may never be done observing.

On the fourth pull, the old mower sputtered, and the engine finally caught.

She straightened up and then looked directly at him.

Fuck.

Her eyes narrowed and they stared at each other for a few seconds before her expression got hard and she began to push the mower back and forth in rows along the driveway and in front of the porch. The lot was tiny and mowing it shouldn't take long.

Though Hunter knew he was made, he couldn't just drive away like he should.

No. Because fool that he was, he and his dick were enjoying the scenery way too much.

Those bright white shorts that clung perfectly to her generous ass, hips and thighs, made her skin tone appear a bit darker than his and he was half Puerto Rican. Maybe she just liked to worship the sun. Suddenly he was very jealous of the sun.

Of suntan lotion. And that bikini top.

She disappeared around back for about five minutes, then came around the corner of the detached garage, the mower now quiet.

She was done. Even though it hadn't taken long to mow what little lawn there was, her skin glistened with perspiration.

Maybe she'd get out the hose next to cool off.

With a grin, Hunter shifted in his driver's seat at that imagery.

He was watching her push the mower back into the dark interior of the garage when his cell phone pinged.

Grabbing it out of the console, he hit the power button to read the message from Diesel.

However, as he was reading, something caught his attention out of the corner of his eye. And that something was moving fast.

His spine snapped straight as he began to turn his head, but he was too late.

Whatever she was carrying shattered his driver's side window.

Before he could open his door, he realized it might not be smart to do so since she was swinging a wooden bat like a Major League baller and now taking it to his windshield and hood.

"What the fuck!" he shouted.

She, of course, didn't hear him because she was doing some yelling of her own. She was screaming at the top of her lungs as the end of her bat made dents in his hood.

"Fuck!" He would just have to take a risk and get the fuck out of his Rover since she was now smashing out his headlights, her hair partially falling out of her top knot and strands of it were flying everywhere, reminding him of Medusa.

Her eyes were wide and wild, and she still screamed nothing that made any fucking sense.

This woman was bat-shit crazy.

Literally. Bat. Shit. Crazy.

But then most hot ones were. "Great in bed, crazy in the head," was a saying that he'd heard all too often in the Army and, fuck him, he found that to be true.

Especially right now.

He kicked open his door and unfolded himself out,

making sure to keep his eyes on her. She was now on the other side of his Rover, decorating his right front fender.

Fuck me.

But as soon as he moved, she hesitated with her arms raised, double-fisting and white-knuckling the bat as her eyes came to him.

Dark eyes like her hair. A dark, dark brown surrounded by very thick, black eyelashes. The strands of hair that had escaped were long, like he suspected. They swept over her chest, which was heaving.

Somebody was pissed.

As he looked at the damage to his vehicle, it was starting to be him.

No, not starting. He was already there.

She was the kind of woman who was difficult to deal with because they acted first, asked questions later.

He had a couple of those in his past. But that's why they had remained in his past. Because who the fuck wanted to walk in the door only to duck flying objects not even knowing why.

No one that he knew of.

He hadn't been fond of ambushes during his tours in the Army, and he definitely wasn't fond of them from pussy who should be greeting him with a kiss, a beer and a fucking blow job.

She blinked. He blinked.

And then it was on.

With a warrior yell, she came at him, bat raised over her head and her tits bouncing dangerously in the scraps of fabric that could barely contain them.

Bat, Hunter, not tits. Eyes on what will kill you. The rest is just attached to the one that will kill you.

He caught the widening of her eyes as he moved forward instead of retreating like she expected him to do. Because the normal thought process would be *get the fuck out of range of a long, heavy item made of wood with a crazy woman swinging it.*

But then, he was tired of this already. That meant he was going to end it.

Her step stuttered as he met her halfway and snagged the bat with one hand as she swung it down and clotheslined her with his other arm.

He heard a gurgle and watched her collapse on the pavement at his feet, hands to her throat.

He whipped the bat across the street with all his fury and it *thumped* unsatisfactorily onto the grass of her yard.

Before she could get up, he dropped to his knee and planted it on her chest to pin her down. The only problem was, her legs were flailing. She was trying to kick him, knee him, scratch him, all the while screaming again. But this time it included words. "Who are you? What the fuck are you doing here? What do you want with me?"

He snagged both of her wrists and held onto them tightly. She jerked and struggled, but he was a lot stronger than her.

Then he shifted his weight until he straddled her thighs so she couldn't kick him. But even so, she did her best to try to buck him off.

Only her best wasn't good enough.

Thank fuck.

Because if she was any stronger than she was, he'd have two eyes scratched out, his jugular ripped out by her teeth and his nuts drop-kicked into the cavity of his body.

He kind of liked all his body parts where they were.

Her teeth were bared, and she was practically snapping at him like an annoyed leopard seal.

"Calm the fuck down."

"Fuck you!" she screamed, her face flushed.

Yep, her eyes were dark brown, almost black. And in her fight, her bikini top had shifted enough that he noticed she didn't have tan lines. Which meant she either sunbathed topless or that was her natural skin tone.

He was guessing with her hair and eye color, and, her name—*if* she was Sucely Hernandez—that she was of some sort of Hispanic descent.

Her temper was another good indicator. While Latinas could be feisty, they could also be dangerous if you simply looked at them the wrong way.

And stupid him had been ogling her as she mowed the fucking grass.

His mistake.

"You done?" he asked as he felt her weaken. She was running out of steam and probably going to crash after that burst of adrenaline.

"I want to know who you are!"

"All you had to do was ask instead of fucking up my SUV."

"Self-defense."

He raised his brows. "Of what?"

"Of whatever you're here to do to me."

"I'm not here to do *anything* to you."

"Let me up!"

"Not until you calm the fuck down." His head tilted as the sound of sirens infiltrated his brain. He gritted his teeth. Someone had called the fucking cops.

Great.

One black and white cruiser came to a screeching halt, diagonally blocking the street in front of the Rover. While another came from the opposite direction and did the same behind. He was now boxed in.

The driver's doors both opened and the cop to his right, who was taking cover behind his door, had a semi-automatic pointed straight at him. The uniformed officer started barking commands.

He glanced down at the woman trapped beneath him. "Now look what you've done."

She sneered and spat at him, luckily missing. "Good, asshole. You're going to jail."

"Doubt that," he grumbled. "And if you spit at me again, you'll regret it."

The cop barked out more commands, which they tended to do as a habit, and Hunter sighed. Releasing her wrists, he lifted his hands in the air and pushed himself to his feet. As soon as he did that, the woman scrambled to hers and rushed him.

He heard "Oh, shit," in stereo from both cops, at the same time he heard it in his own head. They holstered their weapons quickly and rushed toward him, too.

He just had enough time to protect his balls as her knee came up and smashed into his fingers. He heard a loud groan, also in stereo from both cops.

Before he could react, one of them had her hooked around the waist and was dragging her away, though she wasn't going willingly. No surprise there.

"What the fuck's wrong with you?" he heard the tall, dark-haired cop ask.

He glanced at the other one who now stood in front of him, hands planted on his duty belt, shaking his head. Actually, both cops kind of looked alike.

"She do that damage?" the officer with the name tag BRYSON asked him.

"I sure as fuck didn't do it."

The cop's lips almost twitched as he pulled a worn notepad out of his back pocket and a pen from the front shirt pocket of his uniform. He clicked the pen and then tilted his head as he studied Hunter with intense blue eyes.

Then he dropped that gaze. Which was a farce, cause that cop had a way of watching Hunter without appearing to do so. Hunter knew that game. He also knew how to play it.

With pen to paper, Bryson asked, "Name?"

"Hunter."

"Hunter what?"

"Just Hunter."

The cop glanced up with a frown. "ID."

Hunter pulled his wallet from his back pocket, flipped it open and snagged his license, holding it out to the cop between his index and middle fingers. The officer seized his ID and studied it. "Funny how the name Hunter isn't on your license anywhere," he grumbled as he scribbled down the info.

Hunter's gaze slid toward the woman's driveway, where the other officer was questioning her. He looked irritated and she looked equally annoyed with her hands on her hips, throwing attitude. Hunter also noticed that the man had remarkable self-control because he was actually looking at her face as they talked and no lower. Yep, willpower of steel because it was hard to miss those tits in those two turquoise triangles. Hunter brought his attention back to the man before him, who was now tapping the end of his pen on the notepad with impatience.

"Name I earned in the Army."

The officer stared at him for a moment before his body visibly relaxed, and he muttered, "Marines."

Hunter guessed they were now comparing dick sizes. He lifted a brow. "Special forces?"

"No. You?"

"Green Beret."

"Honorable discharge?"

That shouldn't matter but the man was a cop, maybe he thought he could trust a fellow veteran who was honorably discharged over one who wasn't. "Depends what you

consider honorable. The Army and I had two different defi-
nitions."

The cop relaxed even more. "Had that problem myself."

Interesting. "So now that we're best buds, need to be a
bit transparent here so there are no misunderstandings."

Bryson's spine straightened and he dropped the notepad
to his side and jerked his chin up.

Hunter took that as a "go." "Got a Sig .40 in a holster.
Small of my back."

The cop's eyes narrowed as he assessed Hunter's person
as if he had X-ray eyes. "Got a permit?"

"Yeah."

"Anything else since you're being *transparent?*"

"Tactical knife. Right calf."

"Size?"

"Four."

"You planning on pulling it?"

"Not if I don't have a reason to."

Bryson pursed his lips and nodded again. "Why are you
here?"

"Looking for someone."

Every muscle in that cop's body tensed once again and
his gaze became laser focused. "Who?"

"A biker by the name of Brandon Bussard. Goes by Taz."

Bryson's nostrils flared. Only slightly, but Hunter caught
it. "Tasmanian Devil."

Hunter managed to hide his surprise, but barely. "Yeah."

His eyes slid back to the woman speaking with the other
officer when Bryson said, "She's got a protection order
against Mr. Bussard."

So, she *was* who he was looking for. "She Sucely
Hernandez?"

Bryson contemplated the question for longer than
Hunter liked. "Was. Little advice, don't call her that. He

knew her by that name, so she had it changed. She's buried that name and doesn't like when it resurfaces."

No wonder why it had been hard to find her. He had been searching for a woman with a different name. Smart on her part. A pain in the ass on his. "He been around?"

"We haven't run into him, but he's bad news."

"No shit."

"Why are you looking for him? You a bounty hunter?"

"Something like that."

"Licensed?"

"Just doing a favor for a friend. One of your fellow Marines." He figured he'd throw that in to make the cop a little more friendly and agreeable. Sometimes shit like that worked, sometimes it didn't.

In this case, it did.

"He's got a warrant. Hasn't met with his parole officer since his release."

Hunter wasn't going to admit he already knew that. "Maybe he's doing time somewhere other than PA," Hunter suggested, wondering how much these local cops knew. Though, Hunter knew no one by Taz's real name was incarcerated.

"Could be." Bryson scratched his chin. "So, again, why are you here since Bussard isn't?"

"She's one of his victims."

"Of?"

"You know what of. You know she's got a PFA. You guys probably have his mugshot hanging up in your patrol room. You know her real name. I'm not stupid and neither are you," he finished.

"Okay then, why are you visiting one of his victims?"

"I'm visiting all of them."

"Pattern and path," came the murmur.

Hunter didn't answer.

Bryson tilted his head. "Think she's going to talk to you after what happened?"

"She's not going to have a choice."

"How's that?"

"You haven't asked me the most important question yet. Whether I'm going to press charges against her for the destruction of my property."

Something behind the cop's eyes changed. "I'm going to assume no, as long as she pays restitution. And making amends might not be in the form of money."

"Said you weren't stupid, and I was right."

Bryson's gaze slid over Hunter's Range Rover. "That's a lot of restitution."

"Sure is."

"She might not be happy about that."

"Better than handcuffs and a record." Unless those handcuffs were hooked to his headboard.

"Got that right. She can't afford to fight a charge."

"Then she can't afford to fix my SUV."

Bryson snorted. "Hell, I can't afford to fix your SUV." He sobered. "She'll have to agree with that kind of restitution."

"She doesn't seem the agreeable type."

"She's got a temper," Bryson murmured.

"She sting you with it?" Did this cop have something for Hernandez?

"Nope, got my own woman at home. She helps keep me on an even keel."

"Best kind to have."

Bryson's eyes slid to the dark-haired woman, who'd most likely make a man's psyche choppy as fuck. "Damn straight." The cop held out his hand and Hunter took it, giving it a firm shake. "Matt Bryson." He lifted his chin to the other officer. "Adam Bryson."

"Brothers?"

"Cousins. He's also a jarhead."

"Runs in the family?"

Bryson snorted. "You have no fucking idea. Grandfather, father, my other two older brothers. All did their time in the Marines, then Manning Grove PD."

"Served your country, then your community."

"It's in our blood."

"Either deeply dedicated or fucking foolish."

"A little of both."

Hunter grinned. He liked this cop. And he couldn't say that about many who'd crossed his path. This one wasn't easily offended.

"How long will you be in town?" Matt Bryson asked.

"Guess as long as I need to be until I can get her to cooperate and at least fix the headlights on my Rover. Don't want a country bumpkin cop giving me a citation for them." Finding replacement headlights in this area for a Range Rover probably wasn't going to be easy.

Again, Bryson didn't take offense to the tease. "Good fucking luck with both of those."

Hunter was going to need it.

Chapter Four

"What's going on, Frankie?"

"He was watching me."

Officer Adam Bryson jerked up his dark brows. "Maybe because you're wearing a bikini top while you're mowing the lawn. I told you before, you're going to give Mr. Duffy a heart attack."

"It shouldn't matter what I wear."

"And while that's true, you know some men are going to be tempted to look at you." He lifted his hand. "Look, I'm gay and *I* think you look smoking hot dressed like that. You've got the body to pull it off."

One corner of Frankie's lips turned up. "Thanks, Adam." Her smile fell flat as she contemplated the subject of their conversation. "But I have no idea who he is. He's not from around here."

"And Matt'll find out why he's here. But you need to keep your temper in check. That's an expensive vehicle you smashed up. I'd hate to have to cuff you if he wants to press charges."

"He was spying on me."

"It's not a crime to look, but it is to take a bat to a ninety-thousand-dollar Range Rover."

The blood rushed from Frankie's face. "What?" she whispered, panic bubbling up at that cost. "I was just protecting myself."

"From?"

"From whatever he's here for. He looks sketchy."

Adam's eyes slid to the man that Matt had pulled to the side and back to Frankie. "Him watching you mow the lawn could be a little suspect, but he doesn't look sketchy. If Matt was catching those vibes, I'd be able to tell. Matt, of all people, is looking at ease right now."

"Great. Some stranger comes into town, stalks me and you guys make friends with him."

"No one's making friends with anyone."

"Good. You should do your job and arrest him."

Adam brushed a hand over his closely cut hair. "If anyone's going to be arrested, it's you."

"I can't be arrested," Frankie whispered. "Leo..."

"Right. But it's not up to us. It's up to," Adam lifted a hand and waved it in Matt and the stranger's direction, "him. You gave him that power the second you took your bat to his SUV."

"Shit."

"If you were worried about him, you should've called us."

"But if Taz sent him, it might've been over before you arrived."

Adam's chest expanded and contracted as he stared at her. "I understand your concern, Frankie, but this could've ended worse than it did. He could've put a bullet in you and claimed self-defense the second you raised that bat. You used a deadly weapon."

Her and her damn temper. She needed to think before

she acted. That's what got her into this whole mess with Taz in the first place.

"Adam," Frankie began.

Adam once again lifted his hand to stop her. "Stay here. I'll go talk to Matt and find out what's going on." He pinned his eyes on Frankie. "You do not move from this spot until I tell you otherwise."

"But—"

"Frankie!"

"Fine," she huffed, crossing her arms over her bare stomach.

She watched Adam join the other two, then the stranger's eyes landed on her.

No, more like her tits. *Asshole.*

She slid her hand up her stomach and gave him the bird by pressing her middle finger against the bottom curve of her breast. He was sure not to miss it there.

He grinned so large she could see the brightness of his teeth from where she was standing before he turned his attention back to the Brysons.

Suddenly all six eyeballs were pointed in her direction. *Shit.*

Matt shook hands with the stranger. *Again.*

Then so did Adam.

Traitors!

She was a tax-paying resident of Manning Grove, they were supposed to be protecting her. Not having a beer and nachos with someone dangerous.

She saw Adam's mouth moving and the stranger shake his head.

Oh, good. Maybe he decided not to press charges against her.

Though, she couldn't be so lucky.

Then Matt got into his patrol car and drove away. Just like that!

Adam headed back in her direction, the stranger casually following him, the man's stride long, his broad shoulders relaxed and his narrow hips loose. Like he hadn't a care in the damn world.

When they got closer, Adam said, "Gonna get rolling, Frankie. He's not pressing charges. *Yet.* But that doesn't mean he won't. You need to keep your temper on a leash and cooperate with him."

"Why? Is he law enforcement?"

"No. But you owe him for the damage you've done and he's going to work out a payment plan with you."

Payment plan? She couldn't even afford a payment plan. She had a difficult enough time keeping food on the table and the lights on.

Unfortunately, Adam wasn't done. "Make sure you cooperate with him. Don't cut him, don't club him, and, for fuck's sake, don't knee him in the nuts. His generosity is the only thing standing between you and a jail cell. Understood?"

Generosity. Frankie's pressed her lips together. Hard.

Adam pointed a finger at her. "Don't make me come back out here today," was his final shot before climbing into his cruiser and pulling away.

And then there were two.

"You never answered my questions," she said, watching the patrol car turn the corner and disappear.

"The ones you were screaming like a *mujer loca?*"

She swung her narrowed eyes back onto him and studied him more closely. "*¿Sabes español?*"

"Only enough to get by. But I also know a crazy woman when I see one."

"It's not crazy if you're protecting yourself."

"I wasn't a threat."

"So you say."

"Now that you're not wielding a bat, I'm willing to

answer those questions. But not out here since we have to do a bit of negotiating."

"For what?"

"For what the officer said. Damage to my vehicle."

Frankie glanced past him to his Range Rover parked on the street. Shattered glass surrounded it, dents decorated the doors, hood and front fenders. She winced at seeing all the damage she caused, now that fear and anger weren't pumping blood to every inch of her body.

"They also want you to clean up the mess," she heard, and Frankie turned her attention back to him.

"I'll go get a broom and trash can."

As she went to turn, he grabbed her arm. "No. You will take me inside and we can talk first. Then, you can get a broom and whatever else you'll need, and I'll supervise."

She stared at his long fingers wrapped around her forearm and tugged hard. He released her. "You could help."

"I would if I helped make the mess."

Frankie let her gaze roam the man from the top of his head to bottom of his boots. His dark hair was super short along the sides and a little longer on the top, a few grays decorated his temples. He didn't look old enough for that, maybe his late thirties or early forties at the most, but some men grayed early. He'd probably take the gray over a bald spot.

He had a small hoop earring in his left ear and a dark beard covered his lower face. It wasn't bushy or out of control and he didn't let it climb up his cheeks too high. She wondered about his ethnic background since his skin was the color of light caramel and he knew a little bit of Spanish. Not that that meant anything. A lot of people were bilingual.

He wore a black T-shirt that clung to his torso and didn't hide any curve or plane of his chest, abs or arms. This man had no beer belly. The muscles of his arms and neck were defined. He worked out, no doubt.

There was a lump under his tee about midway down his chest. A necklace of some sort.

He was taller than her, but not freakishly tall. Maybe six foot. And his legs were encased in a pair of black cargo pants, his feet in heavy black boots, a plain black leather belt encircled his waist.

The man apparently liked black, since his Range Rover was the same color.

He was well put together and, unlike Taz Bussard, he didn't have a lot of ink she could see. Only a part of one piece peeked out from the sleeve of his left arm. From what she could tell, it looked like a black tribal tattoo.

He didn't look like a typical biker since he didn't wear a cut, both arms weren't solid tats, and he drove an expensive SUV.

But looks could be deceiving.

She'd learned that lesson the hard way.

He wanted to come into her house, and she wasn't sure she wanted to let him in.

In fact, no, she was *sure* she didn't him want him in her house.

"See your wheels spinning and I'm figuring you're a hard-headed woman. But you've got two choices. Jail and restitution, or me." He glanced at her house. "And if you can't afford to paint that house, you can't afford the body work on my Rover."

Damn. That was a low blow.

"And now I see you gearing up to snap my head off. Let me give you a little advice, *loquilla*... Don't. My patience is already thin and getting thinner the longer I stand out here in this goddamn heat looking at my vehicle."

Loquilla.

He was calling her crazy without being obviously offensive. He knew enough Spanish to know that much. It was safe and to anyone listening, it would almost sound as if it was an endearment.

At this point, it wasn't. He didn't know her. She didn't know him.

They were just two strangers staring at each other in her driveway.

"My name is Frankie."

"Heard it. And we're going to talk about that, too."

Frankie blinked. She hadn't been with a man in close to four years. Now she remembered why.

They were bossy as fuck.

Her temper was beginning to rise again, and she swallowed the words she wanted to shoot in his direction like bullets from a machine gun. But between what Adam said and the Range Rover sitting on the street behind him, it reminded her that she needed to keep that in check.

Easier said than done.

She could admit that holding her tongue was one of her weaknesses.

Another one, apparently, was bad boys with tattoos.

Which was why she was back home in Manning Grove living in her childhood home.

The last bad boy with tattoos had changed the course of her life. So instead of moving forward like she originally planned, she ended up moving backward. Or, at least, that was what it felt like.

She had come home to lick her wounds, recover and basically hide in plain sight since bad boys with tattoos were usually not the brightest.

But that assumption might not be true about the one standing in front of her. He seemed to be more of a dangerous man than a bad boy and he didn't appear to be dumb.

But again, looks could be deceiving.

"I just want to get a couple things straight," she began.

"Shoot."

"You expect me to let a man, who I don't even know, into my house."

"Sums it up nicely."

"A man that I don't even know his name."

"Hunter."

"Hunter," she repeated. "That doesn't really fit you."

"It does. More than you know. But I could say the same for the name Frankie."

"It's short for Frances."

"I don't think it's any shorter than the name Frances."

"Let's pretend it is."

His lips remained neutral, but the lines at the corners of his light brown eyes deepened.

"The next thing I need to know before I let a stranger walk into my home is, why you were sitting out here watching me?"

"This is shit we need to discuss inside."

"Why inside?"

"Because, one, I'm sweating my fucking balls off and, two, there are eyes on us." He tilted his head just slightly enough that she caught it and she glanced in that direction.

Yep. Some of her neighbors were conveniently finding things to do outside. "My neighbors are probably just concerned about a stranger on their street. Someone who *doesn't belong here*." She hissed the last part.

"I wasn't just sitting there to take in the scenery, as nice as it is. I'm here for a reason."

"And that reason is me."

"Yes, *loquilla*, it is."

"I'm not so sure I'm happy about you calling me that."

"Probably about as happy as I am about my fucking Rover."

Well, there was that.

"Now, we done here?" he asked, his tone a bit impatient.

Yes, they were. "I'm done. You can go on your way at any time."

"You know that wasn't what I meant." He jerked his chin toward Mr. Duffy, who was outside watering the flowers on his porch. Flowers that were plastic. "Your neighbors not only have eyes, but ears. Big ones. Unless you want them to know the reason I'm here, I suggest you quit stalling and we go inside."

Ice slithered through Frankie's veins. "I'm not liking the sound of this *reason*."

"Like it or not, I need information from you. And now that you owe me, that's going to be part of my payment."

"Part," Frankie murmured. "What's the other part?"

"I'll let you know."

She didn't like the sound of that, either. "How about if you give me your mailing address and I'll send you a check every month until I pay off the damage."

"How about no."

"Adam said you were going to work out a payment plan with me."

"That's correct. But it isn't going to be five dollars a month for eternity."

"It wouldn't be five..." It might be ten. *Shit.* She dropped her head for a moment and stared at the grass-stained tips of her formerly white Keds.

A long finger tucked under her chin and lifted her face. His expression was serious, and, surprisingly, his eyes held sincerity. "I'm not going to hurt you. I just need some of your time."

I'm not going to hurt you.

I'd never hurt you.

Why did you make me hurt you?

She closed her eyes to shut out those words. And when she opened them, this Hunter wore a look of concern.

"I saw your hospital record from when you were admitted to the ER almost four years ago."

She opened her mouth to speak, to deny everything he read, but instead sucked in a sharp breath.

How did he get a hold of that?

"Who are you?" she whispered, fear crawling over her skin and sinking into her bones.

The fear wasn't just for herself.

She jerked her chin from his touch and stepped back quickly. "Who are you?"

"My name's Hunter because that's what I do best."

She shook her head at his words. "I don't understand."

"I'll explain it to you. Inside."

If this man could get to her records, so could anyone else. Her heart was thumping so hard that her pulse was pounding in her ears.

But she wasn't using that name anymore. She wasn't that person anymore.

She had come back to where she grew up and legally changed her name. Taz had never cared enough to know her real last name or about her childhood or family. He never asked details about her at all. He'd only been interested in one thing.

Because of that, she thought she would be safe here. In a sleepy town in northern Pennsylvania. Hours and hours from where she met Brandon Bussard.

Brandon.

Bile worked its way up her throat forcing her to swallow it back down.

She was sure Brandon's mother had high hopes for her son when she picked that name. But Brandon decided to dash them all when he lived as the Tasmanian Devil instead.

If a name fit anyone perfectly, it was Taz's.

Chapter Five

HUNTER SAT at the tiny wooden kitchen table that should have been chopped up and thrown into a bonfire a couple of decades ago. The top was scarred and had nicks taken out of it. It even wobbled a bit.

A swirl of steam rose from the coffee sitting in front of him. The chipped mug stated, "The Pennsylvania Grand Canyon, a GORGEous hike," on the side. He assumed the play on words might be some sort of local joke.

Unfortunately, his sense of humor had fled as he stared at the woman across the tiny table from him, sipping on a diet pop.

She was trying to hide the shake of her hands, but he caught it. And that tremor, even though it was slight, pissed him the fuck off.

This woman was a firecracker.

And someone had tried to snip her fuse.

Not someone.

Taz.

She had pulled a shirt on over her bathing suit top, so that at least helped keep him from being too distracted by her physical attributes. While it covered her generous cleavage, it did nothing to hide her luscious womanly curves. He tried to focus on other things instead...

The house, like the kitchen table, was small. Really small. It was maybe a two bedroom with dormers on the second floor and a stairway cutting up the center from the front door. Those steps divided the house in half, making it feel even more claustrophobic. He didn't like tight spaces, so he didn't like this house already and he'd only seen a very small portion of it.

She had brought him through the back door which led directly into the kitchen, not wanting him to go further. And when she said he needed to stay in the kitchen, the back of his neck prickled.

She was hiding something.

He couldn't blame her for it. She was right. He was a stranger.

And he couldn't imagine she was very trusting with men. Which was a good reason why his Rover was now fucked up.

One minute she was letting her fury fly and the next she was showing fear.

He could understand that, too.

There had been times in his life where he'd been pissed about the situations he'd been forced into, but also scared he'd have to kiss his own ass goodbye. The range of emotions a human could experience in a split moment could be astounding.

Even so, she had nothing to fear from him. Only, she didn't know that.

He lifted his coffee and studied her over the lip of the mug.

Sucely Hernandez aka Frankie Reyes was half-Guatemalan. From what little he pieced together, he knew her mother came to the States to give her unborn daughter a better life and things just went to shit from there.

Life didn't get better for her mother Camila, they got

worse.

But she did her best to save her child, who became a citizen the instant she was born on American soil. Since Frankie was currently sitting in a kitchen in Manning Grove, she apparently remained behind when Camila was deported.

Who raised Camila's daughter, Hunter didn't know. The details were sketchy and when he was searching for Frankie, he wasn't looking into her background, he only needed to know where she lived.

He had been only interested in Taz, not her.

But now he was curious about the dark-eyed, dark-haired beauty who stared back at him. He wanted to know how and why she didn't go back to Guatemala with her mother, and why her path had crossed with one Brandon Bussard.

She in no way reminded him of a woman who would be hanging out with bikers. Especially outlaw bikers, the one-percenters.

But he'd been wrong about shit before.

Once.

A long time ago.

"How did you see my medical records?" she asked. She dropped her gaze to the table and drew her finger back and forth over one of the long, deep scratches.

He couldn't tell her how, because how he accessed them was illegal. Both Hunter and Walker were good at hacking into websites, even ones with firewalls. They had learned that skill during their time in the military and had trained the others. Though Steel, Brick, Mercy and Ryder had no interest in the computer side of shit.

Maybe he shouldn't have told her that, but he needed her to take him seriously and let him in the door.

It had worked.

"I've got a friend," was all he said.

She lifted her gaze and the worry behind her expressive brown eyes pierced his chest. "Taz has friends."

The dread in her voice made that pain even sharper. "Not like mine," he reassured her.

Her throat worked before she asked, "How do you know?"

"Trust me."

"I don't trust anyone," she whispered.

"You trust those cops."

She took a long sip of her pop, put her glass down and said, "I came home so I could surround myself with people who could be trusted."

"Then what you said wasn't true."

"I don't trust strangers," she corrected.

"Fair enough," he murmured and sat back to give her some personal space before asking, "Did you come home after your stint in the hospital?"

Her eyes met his and became guarded. "You're looking for Taz. I don't know where he is. I'm not sure why you're asking questions about me."

He ignored that. "Do you think it was smart coming back to where you grew up?"

She hesitated as if she was considering his question. This was a pivotal moment, whether she would trust him enough to reveal some of her secrets. He just needed her to crack open the door so he could shove his boot in it. Once he did that, he could work on getting her to trust him some more.

"He didn't know a lot about me because he never cared enough to ask, and I didn't bother to tell him." She let her gaze circle the kitchen. "This was the only place I had to go. Maybe I'm stupid to come back home, but it was one place I felt safe."

"Do your neighbors know what your real name is?"

"Was," she corrected him. "Some. Not all. The police know, of course."

He nodded. It was good that the local cops knew her situation. It didn't keep her perfectly safe if Taz wanted to find her, but it was better than nothing.

He watched her carefully when he said softly, "The medical records stated you miscarried."

Color drained from her face. As she shoved her chair back to escape, he reached out, snagged her wrist and tugged her back down into her seat.

"Sit." *Fuck*. He pushed too soon. "Part of your restitution is to answer my questions."

"I'm not sure why you are interested in me if you're only trying to find Taz for whatever reason you are, which you still haven't told me why."

Her temper was returning, which was evident by the spark in her eyes and the tenseness of her body.

She already put her guard back up, so he had no choice but to push forward. "You were pregnant when he put you into that hospital. Was it his?"

Her jaw got tight and she closed her eyes to avoid his.

He no longer needed the answer to that question. She answered it without words.

"Did he know?"

Those thick black eyelashes parted, and her eyes held a pain so deep Hunter felt it himself.

"Yes, that's why I ended up in the hospital."

He did his best to stay in his own chair, not rush out of that kitchen and out of that house to find the motherfucker and beat the life out of him, if he even was still alive. At that moment Hunter hoped he was, so he could be the one to exact revenge on his ass. He had to take a deep inhale before he could manage, "I'm sorry."

"Not as sorry as I was for getting pregnant. It was careless and stupid, and I should've known better. But then everything I did with Taz was careless and stupid. A hard lesson learned. One I swear I'll never forget."

Yeah, Taz had stomped her fire out, but after seeing how she acted earlier, he hoped it had been only temporary.

"Where did you meet him?"

"Is this really necessary?"

"Yes. I'm trying to piece together where he'd been. You weren't his only... victim."

She sank her teeth into her bottom lip before saying, "That doesn't surprise me."

"But you were his last that I know of."

She nodded once. "He did time."

"Right."

"Then I got notice they were releasing him."

"And that worried you."

Her brows furrowed. "Of course."

"But he's had no contact with you."

"No, and I want to keep it that way."

The opening of a door toward the front of the house made her jerk her head in that direction and her eyes widen.

Fear.

It filled her expression.

He surged to his feet, his hand automatically reaching to the small of his back where his waistband holster held his Sig. As he went to pull it, she surged forward, grabbing his arm with a speed that surprised him.

"No!" she hissed, giving his arm a hard tug.

Before he could demand an explanation, he heard a female voice yell, "Frankie!" then footsteps of more than one person coming closer. He kept his fingers wrapped around the Sig's grip.

"Leo was hungry after the park, so we stopped at——" The older woman who stepped into the kitchen came to a screeching halt, her grasp tightening around the toddler's hand and yanking the little boy behind her, as if she would be able to shield him. "¡Dios mío! ¿Es este él?"

"No, I'm not him," Hunter answered quickly. The

woman looked nothing like Frankie. She was short and squat, her eyes a light blue. Her Spanish was good, though she didn't look Hispanic at all. He glanced over his shoulder at Frankie, who was once again chewing on her bottom lip as she stared at the little boy clinging to the back of the older woman's leg. "Who is this?"

"My mother."

Bullshit. That lie slipped out way too easily from her lips. "Your mother was Camila Hernandez. This is not Camila."

Frankie's mouth dropped open and before she could say anything, the older woman spoke first. "Frankie, who is he?"

"I'm still trying to figure that out," Frankie said behind him. She pushed past Hunter and rounded the older woman, to pick up the little boy and clutch him against her.

"Momma," the toddler said, wrapping his arms around her neck and his legs around her waist.

"Yeah, baby? You have fun today with your *abuela*?"

The boy nodded and said very seriously, "Yes. An' we had ice cream."

Frankie gave him a big smile, even though Hunter saw it was forced. "You did? What a lucky little boy you are." She turned her gaze from the boy to the older woman. "How would you like to spend a little more time with your grandmother? Your momma has to take care of a few things. Then, if you're a good boy, we'll get pizza for dinner. Okay?"

"Pizza!" he yelled, then turned his attention to Hunter. "Hi."

Hunter shook himself loose. "Hi. What's your name?"

"Leo." He held up three fingers. "I'm tree."

Hunter's heart thumped heavily. Children trusted people, including strangers, way too easily. "You're very grown up for three."

Leo nodded again.

"Mom, can you take Leo with you? I'll pick him up later

after I grab the pizza."

"Is everything okay? I can feed him dinner if you need me to."

"I want pizza!" Leo yelled, scrunching up his face.

"Well, excuse you, little man!" Frankie scolded him. "Since when do you get to demand things?"

"Since forever," he stated firmly with a sharp nod.

Frankie rolled her eyes. "Uh huh, I don't think so. But I said pizza, so I'll get you pizza."

"Pizza!" Leo crowed again.

"But you have to be a good boy, understood?"

Leo nodded dramatically and said, "I'm always good."

"What did I say about fibbing?"

Leo threw his head back and laughed. Frankie handed him back to her "mother," who took the boy, put him back on his feet and snagged his hand tightly as she eyed up Hunter. "Let's go, Leo. I'll play Legos with you."

"Legos!"

When the woman gave Frankie a pointed look, Frankie gave her a slight nod and her "mother" headed back in the direction where she came from. She threw, "Call me immediately if you need me," over her shoulder.

Hunter waited until he heard the front door close. He took one breath. Two. "Wanna explain what that was about?"

"Not really."

"How about you do it anyway."

"How about no," she echoed his own earlier words.

Leo wasn't any of his business. Hell, *she* wasn't any of his business. She didn't care if she did a million dollars' worth of damage, she was not cutting open a vein to appease him.

She still didn't know *who* he was, why he was looking for Taz and why he thought she might know.

In fact, him searching for Taz and then showing up at her place might put her back on Taz's radar. Something she'd been wanting to avoid.

She learned her lesson from getting involved with a man like Taz and she now considered herself fully educated in that matter. No more lessons needed.

She also didn't want her son caught up in anything that Taz, or this man standing in her kitchen, could bring.

"I'm not giving you a choice."

In the past she preferred men like him, ones who could handle her strong personality.

Until she no longer did.

"Will my debt to you be fully paid if I tell you everything you want to know? And if I tell you, will you leave?"

She knew the answer before he said it.

"No. But if what I'm thinking is true, then you aren't as safe as you think you are. I'm willing to help you in that regard."

"Why?"

"Because I read your medical report. I'm assuming that wasn't the only time he put you in the hospital."

"That was the only time he put me in the hospital," she answered flatly. Only because the previous times Taz put his hands on her weren't as bad and he brushed it off as being her fault.

She knew it wasn't and had begun to separate herself from him quietly before finding out she was pregnant.

And when he guessed she was, he wasn't happy about it.

To put it mildly.

Though she wasn't happy about it either, she refused to take any other measure—like the abortion he insisted she have—instead, choosing to disappear. Unfortunately, he caught her in the midst of trying to do that.

That made him even more unhappy.

There was "no fucking way" she was getting a dime

from him. He wasn't going to be saddled with "one bitch" and her kid for the rest of his life, either.

In fact, he was enraged.

To the point where he ripped out a handful of her hair from her head and threw her down the stairs after punching her in the face and breaking her cheekbone. Then at the bottom of those steps, he kicked the shit out of her in his attempt to cause her to miscarry.

Luckily, her son was as stubborn as his mother.

Also, luckily, the doctor was willing to fudge her medical record to say she miscarried when she didn't, but only after she begged and pleaded with her since not only Frankie's life, but her unborn child's life depended on it.

Leonardo Francis Reyes was a miracle.

A miracle Frankie would do anything to protect.

How either of them survived she didn't know. But they had and she was determined to not let anyone change that.

Not anyone.

Including the man before her. "Why are you searching for Taz?"

"You didn't answer my questions."

"I need to know why you're searching for Taz. I have something precious to protect and he comes first. No, I not only need to know why but what you have planned once you find him."

"What would you have me do?"

The way he asked that made her heart beat a little faster. She moved back into the small kitchen and stood behind a chair, holding onto the back of it. "I don't know you. I don't know what you're capable of."

The man studied her, his head slightly tilted. "No. You don't."

That answer sent a chill sliding down Frankie's spine. "Did he hurt someone you know?"

"Yes."

"Who?"

He didn't even hesitate when he answered, "You."

Oxygen fled her lungs and she frowned. "You don't even know me."

"I knew you the second I read your medical report. I knew you the second I read about your mother. I knew you were strong, brave and a survivor."

Impossible.

She wasn't strong or brave. She only had a temper.

But she was a survivor. Leo was her motivation the second she saw those double lines on her pregnancy test. She knew she would do anything, *anything*, for him.

Including getting away from a man like Taz.

If Leo hadn't survived, she wouldn't have either.

"Did the doctor alter the report to hide the fact that you didn't lose the baby?"

"Yes." Why was she even talking about this? He needed to leave. He was bad news. Anyone connected to Taz was bad news.

This man was probably no different.

But his questioning continued. "And then what did you do?"

If she gave him some information, maybe he would leave. She had no money to pay for the damage to his vehicle, and words were free. For the most part. "Once he was in custody and I was released from the hospital, I hid."

"Did he know you were pregnant?"

"Yes."

"You told him?"

She shook her head. "He guessed."

"Would you have told him?"

Once she saw that positive test, she knew she couldn't. "No."

"Why were you with him?"

She ignored that question. One she didn't want to

answer because she didn't have a good enough reason. One that made sense. Instead she said, "Having Leo was the hardest decision of my life. I knew if Taz found out the baby survived, he might try again, or he might take him from me. Then I might have to deal with his ass for the rest of my life. And if that happened, my son would not have a good fatherly figure in his life. I missed out on having a father. I don't want my son to do the same."

"Try what again?"

"To make me miscarry."

"That's why he knocked you around? To make you lose the baby?"

"Yes. He was pissed I wouldn't..."

Hunter nodded his head, pushed away from the wall he was leaning against and moved to the other side of the small kitchen. He stopped in front of the sink, braced his hands on the edge, leaning forward and staring out of the small window above it. The one with her homemade curtains that overlooked the patch of grass that was her backyard.

"None of this is your business."

He turned his head and his brown eyes were ice cold. "It is now."

"I don't understand."

"I was searching for Taz for one reason. Now I'm searching for him for another."

"And you just saying his name scares me enough that he'll appear out of thin air. If you can find me, so can he."

"Doubt that. I'm pretty good. And I think he's in hiding."

"Why?"

His expression became blank, which made the hair on the back of her neck stand up. "He was a Shadow Warrior."

Every muscle in her body turned to stone.

Taz had hidden it from her. Hidden it until he couldn't. The first night they spent together, she didn't notice those tattoos because they were on his back. But the next morning when he climbed from her bed...

When he walked across the room to "hit the head," as he called it, she couldn't miss those words, those "rockers" he called them when she asked him about it.

She knew nothing about motorcycle clubs. Nothing about bikers or their way of life. She had no idea what that "1%" diamond-shaped tattoo above his heart meant, either.

None of it. He had hidden all of that from her for weeks. For the time it took him to convince her he was interested in more than just sex.

Though, in the end that wasn't quite true.

Because as it turned out, she wasn't the only woman he was sleeping with.

Even so, Brandon "Taz" Bussard liked a challenge and Frankie was one to him. She had turned him down night after night when he came into the bar where she waitressed. But he was persistent. Determined.

And, at first, a charmer.

He wasn't going to quit until he got what he wanted.

Which was her.

She also thought his nickname Taz was just that. A fun nickname that matched the cartoon character tattooed on his right forearm. She mistakenly thought he got that tattoo because he had a sense of humor.

He was handsome under the roughness. His longish brown hair he sometimes wore in a ponytail, his brown eyes, his smile...

It was genuine, until it wasn't.

She didn't mind men with tattoos. And while she wasn't a big fan of facial hair, she didn't mind Taz's longer beard. It fit him. She also thought it was kind of cute that his nickname was short for Tasmanian Devil.

But she did mind once he showed his true colors.

And not just the ones on his back.

Chapter Six

HUNTER COULDN'T TELL her why Taz went into hiding. And he wasn't sure how much she knew about the Warriors. He also wasn't about to admit to what he and his fellow teammates had done to take out that outlaw MC.

That would just be plain fucking stupid.

Her face, when he mentioned that club's name, had frozen and her fingers gripped the back of the chair even harder than they had been.

"You knew that, right?" he asked her.

"Yes. It was hard to miss the ink on his back."

"But he didn't tell you in the beginning? He wasn't wearing a cut when you met him?"

She shook her head as if in a daze. "No. I had no idea."

"You only found out when you saw his back?" He fought the urge to grind his teeth at what that meant. But it happened, and probably more than once, since she had become pregnant with the man's child.

"I asked him about it and he vaguely explained it away. Said it was all in his past and that life was behind him."

Right. "That was his father's club. He followed in his father's footsteps."

Her eyes raised to his. "How do you know?"

"Because one of my veteran buddies is his brother. That's why I'm looking for him."

Suddenly she moved, surprising him as she approached. He held his breath as she reached out and pressed her fingers to his T-shirt between his pecs, outlining his tags.

"Dog tags," she murmured.

He didn't answer.

"You know Leo's uncle."

Then it hit him like a brick over the head.

Leo's uncle. *Fuck.* Slade's nephew. He'd want to know. Slade would also want his blood protected from a psychopath, even if that psycho was his brother.

If Slade knew what Taz did to Frankie, he would have no love for his "long-lost" half-brother. Especially when Taz tried to prevent his own son from being born.

"Yeah. He's a former Marine but now belongs to an MC, just like Taz."

"The Shadow Warriors?"

"No. Their rivals," *or former rivals,* "the Dirty Angels."

"The two brothers are in rival gangs?"

"The DAMC isn't a gang, but yeah. If they ever met, they'd automatically be enemies."

"But if their father was in the Warriors, why did his other son choose to be a rival?"

"Because their father was a piece of shit just like Taz, so Slade never knew him. Buzz didn't take responsibility for the children he put on this Earth, he just made them. He was also a murderer."

Frankie's face paled. "Like father, like son."

Like monster, like son, more like it. "He admitted he killed someone?"

"Since he didn't want to take responsibility for a child, he almost killed me. And Leo."

But he didn't. Thank fuck for that.

Suddenly, with her face paler than normal, she moved away from him and toward the back door. "I need to get my son. And you need to go."

Just like that, she wanted this over.

It wasn't that easy, because at this point, he couldn't walk away. He couldn't leave her to her own defenses if Taz came back to finish what he started, especially because her son was Slade's blood. And, fuck him, for some reason, he wasn't done with Frankie, either.

"I can't go anywhere with my vehicle like that." He needed an excuse to stick around until he figured out how to handle Frankie and Leo. He couldn't in good conscious leave this woman and Slade's nephew vulnerable to a monster.

If Taz was still alive. And until he had confirmation the fucker was dead, he was going to assume Taz only went underground to avoid being picked off by one of the Shadows.

"I can call you a tow truck."

"One you're going to pay for?"

He couldn't miss the panic on her face, though she tried to hide it. She was clearly struggling financially.

That was her weakness. That's what he'd need to use to convince her to cooperate with him. Well, that and Taz.

"I can take you to a motel in town where you can wait for your vehicle to be fixed."

"One, do you think any body shops around here will be able to fix my Rover that quickly? And two, you still haven't answered all my questions."

Her hand was on the door knob and she was like a bird ready to take flight. "I need to pick up pizza and get my son."

"They only left a few minutes ago."

"But he's my son," she said in a broken whisper.

He approached her and curled a hand around her neck,

looking down into her worried brown eyes. "I get it. He's your everything and you want to protect him. But helping me will protect him. I need to find Taz. Once I do..." He let that drop.

A little light flickered behind her brown eyes once more. That light equaled hope. "Once you do, I won't ever have to worry about him again?"

He couldn't guarantee that. But... "That's the plan."

"Are you my only chance of living the rest of my life in peace?"

"I can't guarantee you won't have problems from anyone other than Taz. As you know, life's unpredictable. But any problems you have won't be from him."

She released the knob and turned, his thumb sliding along her pulse. *Fuck*, he wanted to be the one to wipe that apprehension out of those eyes. Which surprised the fuck out of him. He didn't even know her.

His only concern should be finding Slade's brother, not protecting Frankie from her former lover.

But her next words touched his very soul. "I'm tired of being scared. I hate that he holds that much power over me just by existing."

This woman shouldn't have to live her life in fear just because she slept with the wrong guy. A decision which ended up becoming a life-altering mistake.

"Look, I'll get out of your hair for now. Drop me off at a motel, get your pizza, spend time with your son and think about it tonight once he goes to sleep. I'll give you my number, so you can call me tomorrow. I'm going to find him one way or another. With or without your help. But I do have more questions when and if you're ready to answer them."

The woman was not good at hiding her emotions, which was currently relief. He wanted her to chew on why he was in town and maybe she'd be more accommodating.

She nodded. "I can drop you off. But I still have to clean up all the glass."

"I'll help you do that. Then I'll hit the motel, find a tow truck and someone who can fix my Rover."

"We never finished working out the payment details."

Right. "Let me find out how much it costs to fix my vehicle first."

"It's going to be a lot." The worry was creeping back into her face.

"Probably best to think before you act," he reminded her. And he got the reaction he hoped for. The hard-headed woman was back in full force.

She set her jaw and yanked open the door, heading outside. He followed with a grin and helped her clean up the glass.

She then dumped his ass as fast as possible off at some motel on the west side of town.

He did discover something about her during that time, though. She liked to hold onto grudges, so that might just work in his favor.

———

Sitting on the bed, Hunter flipped the cop's business card over and over in his fingers. He paused, read the name on the front one more time—*Matt Bryson*—then he dialed the cell phone number the cop had scribbled on the back.

His call went straight to voicemail.

"Bryson. Hunter. Just giving you a heads up. Staying in town for a bit at The Grove Inn. If you hear anything about Brandon Bussard, get ahold of me right away." He rattled off his cell phone number.

Hunter ended the call, then sighed. Since the moment he'd stepped into the tiny motel room that looked like it had been updated once—back in 1978—he'd been on the phone. He found a tow truck that would haul his Rover down to the nearest dealership, which was all the fucking way in Harrisburg, a good two and a half hours south.

He called the dealership, warned them it was coming and instructed them to do whatever was needed to get his baby back to her original splendor. No matter the cost.

He called around for a rental car. One would be delivered in a couple of hours.

He called Walker to have him keep digging when he had the chance and also caught him up to date with what Hunter knew so far. He talked to Diesel, leaving it up to his boss whether to tell Slade that he was an uncle. He also let D know he wouldn't be back in Shadow Valley for a bit.

How long that "bit" was, Hunter didn't know.

It all depended on the dark-haired, dark-eyed spitfire who had gotten under his skin in a very short amount of time.

He really should just jump into the rental car once it was delivered and roll out of this town. However, Manning Grove was the last spot on his list to gather info. He relied on what Frankie might tell him to take his next step.

What he needed to know was, where she met him. He knew she ended up in a hospital in Lancaster County, but that didn't mean that was where the two met.

Once he had that info, he could head in that direction and do a little more sniffing around.

In the meantime, he would wait for the car to arrive and maybe catch a nap. That nap being enhanced with a little fantasizing about one Sucely Hernandez aka Frankie Reyes.

He had to hand it to her, it was smart to change her name. But he wasn't so sure if it was smart to return to her hometown. Though, Taz probably didn't know or care about her history. He probably wasn't the kind of guy who wanted to know where she was born or where she graduated high school, or even what her hopes and dreams were.

For some strange reason, Hunter wanted to know all of that about Frankie, even though he'd only known her for a few hours.

Taz knew her long enough to get down her pants and knock her up, but he hadn't given a fuck about her. If he had, he wouldn't have done what he'd done. Even if the man didn't want to be responsible for a child, he didn't need to go about it the way he had.

Enough about that fuckwad Taz. Hunter glanced at the old clock radio—one which the plastic tiled numbers actually flipped in a circle—surprised it still worked. If it was accurate, he still had an hour and a half before the rental car company dropped off his temporary ride.

He could do a lot in an hour and a half. While he should be on his laptop doing more research, the place didn't have Wi-Fi and he'd have to use his cell as a hot spot. And being in the valley where he was, his cell phone coverage was barely good enough to make phone calls, forget data coverage.

Which meant there was only one thing left to do...

Strip the bed of its worn-out, thin bedspread and settle onto the hopefully clean sheets to pull one off.

All he had to do was replay Frankie attempting to start her lawnmower on a constant loop in his head.

Was it wrong? Probably.

Would that stop him? Probably not.

The only ones who would know would be him and his fist. And his fist wouldn't be talking.

He set his cell phone on the old scratched up nightstand, then leaned over with a groan to unlace his boots. Once he had them pulled off, he lined them neatly next to the bed, tucked his socks inside, got to his feet and unbuckled his belt, unhooked his waistband holster and placed his Sig next to his cell phone. After yanking off his T-shirt and dropping his pants, he tossed them to the other side of the bed and sat on the edge of the mattress to unstrap the knife sheath he had wrapped around his calf. He put that next to the bed within reach, too.

He got up to dig into his duffel bag, took out his toiletry kit and searched for something to use as lube. Nothing.

Fuck. He would just have to dry fist it.

Once he got his rental, he would pick up lube somewhere because if he stayed in this town for any length of time, he would need a lot of it. Especially if he was dealing with Frankie.

Most motels had at least a little bottle of lotion. Not this dump. He wondered if she picked this flea bag motel for a reason since it couldn't be the only place to stay in town.

On tomorrow's agenda: Find lube and a better place to stay.

On the immediate agenda: work out some tension.

As he settled on the bed, he leaned back against the headboard, making it creak loudly as he put his weight on it. Then he shoved his boxers down just enough to tuck them under his balls, gave them a slight squeeze, and closed his eyes.

Fuck yeah.

He hit the replay button over and over of Frankie's tits as she bent over and then yanked the starter cord of the mower.

Once. Twice. Three times.

The faster she pulled, the faster he pulled.

His balls got tight, the pressure built, his hips jerked and...

Yeah, he was glad he took off his shirt.

He opened his eyes to see the mess he made all over his stomach and up his chest.

Now he only had one hour, twenty-nine minutes and thirty seconds left until his car was delivered.

Fuck.

He hated not having a vehicle. He hated being stranded. But if it got to be too much, he could hoof it somewhere. Being right outside of town, it couldn't be too far to get to any kind of civilization. Hell, he'd marched for miles in the Army carrying a heavy rucksack. He wasn't opposed to using his two feet.

He glanced down at his gut. Once he cleaned up his DNA spill, that was.

He eyed the socks he'd tucked in his boots. No. He had no access to a washing machine, and he didn't feel like packing stiff socks back into his duffel. He leaned over and jerked open the drawer of the nightstand. It didn't budge.

He tried again, yanking harder. The knob almost ripped off in his hand but the drawer broke free and he glanced inside.

A bible.

Great, he wasn't in the mood to rip out pages of the "good book" to clean up his cum.

But, thank fuck, in the back of the drawer was a box of generic tissues. They were probably from 1986 and about as soft as sandpaper, but they'd do to wipe up the load enough so he could wash off the remainder in bathroom.

He pulled one, two...

Fuck. Two tissues left. They would have to do as long as they didn't disintegrate.

He scooped up the thick streams, threw the tissues onto the nightstand, and pushed to his feet, yanking his boxers back up and adjusting everything back into place.

In the bathroom, he cleaned his stomach off with a washcloth that, if possible, was rougher than the tissues and, with a yawn, headed back out into the maybe twelve by twelve room.

A cell. Not much bigger than a fucking cell.

He pushed that thought out of his head.

He didn't need those wood-paneled walls closing in on him.

He didn't need a full-blown panic attack. He needed to get dressed and head outside until it passed.

But before he could tug on his clothes, a knock at the door filled the tight space.

His eyebrows dropped low as he glanced at the old clock radio again.

Had the rental company arrived early? Impossible. They would've had to drive at warp speed.

He snagged his Sig off the nightstand and in two steps had his eye pressed to the peephole. His heart flipped because the subject of his jerkoff was standing on the other side of the fucking door.

Fuck!

He blew out a breath and held his gun to the small of his back. With one hand, he slid open the joke of a security chain and unlocked the door before opening it only enough to see her and give her a view of only a sliver of him.

She held something in front of her like a shield. A plastic container.

His gaze slid back up from her hands, slowly over her chest, then up to her face. Well, he didn't feel so bad now, she was staring at his chest, too.

Or what she could see of it.

Hell, if she wanted to eye him up, he wasn't going to discourage her. He opened the door wider to give her that chance. "Thought you were getting your son pizza."

"I did." Her dark eyes lifted and met his.

He cocked a brow.

He noticed she mentally shook herself before saying, "I dropped it off at my mom's and felt bad about attacking you, so I brought this for you. I figured you might be hungry and there aren't any restaurants nearby." She shoved the container into his bare chest.

He didn't grab it because he still had one hand gripping the door and one on his gun. And, more importantly, if he accepted it, she might turn around and leave.

He stepped back and opened the door even wider, jerking his chin toward the interior.

Her gaze shifted to over his shoulder, then back to him.

She was unsure.

No shit, Sherlock. Of course, she would be. He was still a stranger, something he wanted to change, and she'd be alone with him, a man who was only wearing boxers, in his fucking motel room.

Not to mention, he just shot a load with her in his mind's eye.

But he took a chance and told her to "come in," anyway. And, fuck him, she tentatively stepped inside.

He quickly closed the door, leaving the chain hanging and only twisting the lock.

She surveyed the tiny room. "I didn't realize it was such a dump."

Sure, she didn't.

He moved back to the nightstand, putting down his Sig. Her eyes followed his motion and landed on his gun and knife, then slid to...

Fuck! The sticky wad of tissues next to them.

He quickly stepped in front of the nightstand to block her view, reached behind himself as stealth as possible and snagged the tissues within his fingers. He tried not to make a face when they squished in his hand.

That had been one hell of a monster load.

Now he only needed to discreetly get rid of the evidence. Easier said than done.

Leaning back slightly, his fingers found the edge of the cockeyed drawer so he could slide it open just enough to drop the tissues in and work it closed. Of course, none of that was done silently. Fuck no. The scraping of the wooden drawer had sounded a thousand times louder in the small room than it should've.

Did her lips twitch?

Yep, she was fighting back her amusement. Until her gaze dropped, and the slight curl of her mouth flattened out.

His lungs emptied of air as she studied the puckered scar on the lower left of his stomach, just above the waistband of his boxers. Then her gaze dropped even lower to the matching one on his right thigh.

When it lifted, she stared at his dog tags.

He cleared his throat to catch her attention.

It worked. She unfroze herself and held out the container again. "It's still warm." When he didn't take it from her, she tilted her head. "It's just some leftovers I reheated."

She brought him food. As a peace offering? Or was she here to poison him? "What is it?"

"Stuffed peppers. Believe it or not, one of Leo's favorites."

"You made it?"

She nodded. "I grow my own peppers, too."

Oh great, now he had a picture in his head of her bending over in some veggie garden wearing that fucking bikini top. He cleared his throat. "Kid's got good taste."

Mentioning her son made her lips curl slightly again. "I'm lucky he's not a picky eater. But he still loves his pizza, hot dogs and mac and cheese."

"Can't blame him there." He finally took the container. "I don't have any utensils."

She reached behind her and produced a set of plasticware she must have tucked into the back pocket of her shorts.

He took them, sat on the edge of the bed, and popped open the lid. He didn't have to lift the container to his nose, his mouth watered and his stomach growled from the unbelievable smell wafting up.

If it tasted as good as it smelled...

He lifted his gaze to the woman who stood between him and the door with an unsure look on her face.

If she tasted as good as she looked...

He closed his eyes for a moment, willing his blood not to rush south again.

"You don't like stuffed peppers?"

He fucking loved stuffed peppers. The spicier the better. And they smelled as if they might burn not only his lips but his stomach lining.

"I added an extra kick to yours. I keep Leo's a bit bland."

He wondered how much spice she liked.

Jesus. He shook himself mentally. "You just gonna stand there?" he asked more roughly than he meant to. At least his voice didn't break like a fucking teenage boy crushing on some busty cheerleader.

Her eyes widened. "No, I'll leave..."

His next words stopped her. "No, I meant you can have a seat."

She glanced around the room. There wasn't one fucking chair in that room. That was because there was no space for one. The room was fit for a hamster.

"I'm not so sure that's a good idea."

"It's a good idea," he confirmed, then used the plastic fork and knife to cut into a red pepper and made sure he got a good chunk of the filling before shoving it into his mouth.

Damn. This woman could cook. And, fuck yes, it was spicy as hell. It was perfect. His favorite foods were ones that burned on the way in and then burned again on the way out.

As he chewed, he watched her take a step closer to the bed. "Sit," he said around his mouthful, trying not to pant from not only the heat of the food but of the woman in front of him.

She probably wasn't one to take orders, so he was surprised when she perched on the edge of the bed next to him.

"You eat?"

She shook her head, her long, dark hair sweeping over her bare shoulders. She was now wearing a snug pink camisole-type thingy that clung to those tits he didn't think he'd ever forget and a navy pair of linen shorts that were short enough to give him a generous eyeful of her thighs. "Not yet. I'll grab something when—"

He cut off another piece of pepper and lifted it to her lips, cutting off her words. She stared at the fork for a second, then him for another, before opening her mouth. Her luscious mouth closed around the bite of food, and he slipped the fork from her lips so she could chew.

"Best stuffed peppers I ever had," he murmured, watching her mouth move. When she swallowed, he couldn't pull his eyes from her delicate throat.

He would like to see it arched with her head thrown back on his pillow. He would love to see the feminine lines of her throat vibrate when she screamed during an orgasm. He would love to hear his name on her lips as he buried his face between her thighs.

But not here. Not in this dump.

"While I appreciate you bringing me this, I told you to sleep on your decision."

She licked her lips and he had a hard time dragging his gaze away and back to the contents of the container.

"I didn't need a night to sleep on it. I only had to see him."

Him?

It hit Hunter who she was talking about when she continued. "His innocent face, his smile. Hearing his

laughter and his bossy little three-year-old self. I realized..."
Her breath hitched. "I realized I can't risk losing him. I
would die if I did. You're right. He's my everything. He's my
heart, he's the blood in my veins. I'm willing to help you in
any way I can."

He placed the fork into the container and considered
what she said. "He's your son's father." Taz might not be a
real father to Leo, but she had to be sure.

"He's no father. No real father would want to kill their
unborn child by killing that child's mother."

Hunter agreed. However, this talk of Taz was making
him lose his appetite.

"You're not hungry?" she asked.

He dropped his gaze to his half-eaten food and unlocked
his jaws. "I'm full," he lied.

"A man like you eats more than that."

A man like you.

He grunted. She knew nothing about a man like him.

"I pay my debts. Just tell me what I need to do."

What she needed to do was let him enjoy the rest of the
meal she brought him before talking business. He wouldn't
want to let what she so thoughtfully made him go to waste.
Leftovers or not. Appetite or no appetite.

He never had stuffed peppers this good and probably
wouldn't again.

He shoveled in the rest of the meal, popped the lid back
on and handed her the container. She accepted it and
gripped it in her lap. He wanted to take the container back,
throw it across the room and smooth out her clenched
fingers.

Instead, he curled his into fists to avoid reaching out to
her. "For starters, tell me where you met Taz."

"A bar called The Boneyard outside the city of
Lancaster."

The Boneyard. "You hung out there?"

She shook her head. "I worked there. I mostly served drinks and food so I could make tips. Sometimes I filled in behind the bar if my boss was short a bartender. I occasionally worked in the kitchen when he was short a line cook. I took all the overtime I could get. There were nights I stayed until the early hours to mop the floors and wipe down tables to make ends meet."

He was right about her. She was a survivor. Someone not afraid of hard work. She did what she had to do to make ends meet and now take care of and protect her son.

"Taz was a customer?"

"Yes. He showed up one day and became a regular. He was in there almost every night. He always sat in my section, tipped me well, told me jokes, anything to keep me at his table."

"He was charming."

She stared across the short expanse of room toward the door, saying flatly, "Until he wasn't."

The man tried to kill her, snuff out her light. For what? Because she accidentally became pregnant?

Taz also bore some responsibility for that.

"Some men are like that, *loquilla*, they work hard to get a woman to trust them, gain their interest. But their true colors don't come out until they have that woman hook, line and sinker." He hadn't meant to call her that nickname again, but it slipped out. He didn't mean anything bad by it and he hoped she didn't take it as such. He needed her to cooperate, not storm out pissed.

But it wasn't anger that fueled her next words, it was regret. "You mean crazy fools like me."

"It can happen to anyone. Some people are great liars. Slick. They have skills. He never wore his colors?"

"The Boneyard didn't allow colors. The owner kept a sign out front stating that colors weren't allowed. So, I had no idea he was part of a biker gang until, like I told you, I saw his tattoos, but even then, he said he'd parted ways with them."

"Normally, I'd correct that misconception, but the Shadow Warriors were no better than a fucking gang. They were the type of club that did nothing positive."

"Were?"

"Yeah, the club is defunct now." But was it really? If Taz was still wearing his SWMC cut on his back, then the club was still living and breathing. And it could rise again with just one bad seed.

They needed to make sure that seed didn't take root anywhere and flourish.

"I might go to hell for this, but it'll be worth it. I'll do whatever you need me to do so you can do whatever you need to do. This way Taz is no longer a threat to me or my son. I never want that man to touch Leo with his darkness. My son has a light inside him that I will do *anything* in my power to keep burning brightly."

Hunter stared at the woman next to him. Her knuckles had turned white from how hard she was gripping the plastic container. Her eyes held a determination, her face a fierce expression.

She was a fighter.

She probably fought that motherfucker when he was trying to beat her down, extinguish her own light, the one she passed on to her son. And Taz almost won that fight. But the war wasn't over yet.

Hunter was now leading the next charge. He had good men at his back and more reason than ever to find the man who went underground to avoid the total annihilation of his club.

Slade's brother or not, Hunter's sights were now more sharply focused on one Brandon Bussard.

Frankie and her son would never be completely safe with

Taz walking the Earth. That meant Hunter had to make sure that stopped happening.

But he had to find him first.

He needed to head to Lancaster, snoop around, hang out at The Boneyard and strike up some conversations with the employees and regulars there. Someone who might know something about the man who chased a woman and once he got her, he broke her.

Men like that didn't see women as human beings, they were objects. Disposable things which, when they were done with them, they threw away.

Or down a flight of steps.

Taz learned that behavior from Buzz. From watching his father beat the shit out of his mother. Something that became a normal occurrence.

Hunter's own father was a drunk.

And there had been plenty of times Danny Delgado, Sr., had struck his mother. Too many times than Hunter could count. Alcohol could be an evil mistress because whenever his father was sober, he thought the sun rose and set in Hunter's mother, Lena.

But it was the times when Senior hit the bottle that things got dark and ugly. And Hunter was too young and weak to do anything about it. Instead, his mother would just tell him to hide.

Hunter was no longer too young. Or too weak. Nor would he ever hide again from an abusive man. If Danny Sr. hadn't hung himself in that fucking cell, Hunter would've probably broken his neck for him. He also wouldn't have shed one fucking tear after doing it.

Not fucking one.

And he certainly wouldn't shed a fucking tear when he got his hands on Taz.

Chapter Seven

FRANKIE ROLLED over and rubbed the sleep from her eyes. She glanced at the time and cursed. Her mom had convinced her to let Leo spend the night at her place after they ate pizza and played Legos. He had actually fallen asleep and she didn't want to disturb him.

Frankie didn't argue. She actually looked forward to sleeping in. Have a rare morning where her little monkey didn't climb into bed with her and wake her up, demanding his breakfast. Oftentimes at five in the morning.

Occasionally she could convince Leo to curl up with her so she could sleep just a little bit longer. But only occasionally. Most times, she got up and made him breakfast. She probably spoiled him way too much, but she wouldn't have it any other way for her miracle kid.

However, this time it wasn't Leo interrupting her plans to sleep in this morning. No. Someone was banging on what sounded like the front door at seven a.m.

Seven. Fucking. A. M.

She tossed the covers back and with another curse, she tucked her breasts back into the tank top she wore to bed, since at least one always managed to escape during the night. She hiked up her pajama shorts and headed downstairs.

Each step down the stairs, as well as each pound on the door, got her blood boiling even faster. She was going to kill whoever it was.

There was no way it was her mom delivering Leo back to her this morning. In fact, she said she'd drop Leo off at daycare, so Frankie didn't have to do it before work.

And she wasn't due at work until ten forty-five for the eleven to seven shift. So, whoever was at her front door was already fucking up her day.

With a growl, she twisted the deadbolt and yanked open the door.

Then stopped breathing.

Light brown eyes narrowed on her with irritation. "You didn't even fucking ask who it was or check your peephole before you opened the door, did you?" Then the man on her stoop made the shape of a "gun" using his hand, pointed it at her and said, "Boom. You're fucking dead."

Air rushed back into her lungs as she sucked in a sharp breath and slammed the door shut in his face.

The nerve of that fucker!

As she stared at the front door, she realized she'd better lock it. As she reached to do just that, the front door swung open and his big body bumped hers, knocking her off balance. Before she could catch herself, he had the door slammed shut, locked, and her pinned against the wall by her neck.

Shit. The man could move fast.

His eyes hit hers. "And now, the person who just broke into your house because you had a hissy fit about being woken up is going to rape you and leave you for dead."

Her eyes widened at his words. *What?*

The fingers he had wrapped around her throat loosened and he dropped his hand, stepping back, shaking his head.

"Stupid, Frankie, completely fucking stupid. You had no idea who was out there and flung open the door ready to give me a piece of your mind. You once again acted irrationally before you thought rationally. You not only risked your life, but your son's."

Shit. He was right.

The blood drained from her face before rushing back into her cheeks as she became aware of the man standing before her.

Like... completely aware.

Very aware.

Super aware.

Holy shit.

She swallowed the saliva that had pooled in her mouth in an attempt not to choke.

She thought he was freaking hot yesterday in his motel room when he only wore boxers.

His naturally darker skin, his gold-flecked brown eyes, his... *muscles*... The large black tribal tattoo that covered his left arm, left side, and crawled up over his shoulder. His dog tags. She didn't think the man had an ounce of fat on him, unlike her, who had plenty to spare.

But his boxers had been loose enough to hide things. What he wore now did not.

The silky black fabric of the shorts he wore—and she hadn't seen shorts that short on a man in maybe... *never*— clung to things that might be considered obscene out in public. Furthermore, those shorts appeared damp and even more clingy than normal. So, they hid... *nothing.*

Almost *nothing* was left to her imagination.

He didn't wear a shirt this morning, either. Maybe he had something against shirts. Or pants. Or...

Hell, she wasn't complaining.

His caramel-colored skin shone with what she could only assume was sweat because some beads were gathered on his forehead, his hair was damp at the sides, and he smelled... hot and metallic, like he'd been exerting himself.

Besides those little shorts, he only wore a pair of short athletic socks and sneakers.

"Did you run here?" she managed to squeak out.

His forehead crinkled and he shook his head again. "We're not done having a discussion about how you opened the door."

"Got it. Opening the door without knowing who is on the other side equals bad. Okay, that conversation is over. Did you run here?"

Of course, he did. Was it wrong that she wanted to lick the drop of sweat now sliding down his temple? Or taste the salt on his damp skin around his small, dark tightly-beaded nipples?

Yes, Frankie, that's wrong. Wrong, wrong, wrong.

Maybe he wouldn't mind, though?

She could ask.

She closed her eyes and tried to rein in her wildly spinning thoughts.

"You okay?"

She opened one eye. Yep, he was really in her house, wearing just... whatever he was wearing, and she wouldn't mind having him for breakfast.

She sucked in a long breath through her nose.

She wasn't going to make that mistake again. Sleeping with some "bad boy." *That was a hard-learned lesson, Frankie. Don't make that mistake again.*

"You need to sit down?" he asked, concern coloring his tone.

She popped open her other eye. She probably should sit down since she was feeling a bit light-headed. "Why are you here?" She winced when that question came out way too breathless.

"Been thinking about how you can pay me back. I'll take a few meals as partial payment."

"You're here for breakfast?" she squeaked in surprise.

"If you make breakfast like you did stuffed peppers, then yeah."

"Now?"

His eyes narrowed. "It's the morning, so yeah."

"You woke me up."

He glanced at his black—*of course*—watch. "It's seven."

"Barely."

"Kid's probably up already."

"Leo's not here."

His head lifted, his eyes slid to the side, landed back on her and then he pursed his lips as he looked at her.

He didn't just look at her, he *looked* at her.

Like suddenly his breakfast plans had changed.

She glanced down to make sure one of her wayward breasts hadn't escaped again. It hadn't.

Though, for some reason, they began to ache.

For his fingers, tongues and lips.

Down, Frankie, down.

But the way he was staring at her wasn't helping. And it wasn't because he was hungry for pancakes.

However, he wasn't getting anything other than pancakes. Or eggs and toast. She opened her mouth to ask, "What are you hungry for?"

His eyes darkened and her gaze landed on his lips as they parted. She waited on bated breath for his answer.

And waited.

"Can I shower first?"

Huh? "Shower?"

"Yeah, your shower. I'm all sweaty."

Hold up. This man was going to be naked upstairs in *her* shower? He was practically naked now, but add a bit of soapy water and a whole bunch of him touching himself as he scrubbed...

She reached back and braced herself using the wall behind her.

"You sure you're okay?"

"I... I just need coffee."

He nodded. "So, shower?"

"Yes, please... I mean..." She cleared her throat and looked at something neutral, like his sneakers.

His finger tucked under her chin and he lifted her face. His lips were moving again. What happened to the sound?

"What?" she whispered.

"Towel?" He was wearing a crooked grin. That grin no longer made him look like a bad boy, it made him look... doable. Completely, utterly doable.

"In the hall closet."

With a nod, he dropped his hand and stepped back. "Frankie."

"Huh?"

"I'm gonna go take a shower. You go make breakfast. Make whatever you want. I'm sure it'll taste good."

I'm sure you would taste good, too. "Mmm hmm."

"Coffee, too, since you're having brain freeze."

No, it was more like her brain was overheating. Among other things. She needed to crank the temp lower on the A/C unit in the front window. Like to zero degrees.

"Frankie."

"Yeah?" she breathed.

"Breakfast."

She nodded and watched as he disappeared, bounding up the steps like he lived there.

Then she tried to remember the last time she cleaned the bathroom. Even if it had been a month, it had to be better than the bathroom at the motel. She had used it before leaving his room yesterday and she cringed when she did so. So, no matter what condition her bathroom was in, it probably looked like the Ritz compared to the one in his tiny room.

It took her a few seconds to unstick her feet, and she moved until she stood at the base of the stairs, staring up them.

She was torn. Go up and help him shower. Or fight that urge and go make breakfast.

She didn't need a new mess in her life.

She didn't need to get involved with a man who could possibly be dangerous.

Though, it wasn't like they were going to date or anything.

And Leo wasn't home.

She hadn't been with a man since Taz. And, to be honest, that experience was far from stellar.

She wondered how stellar Hunter was in bed.

She had a son to worry about now. It wasn't just her anymore.

He was right. She needed to think before she acted. Her sprinting up the stairs and tackling him like a starving bear that just woke up from hibernation wouldn't be her thinking "properly."

She'd already done enough in her life she regretted. She didn't want to add to the list willingly.

Therefore, she blew out a breath and when she heard the squeaky faucet in the shower turn on, she headed toward the kitchen to make breakfast.

———

She sensed him before she smelled him. Her body wash was mango scented and he had no choice but to use it since his only other option was Leo's bubble bath.

She continued to chop up the peppers much more carefully now, because, for some reason, her fingers had a slight shake to them. She had a small pile of red, green and yellow peppers, and even jalapeños on the cutting board to add to the mushrooms, diced homegrown tomatoes and shredded cheese she was going to use in the omelets she planned on making.

While he showered, she had also picked some fresh parsley and chives from her small collection of herb pots.

She had a full pot of coffee made, but her mug sat ignored at her elbow. Her stomach had been too busy doing flips to risk adding caffeine to it.

The whole time he was upstairs, she found it difficult to concentrate. Mostly because she had to keep talking herself out of joining him.

But she'd been strong enough to resist. She was proud she'd managed to talk herself out of it at least fifty times.

Now, he stood in her kitchen.

She began to beat the eggs in the bowl with a fork and added a bit of salt and pepper. "Coffee's ready. Mugs are in the cabinet above the coffeemaker."

No answer. Had he left the kitchen?

She glanced over her shoulder and, once again, it felt like someone kicked her in the solar plexus.

Of course, he wouldn't have anything to change into. So, *of course*, he would only be wearing... *a... damn... towel*.

And, of course, it wasn't like she had anything to offer him to wear. He certainly wouldn't fit in a pair of Leo's Iron Man Underoos.

No, because between seeing him in those damp clingy shorts and now a damp clingy towel, she knew one hundred percent he could not fit.

She turned back to stare at the cutting board, heat flickering at her center, her nipples pebbling painfully. Her body a complete traitor.

She should've run up those fucking stairs.

"You're doing this on purpose," she muttered under her breath.

"Doing what?"

She jumped because she didn't think he'd be able to hear her. When he asked that question, his warm breath had slid over her skin, making her shiver. He was right behind her.

Right.

Behind.

Her.

His heat beat against her back, even though they weren't even touching.

"What am I doing?" he asked so softly and so close to her ear, she almost melted into a puddle at his feet.

Tempting me, that's what you're doing. And you know it.

Think before you act, Frankie. Think!

"Sorry for only wearing a towel to breakfast, but my shorts are still sweaty, and I didn't want to put them back on until they dry." His voice was deep, low, masculine.

He wasn't sorry.

But then... neither was she.

She gripped the edge of the counter to keep herself from turning around. Because if she did, they would be toe to toe.

Chest to chest.

Skin to skin.

Tucking her bottom lip between her teeth and biting down hard, she stifled a groan.

She was stupid to let him stay for breakfast.

But she owed him. She owed him big time. Not just for damaging his vehicle, but because he might remove any threat of Taz from her and Leo's life.

And that right there was priceless.

She would do almost *anything* for that.

His arm brushed against her as he reached for her mug. "Do you want me to heat up your coffee?"

"No," she managed to say, still staring at the wood cutting board.

She warred with herself. This thinking before acting shit was for the birds.

"No? You like your coffee cold?"

"No," she murmured again.

Okay, she *thought* about it and now it was time to *act*.

"No," she said again and turned. "No point in heating it up. It'll only get cold again."

As his brows furrowed and he opened his mouth—probably to ask what the fuck she was talking about—she surged forward the few inches separating them. She grabbed his face and closed her eyes just as she caught his surprised expression. And then smothered his "Frankie" with her mouth against his.

He fell back a half-step, but she went with him, sealing their lips together more firmly, sweeping her tongue into his mouth. Letting her left hand slip from his cheek to his warm, hairless chest. Her right hand slid from his other cheek, down his throat and she wrapped her fingers around the back of his neck, keeping him right where she wanted him.

It seeped into her brain that he wasn't kissing her back, he wasn't touching her, his arms hung by his sides, his mouth remained motionless.

But with her palm pressed to his chest, she could feel his thundering heartbeat and his quickness of breath.

She stilled, then stepped back, heat climbing into her face. "I'm sorry... I... It's been... You..."

Nothing she could say would make it better. She just molested the man in her kitchen. She couldn't look him in the eye, so she stared at his chest instead until she realized that wasn't a good idea, either.

She began to move away but he snagged her wrist and pulled her back until she was standing in front of him, her ass pressed against the counter.

"I don't want you to pay me back this way. I won't accept sex as payment."

What? Her mouth opened, and her breath hissed out. Is that what he thought?

"That wasn't my intent," she whispered. "I would never sell myself like that. I would rather work two jobs to pay you back before doing something of that nature."

He tucked a hand along her jawline, his fingers sliding into her hair. "I just didn't want you to feel obligated."

"This has nothing to do with obligations." It had to do with silky shorts, and damp towels, defined muscles, a large tribal tattoo, lips she wanted to taste, a deep voice she wanted whispering words into her ear, and light brown eyes that didn't miss a thing. All of that and more which made her feel things she hadn't felt in a long, long time.

One of his dark eyebrows rose. "No?"

She shook her head, staring into those eyes which seemed capable of swallowing her whole.

Her tongue swept along her bottom lip and his eyes followed the movement.

"I only came here for breakfast. I swear."

She believed him because he had no idea Leo wouldn't be home.

But the point was, Leo wasn't home, and they were two adults standing in her kitchen and he was only wearing a towel.

She was interested, so if he was... Would there be any harm?

Probably.

It probably would be a big mistake.

She had thought the same thing with Taz and look where it landed her. As a single mother who worried about her son's safety. She had to change her name to "hide" from the man she so stupidly got involved with because she didn't think there would be any harm in it.

"I should be making breakfast," she murmured, hoping that reminder would knock some sense into her.

"I said I liked spicy foods, *loquilla*, but it's not the only thing I enjoy spicy."

She should groan and roll her eyes at that, but she didn't. Instead, his words made the heat swirl through her even faster.

He suddenly released her and stepped back. "But breakfast *is* the most important meal of the day."

She blinked.

He grinned and tipped his head to concentrate on re-securing the knot holding his towel together.

Frankie wasn't sure what happened next.

If anyone had been watching, they might have said she rushed him and knocked him backwards. And they might have witnessed him grab her around the waist before they both landed hard on the floor with a grunt, his head narrowly missing the corner of a chair. Then Frankie could have scrambled to straddle his waist, which he didn't fight... not one bit... before she took his mouth again.

They just might have seen all of that.

However, this time they both groaned when their tongues tangled and clashed. Frankie kept hold of his face as Hunter held onto hers, neither wanting to break the kiss.

He tasted like toothpaste, and she vaguely wondered how or why he brushed his teeth.

But, at the moment, she really didn't care. What she did care about was that he was a great kisser. Every time she took control, he stole it back.

Every time she tried to pull away, to catch her breath, to pick her scattered brain cells off the floor, he held on tighter.

Yes, there was no doubt he wanted what she did.

Unfortunately, that made keeping her head on straight and thinking rationally before she did something stupid even more difficult.

And the last thing she wanted was to become the single mother of *two* children.

Even though she and Taz had used protection, it obviously hadn't been a hundred percent reliable. Which, in the end, got her in the predicament she was currently in...

Straddling a practically naked man, who she only met the day before, on the floor of her fucking kitchen.

The man who was only there to help clean up her mess from another man.

Fuck. Fuck. Fuck.

But, *dammit*, she couldn't stop kissing him. And now his hands where sliding up her bare thighs and burrowing into her PJ shorts. She did a quick mental check on when the last time she had done a little landscaping down there and couldn't remember.

She only hoped his fingers didn't become lost in a forest.

But, hey, it had been a long time since anyone had seen that part of her besides her gynecologist. So, whatever. He could deal with it. If he couldn't, he could eat his breakfast elsewhere.

Hopefully, he was a man who didn't mind fighting his way through a little overgrowth. Not to mention, she hadn't had a chance to shower or brush her teeth yet.

Since he was still kissing her, she took that as a good sign.

Maybe he was desperate like her and hadn't gotten any in a while. Though, as she pictured him in those shorts, she couldn't imagine he didn't have women throwing themselves at him.

Like she had.

And was still doing.

She felt no shame because—

Yes, because he was now drawing a finger through her wetness. She shifted forward, encouraging him to do more, all still without breaking the kiss. Because if he released her mouth, she was going to start begging him to take her right there on the worn linoleum floor of her tiny kitchen and it would not be pretty.

He pulled back just enough to say against her lips, "Fuck, Frankie, you normally get this wet?"

Fuck no! But then, I've never tackled a man who looked like you.

In reality, she wasn't sure how to answer that question. Sex had been the last thing on her mind for the past few years as she struggled to raise her son by herself.

At least, until Hunter showed up at her door this morning. Now, sex was all she could think about.

Especially once he slipped two fingers inside of her. And then his thumb did some wicked things to her clit.

His other hand had slid under her pajama shorts and now clutched her ass. Each fingertip dug into her flesh like he was clinging for dear life.

Maybe he was.

She planted her palms on his chest and pushed herself upright, her knees on the floor taking most of her weight.

Oh, wait. She forgot something...

With a grin, she leaned over again and sucked one of his small dark nipples into her mouth, causing his hips to surge upward. She finished with a scrape of her teeth over the tiny hard tip and then did the same to the other one.

Fuck yes, this was the breakfast of champions.

She face-planted into his chest as his long fingers slid in and out, drawing even more wetness from her. His chest rumbled when he groaned, "Fuck, Frankie."

She assumed that was a good, "Fuck, Frankie." But he needed to lose the comma so it became "fuck Frankie" and soon. They needed to move this along.

Even with her body like rubber, she managed to sit up

again. His eyes were dark and glued to her, so she grabbed the hem of her tank top and yanked it over her head, tossing it behind her.

"Fuck, Frankie," he murmured again, his gaze dropping to her breasts.

Was that all he could say?

"Yes, please," she answered.

His brown eyes flicked up to hers, a frown creasing his forehead. "I'm not prepared."

She peered over her shoulder to the towel that was now cockeyed and tented.

Um, yes, he was.

Then it hit her. *Oh fuck.*

Unless he normally tucked one into his sneaker when he went for a run, he had no condom.

Oh fuckity fuck. She did a quick mental inventory of her nightstand drawer. Of her linen closet. Of the medicine cabinet.

Of course, she had no fucking condoms! What was the point of them if you weren't having sex? Use them as expensive water balloons?

She face-planted again onto his chest and bit back a frustrated scream.

Then his body shook beneath her.

She lifted her head just enough to see his face. "This isn't funny."

"You didn't think before you acted... *again.*"

"Shut up," she muttered. "You had the same idea."

"Yeah, but I'd expect you would be prepared. It's your house."

She hissed, "I don't have sex."

He hesitated before asking, "Never?"

"Not with another human being and not since Leo was conceived."

His fingers stopped working their magic, which made

her want to scream again. "There are ways around our predicament."

"Yes, but that's like eating apple pie without the vanilla ice cream."

"I eat apple pie without the ice cream," he said in a serious tone.

She stared at him. "You don't look like you eat any pie."

"I eat pie," he confirmed, the lines around his eyes crinkling more.

That was encouraging because she had a pie he could eat. "As you can tell, I eat the pie *and* the ice cream."

"And I like women who like to eat. I want a woman's thighs to be soft when I'm lying between them. I don't want them to be able to break me in two."

"Mine are definitely soft."

"I know. They're hugging my waist." He slipped his hands from her PJ bottoms and squeezed her upper thighs. "I also don't like when a woman shaves her pussy bare."

"You're safe there."

His lips twitched. "I figured that out on my own."

She pressed a finger to his lips, quieting him. "Let's not go there. I just said I haven't had sex in forever."

"And I would love to break that streak for you, but not without protection."

Damn. "You could borrow my car and hit the Old Towne Pharmacy," she suggested.

"That I could, though they might not appreciate me shopping in a towel."

"They just might. Depends who's at the register. You might even get a discount."

"Or I could borrow your car, go back to the Bates Motel, change into clean clothes, grab a condom and hope one of the Bryson Bobbsey twins doesn't pull me over when I speed back over here."

"You have condoms in your motel room?"

"Of course."

"More than one?"

"Yeah."

"And you're only bringing back one?"

His face split into a smile. Then he hooked his leg around her hip and knocked her off balance, somehow rolling them—without crashing into the table—until he was on top. He planted his palms on the floor on either side of her head and dropped his face until they were almost nose to nose. "How many do you need?"

Somehow, someway, the knot on his towel had given way and his erection was now settled at the crux of her thighs. This in no way helped her with thinking before she acted.

"How many do you have?"

"I haven't checked lately."

"Good answer."

He closed the gap between them, giving her a quick kiss and then he was up and on his feet. Like magic.

Or more like a routine from *Magic Mike.*

But without the towel, this was so, so, *sooooo* much better than the movie.

Holy shit.

She licked her dry lips. "How fast can you get there and back?"

"How fast can you shower, brush your teeth and do a little bushwhacking?"

She grinned.

He grinned.

He grabbed the towel and was gone.

Chapter Eight

AFTER LOCKING THE DOOR, he hung her house and car keys on the hook by the front door and turned to stare up the narrow steps.

He hated this house. He almost had a panic attack in her tiny bathroom earlier. The single bathroom in the house only had space for a sink, the toilet and a combo shower and tub. How she tended to her son in that bathroom, he had no fucking clue.

They were about to have sex and, guaranteed, it would not be in that fucking shower. And he sure as hell hoped she had a bed larger than a twin-sized in a bedroom bigger than a closet.

He lived in a spacious studio-like condo in Shadow Valley and if he ever built a house, it would need to have an open floor plan like Mercy and Rissa's.

He could never live in a house like this.

But then, he wasn't moving in. He was just moving in on the woman who lived here.

He was only here to break the seal, then he could leave, head back to his motel and plot his next steps in finding Taz.

But the fantasies he had about Frankie before she

showed up at his room yesterday and again after she left were about to go three-dimensional and high definition. No fantasy, all reality.

"*Loquilla?*" he called up the steps. Was she ready and waiting for him?

Fuck, he hoped so. He was lucky he didn't crash her piece of shit car on the way to the motel or on the way back since he couldn't get the picture of her naked and writhing on her bed out of his head. Which made for very distracted driving.

He might have even run over a squirrel, but he didn't bother to slow down to check.

Rest in pieces, little buddy.

He came prepared this time, though. His Sig, his Buck tactical knife and six of what was left of the twelve-pack box of condoms he'd usually carried in his always-prepared duffel bag. However, no one but him needed to know where he'd used the other six.

That was classified information.

He couldn't imagine they'd need all six this morning. But he'd give it the old college try. He learned perseverance in the Army and was never one to give up until he reached his goal.

But a realistic goal would be two. *Maybe* three.

He grinned and called up the stairs again, "Frankie."

His mouth snapped shut as she appeared at the top of the steps, hands on hips, head tilted, her long dark brown hair draped over her shoulders and down her chest.

His eyes may have bugged out of his head because she wasn't just standing there looking a little miffed. She was standing there completely naked.

"Why are you wasting energy by yelling my name? You need to use that energy for other purposes."

As soon as the breath rushed back into his lungs, he asked, "Like what?"

She flung a hand out and her full tits bounced with the movement, catching his attention. "If you had actually come up the steps instead of standing at the bottom and yelling like a three-year-old, then you'd know. Did you bring the condoms?" Her eyes widened when he held up the strip of six. "Aren't you being a little optimistic?"

"You said you hadn't had sex in 'forever.' I figured you may want to make up for lost time." He'd gladly volunteer for that.

"Well then, why are you still down there and I'm up here?"

He pressed his lips together and bounded up the steps two at a time. He was lucky he didn't tackle her to the floor like she did to him earlier. But he wasn't in the mood to have their first round of sex in the narrow hallway or on the floor, which wasn't as clean as he kept his own place.

Instead, he went toe to toe with her and stared down into her upturned face. She was so fucking beautiful. Her dark eyes, her thick black lashes, her full lips...

"How are you not out of breath after doing that?"

He cupped her cheeks and said, "The only thing that's stealing my breath is you standing here naked, knowing that I'll soon get to taste and touch every part of you."

Who just said that? Was that him? He didn't say shit like that. But he was glad he did when her eyelids lowered and her lips parted.

"I assume your bedroom is to the right, since it doesn't have Marvel stickers all over the door."

"I like Marvel, too," she murmured. "There's something about a man in a tight costume——"

He swallowed the rest of her words when he took her mouth, sweeping his tongue through it, capturing her groan and keeping it for himself.

When he released it, he grabbed her shoulder to turn

her in the direction of her bedroom and slapped her ass. "Go."

Her head twisted to glare at him. "Go?"

"You heard me. Go." She opened her mouth, but he cut her off. "Look, we have six condoms. What time does your son get home?" He needed a plan of attack.

"I pick him up from daycare when I get off of work."

Work? Well, that might put a kink in his plans. "You work today?"

"Yes."

This was news. He glanced at his watch. "What time do you work?"

"I need to be there at ten forty-five."

That was an odd time. "Who fucking starts their work day at ten forty-five?"

"Someone who's a server at the only semi-fancy restaurant within a thirty-mile radius."

Fuck. It was now after eight.

"How long does it take you to get ready for work?" He saw his window of opportunity closing to use at least three of those condoms.

"About a half hour, give or take fifteen minutes."

What? "Fuck," he muttered.

"That's what we should be doing instead of standing out here in this hallway discussing how long we have until I have to leave for work."

He pointed toward her bedroom. "And I told you to 'go' and you had to sass me."

Her eyebrows shot up her forehead and her head jerked back. "I *sassed* you?"

There it was. That fire. "Yeah, you gave me and are still giving me that *loquilla* attitude."

"If you don't watch *your attitude*, you're going to be leaving with the same number of condoms as you walked in with."

"And your dry spell will continue," he reminded her.

She pursed her lips and tilted her head. "Good point," she muttered, then turned and strutted that curvy ass of hers right through her bedroom door. "Hurry up!" she called over her shoulder.

She might not want to encourage him to hurry anything. It had been a few weeks for him, and he was raring to go. He hadn't realized how long it had been until he found his condoms buried deep at the bottom of his duffel.

He had been slacking on finding female companionship since this search for Taz had been taking up most of his time, with working out at Shadow Valley Fitness the rest.

Good thing that was going to be corrected here this morning. If he stopped standing at the top of the steps like a dumb ass.

When he walked through the doorway, a hand reached out, grabbed the waistband of his jeans and hauled him inside as the door slammed shut behind him.

"About time," she said dragging him across the room toward the bed. He was relieved to see she had a decent-sized mattress. Maybe not a king, but a queen was good enough, and he was just glad it wasn't a single, otherwise he'd just be bending her over it.

He grabbed her wrist, planted his heels and jerked her to a halt. "Let's get one thing straight."

Her dark brown eyes hit his. "Just one?"

"Yeah, it's an important one. I said I like spicy, *loquilla*, but that does not mean domineering, remember that."

She smiled and lifted one shoulder. "Okay."

That was too easy.

"I'm fine with you driving the bus, but let's get on board," she encouraged him.

While she climbed onto the bed and propped herself up with the pillows, he moved to her dresser and unclipped his holster, setting it on the top. He kept his eyes on her, letting his gaze roam over every curve and peak of her. Her tits were big enough to fuck. Her ass was big enough to fuck. And so was her mouth.

And, *damn*, he didn't know where he wanted to start first. Once his head was free of his shirt, his eyes landed on her again and he knew exactly where he would start.

Her knees were cocked open, one hand cupped her own tit, and the other was sliding down her belly to...

Fuck. She had bushwhacked all right. The hair right above her pussy had been trimmed in the shape of an... arrow. Which pointed right at his first target.

"I have a good sense of direction, didn't need the visual, *loquilla*."

"Well, I figured just in case you got lost."

His hands went to his belt buckle. "I've got a pretty good compass."

"Men don't like to stop and ask for directions."

"I'm not most men."

"I hope not," she whispered as she watched him unzip his jeans to relieve the pressure his erection was causing.

"I never fed you breakfast," he heard as he bent over to unlace his boots and toe them off. "You must be hungry."

He grinned at the floor, then straightened and shoved his jeans down his legs and over his knife holster. "Starving." He stepped out of them, removed his Buck knife, putting it next to his Sig, then slipped out of his socks and boxers.

Her eyelids were heavy as she played with herself, watching him strip down. She liked what she saw.

Good. He liked what he saw, too. A flush crept from her chest into her cheeks. Her dark nipples were puckered, just waiting for his mouth. But they would have to wait.

He needed to follow the arrow first. His mouth watered at the thought of tasting her there. Of burying his tongue inside her before burying his cock.

Which he fisted once, twice, as he approached the bed,

his actions drawing her eyes. He tossed the strip of condoms by her side so they were within reach, planted his knee into the mattress and climbed onto the bed.

Then he dropped to his belly and buried his head between her thick thighs, tracing the tip of his tongue along both creases where those thighs met her pussy. Her nails dug into his shoulders painfully and he allowed it because he liked it.

He tipped his eyes up to hers when he ran the flat of his tongue up one plump, slick labia and then the other.

Fuck yes, this woman could get wet. She was probably ready for him now, but he didn't want to rush their first time.

Using the V of his fingers, he separated her and lightly blew on her clit. He grinned again when her hips jerked, and her nails dug even deeper into his shoulders. The slight pain kept him from losing it and just taking her like he really wanted to do. Kept him there in the moment.

The last time he had sex, it was a quick fuck in a bathroom stall in a bar in downtown Pittsburgh. The blonde was shallow, had big, fake tits that hardly jiggled and she probably only fucked him so he'd buy her drinks the rest of the night.

He didn't.

There was nothing fake about Frankie. No plastic surgery. Her hair didn't seem to be dyed. No fake eyelashes, no fake nails, those were all real. She probably couldn't afford to pamper herself.

But he liked what he saw. She didn't hide the curve of her belly and her tits jiggled and bounced when she moved. Her hips were wide, but her waist defined. But it was her ass and thighs he couldn't get enough of. The first time he took her, she would be on her back. The second time he would have her on her belly or her knees.

But this time... this time he wanted to watch her face, her reactions.

He wanted to study the arch of her throat, taste the tight beads of her nipples, lick along her pulse, kiss her lips, explore her mouth. Stare into those dark eyes when he buried himself deep and came.

He wanted it all.

She seemed to be a woman who would give it all. *If* she wanted to give it to you. If not, you were shit out of luck. She had two speeds... Go and stop.

Her head was tipped up and she looked a little annoyed. "Are you just going to breathe on me, or are you going to make me come?"

He lifted his head. "A little fucking impatient, are we?"

"Well, it's been over four years."

"Did he make you come?"

Her expression made it evident she wasn't expecting that question. And he wasn't sure why he asked it. Because, truth be told, he really didn't want to know.

"Occasionally."

He could live with that answer. "With me it won't be *occasionally*." Because, fuck it... *¿Quién es más macho?*

With a curl to the corner of her lips, she dropped her head back onto the pillow and said to the ceiling, "Good."

"Good," he murmured and flicked her clit with the tip of his tongue. Then he got to work.

———

FRANKIE'S BRAIN had stopped working. She couldn't think at all. All she could do was feel what he was doing to her. His mouth was latched onto one nipple and he was not gentle at all. It was almost painful.

Almost. But not quite to the point of telling him to stop.

"Yes," she hissed. No, she was encouraging him instead.

He had her wrists pinned above her head and he was powering deep. His hips like pistons as he pumped hard, fast, relentless.

Her eyes rolled back, and she cried out for the hundredth time when he adjusted the tilt of his hips *again*, making sure he couldn't take it any deeper.

Oh fuck, he couldn't.

Could he?

He needed to release her arms so she could grab his ass and see if it was possible. Every thrust pushed the air from her lungs, and as soon as she'd suck in another breath, he'd slam it right back out of her.

She was close to coming a third time. There was something about his hips. Whatever he was doing...

Fuck. Whatever he was doing, he needed to continue.

The twinge of pain he caused with his teeth and mouth only enhanced what those hips were doing. He was a powerhouse.

And he didn't treat her like she was some delicate flower. He gave her his all.

Because if this wasn't his "all" he might be able to do some damage.

With a last nip to her breast, he surged upward, taking her mouth again, forcing her lips open, taking control.

He swallowed every one of her gasps and she couldn't stop them from coming.

She only wished she could watch him move, his back, his ass, his thighs. Just imagining his muscles bunching as he drove hard and deep, took her to that point of no return.

And she didn't fight it. She let it happen. She broke her mouth free and rolled her head back as she cried out, pulsating around him, which drove him to pump even faster.

He finally released her wrists, but she couldn't move, she was only a boneless shell as he cupped one of her breasts and kneaded it, then twisted the nipple. His other hand wormed between them and found her overly sensitive clit to thumb it roughly. And suddenly, she was back in the game, digging her fingers into his ass, lifting her hips to meet him thrust for thrust, their damp cheeks glued together, his grunts filling her ear.

And, *Jesus*, if this man pulled a fourth climax from her...

Moments later he did just that, as he shoved his face into her neck and groaned, his body flexing and curling as he drove deep one last time.

After she began to come down from her orgasmic high, she closed her eyes and tried to wrangle her out-of-control breath, but she gave up on that and figured if she hyperventilated it was well worth it.

Especially when he left his face buried against her throat while his body relaxed, and he gave her some of his weight.

Not all of it, though, because he was bigger and built from solid muscle and while she was curvy, he still weighed a lot more than her.

Or, at least, she hoped he did.

Didn't matter. He hadn't been turned off by what he saw. When she stood at the top of the steps in all her glory, his eyes had become heated and hyper-focused, leaving no doubt he wanted her.

She was a single mother who'd pushed out a kid three years ago and still carried that extra baggage. She wasn't a gym bunny and never would be, and you wouldn't catch her going for a jog through town. No, instead you'd see her sneaking back into the kitchen at The Carriage House and standing next to the chef to taste his newest masterpiece as he explained to her how to make it.

She liked to eat, but she *loved* to cook. That had been her dream, to be a chef. She wanted to express herself through food, but never got that chance.

However, the man whose breath was starting to beat a

little slower against her damp skin seemed to enjoy her stuffed peppers yesterday.

He probably would have liked her omelet, too.

She was sure he liked what he got served instead better.

But Hunter was clearly athletic and had just spent a lot of energy making her lose her mind, so he was probably hungry.

As much as she wanted to feed him, she also didn't want to move. She liked right where they were.

It was one thing to have her wiggly son in her bed in the morning, it was quite another to have a man like Hunter nailing her to the mattress.

And nail her he did.

She smiled up at the ceiling.

She would be sore and possibly work her whole shift at The Carriage House bow-legged. But she'd manage.

She turned her head just enough to look at the nightstand. They still had five condoms left. Even with all what they did, they managed to only use one.

She wondered how long he would be in town...

"Frankie," he murmured against her skin.

"Hmm?"

"I need to get rid of the condom, but I'm liking where I'm at right now."

She was liking where he was at, too, but... "I was thinking about making you that omelet. Maybe I can run down and do that while you take care of business."

He lifted his head and glanced at her alarm clock. "How fast can you make an omelet?"

She did a half-shrug. "I had everything prepared. No more than fifteen minutes."

"That might give us time for one more round before you get ready for work."

She covered her mouth and coughed. "My throat is

suddenly scratchy, and I'm congested. I think I came down with the work flu."

He lifted his face from her neck, and she could see the gold flecks in his light brown eyes now that the sun had risen higher and was beaming through a gap in her curtains.

"Will that get you in trouble?"

"I hardly ever take off, even with having Leo. If the daycare can't take him, my mom steps in when she can."

He rolled off her, slipped the full condom off, tying it and tucking it into a tissue from her nightstand. Then he rolled back, facing her, his head propped in his hand. "Why do you call her your mom?"

Frankie let her gaze run down the line of his body, and it stopped at the first puckered scar. He most likely got shot while in the military, but she wondered about the circumstances.

It wasn't any of her business, just like her calling Diane "Mom" wasn't any of his. "Because she's my mom."

"She's not your birth mom. Camila Hernandez was murdered in Guatemala while her baby girl was left behind in the States."

Frankie pushed to a seat and stared down at him. "Thank you for killing my afterglow."

"It wasn't meant to kill it. I was just curious. Could do some digging myself, but I'd rather hear it from you."

"Why? Why do you need to know? This is just a," she waved her hand over the bed and over the two of them, "thing. You're leaving town soon, I'm sure. And I have a son who means the world to me. I don't bring random men home and don't plan on starting."

"I'm not some random man."

"No?"

He didn't answer her, instead he jackknifed up and off the bed, grabbed the tissue-wrapped condom and stalked naked out of the bedroom.

She sat there in bed, staring at the open doorway, wondering whether she should get dressed and make him breakfast, or tell him to leave.

But before she could decide, he was back, his jaw tight as he bent over to snag his boxers and pull them on. Then he started talking. "This is how it's going to go. You're going to call off sick from work, then haul your ass downstairs and make me breakfast. When we're done eating, you're going to clear off the table so I can fuck you over it. Then we're going to spend the rest of the day up here in your bed, so by the time your son needs to be picked up from daycare, you'll have to send someone else to pick him up as you won't be able to move. Then I'm leaving, spending the night in the roach motel and heading to Lancaster first thing in the morning. And I don't want to hear one fucking word about the fact that I'm bringing one of my... *coworkers*... up here to keep an eye on you while I search for Taz."

The whole time he was talking, she just stared at him as she waited for him to take a breath. And when he did, all she could ask was, "Is that right?"

"That's fucking right. By the time I leave here later, I will no longer be some random man in your bed and in your fucking pussy. Do we have that straight?"

She didn't think she had ever been speechless in her life. Not once. Even when Taz was taking out his temper on her. Not once had she been quiet, which was one of her problems.

But at that moment, her mouth hung open and she couldn't find any words.

Other than, "Okay."

Chapter Nine

HE WAS anxious to get back to Manning Grove. He had called Steel to come up and keep an eye on Frankie and her son while he was gone. Steel wasn't happy about it, but he did it. Hunter then met Walker in Lancaster and they spent three days searching for any sign of Taz or at least for a clue as to where he might have disappeared.

Lancaster was a bust; they didn't get shit.

They had talked to everyone who worked at Frankie's former employer, The Boneyard. They had a conversation with Frankie's old landlord. Also with the manager of the fleabag motel where Taz lived temporarily before landing behind bars.

He checked with Lancaster City PD, some local police departments surrounding the city and also the State Police in that area. Nothing. Besides his arrest for assaulting Frankie, he'd kept his nose clean while in that area. Not even a fucking parking ticket.

They also ran across a couple members of the Sons of Satan MC, a support club for the Pagans. Since that outlaw club was based out of Lancaster, he wouldn't put it past Taz to have tried to weasel his way into their midst.

They didn't know shit about any Tasmanian Devil. Nor were they open for any further discussion. But after staking out their clubhouse for two nights, no one who looked like Taz came or went.

The obvious conclusion was Taz was no longer in the area and probably left once he got released. His parole officer hadn't seen him either, which was why he had an open warrant for his arrest.

But Hunter wanted to find him before law enforcement did. If Taz ended up behind bars again due to breaking his parole, he, or any of the Shadows, would have a tough time getting access to the man.

They *could*, but it wouldn't be as easy as if Taz was free. Plus, if D's crew could make him disappear, then no one would be the wiser. Any death in lockup was investigated, even if it appeared to be suicide.

Here Hunter was already planning the motherfucker's demise, even though no one had talked to Slade and told him the details of his brother, or the situation involving the mother of his nephew. Hunter was leaving it to Diesel, who was oddly sitting on his hands.

His boss probably had a reason, but to ask the big guy what it was was futile. He'd probably grunt and hang up the phone, so Hunter didn't push it.

They'd deal with it when they had to deal with it. Right now, they still had to find the slippery fucker.

On his long trip back north, he stopped in Harrisburg to check on his baby at the dealership. She was in pieces as they worked on her, restoring her to her former beauty.

Now, if he was going to shed a tear over anything, that sight would've caused it.

But by the time he drove past the painted wood sign that read, "Welcome to Manning Grove," his irritation about the destruction Frankie caused had waned.

Lucky for her. Because his palm had itched to spank her

ass as he stood in the bay at the dealer's body shop while witnessing the damage all over again.

She'd probably fight him if he tried to take her over his knee, but that would be a challenge he'd welcome. Because the woman would never go down easy.

Which was why it surprised him to no fucking end Taz got away with abusing her. If anything, Hunter would have expected her to stick the biker between the ribs with a fucking kitchen knife in the middle of the night while the asshole was sleeping.

He never understood women and wasn't even going to try. It wasn't worth the headache.

But a sharp pain stabbed his temples when he pulled into Frankie's driveway and saw Steel's blacked-out custom Fat Boy parked in front of the garage.

Son of a bitch.

He was supposed to be keeping an eye on her, not making moves. That being said, Steel had a short fuse and Hunter couldn't imagine him tolerating Frankie's back-talking, act-first-think-later, hot-tempered attitude.

Nope, all that sass needed a man with a lot of patience. Hunter wasn't the most patient man himself, but after spending a day in bed with the woman, he might be willing to dig deep for a little extra to deal with her.

Because at the end of that day, minutes before Frankie's "mom" dropped off her son, Hunter had left with a grin and nothing but prunes left for his nuts. If he came one more time, it would've simply been a puff of smoke.

That night he'd gotten the best sleep he'd had in a long while. In fact, he'd even slept in the next morning and skipped his early morning run.

He was also surprised he hadn't lost ten pounds with all that cardio.

And, fuck him, he couldn't wait to do it again.

Her pussy was like hot silk, her mouth like a Dyson

vacuum, her tits and ass were perfect for all kinds of extracurricular activities.

And the woman hadn't said no to any of them.

"Fuck," he muttered into the quiet interior of his rental SUV. Then he adjusted his hard-on and thought back to his time trapped under a pile of rubble in Baghdad so the blood would recede from his dick.

But bringing that memory back to the surface made him scramble quickly from the interior of the vehicle. He didn't need to go into a full-blown panic attack due to being in an enclosed space.

As he approached the front door, it swung open and Steel filled the doorway wearing a snug, white wife-beater with an unfolded paper napkin tucked into the neckline.

Hunter's step stuttered as he took in his fellow Shadow, who was also wearing a shit-eating grin.

"What the fuck are you doing?" Hunter collected his composure and climbed the steps onto the porch.

That wide grin didn't even waiver. "Eating. The fucking bitch can cook."

Hunter stopped on the welcome mat, dropped his head and stared at his boots, trying not to take offense at Steel calling Frankie a bitch. He knew the man didn't mean it as an insult, but Hunter had a strong dislike for it.

"Brother, can see your panties just got in a wad, but get over it. You calling her *loquilla* isn't much better."

He raised his gaze. "She told you that?"

"Told me a lot of things."

Fuck. She probably ran her fucking mouth. "Like what?"

Steel's grin turned into a full-blown, smart-ass smile and he stepped back as he shrugged. "Said she had a hard time finding your dick and had to get out the magnifying glass and a pair of tweezers."

"Big enough to make you gag," Hunter muttered as he pushed past him and into the house.

"Then good thing I don't like sucking dick," Steel announced as he shut the front door and twisted the deadbolt.

"That's not what Brick told me," Hunter threw over his shoulder as he headed toward Frankie's kitchen.

He slammed on the brakes when he discovered not only Frankie stood at the counter in a pair of olive-green *short* shorts clinging to the bottom curves of her luscious ass, but she wore a bikini top, this time the color of the sun.

"What the f—" He swallowed his curse as his gaze landed on Leo sitting at the table in a booster seat, his curious dark brown eyes glued to him.

The kid had an elbow macaroni stuck to his cheek as he smiled at Hunter and said, "Hi," then waved a hand at him, which was covered in what looked like cheese.

"Hi," Hunter returned automatically.

"This sh— *stuff* is the fu— *freaking* best mac and cheese I ever ate," Steel said, now sitting at the same table as Frankie's son and shoving a forkful into his mouth.

Frankie turned around, giving *everyone* in the room a great view of her cleavage, as her gaze slid through Hunter to give Steel a warm smile. "I'm glad you're enjoying it." Her smile was gone when she finally turned her attention to Hunter. "Sit. I'll get you some dinner."

Sit. I'll get you some dinner? That was his welcome after busting his ass for three days searching for her abusive former lover *and* after he fucked her into oblivion the last time he saw her?

Fuck. That.

In two long strides, he had her hooked by the elbow and was tugging her toward the kitchen door that lead to her backyard. "Watch the kid," Hunter tossed over his shoulder at Steel and continued to "escort" a surprised Frankie out the back door, not waiting for an answer from the other man.

As soon as the door closed behind them, he pulled her across her postage-stamp-sized backyard and behind the not much larger garage.

"Problem?" she asked, her attitude already bubbling at the surface.

Right now, she wasn't the only one with an attitude.

He spun her until her back was to the garage wall and dropped his hands to his hips. He forced himself not to get in her face when he growled, "Yeah, I got a problem. First off, your kid has the courtesy to say hi and you don't?"

"He says hi to rocks in the yard and bloated roadkill along the berm."

He ignored that. "And second, why the fuck are you wearing that around Steel?"

"What?"

She was playing dumb, which was not helping his blood pressure. "That top." No, it couldn't even be called a top. It only covered her nipples. And even then, barely because he'd seen firsthand how large they were. Perfect for *his* damn mouth, not Steel's.

"Well, maybe you haven't noticed, it's blazing hot outside and I needed to water my garden."

His eyebrows shot up his head and he was surprised they didn't launch to the moon. "You were outside in that with your hose?" He wanted to close his eyes to fully appreciate that image.

But he couldn't because while his eyebrows had gone high, hers went low. "A hose is what you use to water. So, yes."

"With Steel here?"

"Yes, he played with Leo outside while I watered."

"I'll just bet he did."

Of course Steel was going to watch Frankie watering her garden with her tits barely contained in a couple scraps of fabric. Tits which were proportioned to her ass and thighs.

The only woman he'd met recently who might have bigger ones was Rissa. And all his teammates had a difficult time not having a full-blown conversation with them when she was in the room. The struggle was real, and the only reason why they succeeded was because Mercy saw *everything*.

"Since you're sharing your 'problems,' then so will I... One, I didn't need a babysitter. I certainly didn't ask for one. But, for some reason, I got one. Also, for some reason, us sleeping together *once,* mind you, suddenly made you the boss of me. I'm not sure how that works. Oh wait...," she lifted a finger, "it doesn't."

Hunter's head jerked back. "I'm not the boss of you." And they didn't sleep together only once. He lost count of how many times, it had just been all been packed into *one day*.

"Then stop acting like it. I've survived the last four years without you."

While that was true, there was a good reason why she'd been safe before now. "Frankie, Taz got eighteen months for what he did to you, then had twelve more tacked on. You think that made him happy? And he was released only a few months ago. If he's out to find you, it's going to take him longer than you think to do so. It took me a while and I know what the fuck I'm doing. Let me remind you, him doing extra time for bad behavior and then skipping out on his parole officer is a sign he didn't find Jesus while inside or that he's on the straight and narrow. He's gone ghost for a reason. My guess is to find you or avoid us."

Her head tilted and her hands planted on her hips. "Which you never explained why he would need to avoid you. You'd think he would want to reunite with his long-lost brother, not hide from the men trying to reunite them."

Hunter's mouth snapped shut.

She threw her hands up at his non-answer. "Right. Luckily, Steel decided I needed to know the truth."

Fucking Steel. Was his teammate trying to get in there? Well, he wasn't going to get in there. Fuck no. Hunter had already been in there and marked his territory.

He closed his eyes and bit back a curse. *What the fuck.*

He hardly knew the woman, had sex with her once... *Fuck*, for *one day*, and now he was claiming his territory?

No. Just fucking no.

He did not need the burden of a regular piece or her kid.

Who, he reminded himself, was Slade's *nephew*.

He opened his eyes and stared at the woman before him. But that didn't mean he didn't want to get in there again.

Maybe Steel could take Leo to the park.

Jesus. He shook his brain free of that selfish thought.

Suddenly, the strong woman who stood with her back to the garage crumpled before his eyes. Her face twisted seconds before she covered it with both hands.

Damn. He hadn't been ready for that.

"He can't find out about Leo," came muffled from between her fingers.

Like her face, something twisted deep inside him and he wrapped his arms around her shoulders, pulling her into him. She planted her face in his chest and he dug his fingers into her hair, which was up in a messy knot on top of her head, to hold her against him as a few sobs wracked her body.

He dropped his lips against her hair and whispered, "That's why I need to find him, Frankie. For your safety and Leo's, too."

She sounded too vulnerable for his liking when she asked, "Do you really think he's searching for me?"

Hunter wished he knew that answer. "I don't know. I don't want to risk it by waiting."

"Why would he care about finding me or the son he

didn't even want in the first place?" Her tears were turning into anger.

He needed to be completely honest with her. "If he is, and we don't know for sure, it's because he spent over two years in county due to you. And all that time he sat in a cell, probably in an overcrowded jail, blaming you every fucking second while in there and letting that anger fester."

"I didn't cause that, he did!"

"And you'd be correct, but he's the kind of guy who'd blame you for his problems."

She closed her mouth, pulled her head back and stared up at him for a moment. Her dark brown eyes, even though now fiery were still rimmed with tears. "I was always to blame for his ugly behavior."

"That's how abusive fucks manipulate the people they hurt. They push the fault onto the other party."

"He did that," she mumbled. "Every time."

Every time.

Fuck. That just confirmed it wasn't only the one time she ended up at the hospital. A muscled popped in his jaw. "How many was that?"

She didn't answer. The little he'd learned about her in the short amount of time he'd known her, he knew she wouldn't willingly stay with someone who knocked her around like that.

That was not Frankie.

She was not a woman who would flinch when a hand was lifted, she'd strike first. She was not a woman who would cower when a voice was raised, she'd yell back. And if she was cornered, she'd fight first and ask questions later.

Unfortunately, resistance usually wound a man up even more who couldn't contain his violent tendencies. Made that abuser more determined than ever to bring that woman to "heel." To strip her of her power. To dominate her.

To be king. God. And the Almighty.

Frankie would be the kind of woman who, if she didn't walk away, would end up dead because she'd never stop fighting back no matter how many times she was beaten down.

That fucking stubbornness was embedded deep within her soul.

Hunter saw it from the very start. It was her tits that first caught his attention. But it was her spirit that kept it.

And still held it.

But he understood her current fear. It wasn't just her anymore. She had a toddler who depended on her. A son she carried inside her for nine months even after almost losing him.

A child who was determined to be born.

Hunter didn't believe in miracles but if there ever was one, it was Leo.

"Frankie," he lifted his head and then tucked two fingers under her chin to raise her face. "How many times was it?"

No matter what her answer, his blood would rage. But he needed to hear it. He shouldn't need to, but he did.

"Just a couple other times," she said her voice a bit ragged, her eyes sliding away to avoid his. "Nothing like the last time, though."

"But you stayed with him." Again, this surprised him, knowing what he knew about her.

"I was making arrangements to leave town."

"You weren't even living together."

Her eyes met his. "No. But he knew where I lived. He'd show up in the middle of the night pounding on the door, causing my neighbors to complain to my landlord. I would let him in just to quiet him down."

"You should've called the cops."

Her jaw tightened. "I should've but I didn't. I didn't want to find myself out on the street. It was faster to let him in."

It was probably smart she didn't come home to Manning Grove until after he was arrested. Otherwise, he might have followed her.

"Frankie," he murmured.

"Yes?" Her dark brown eyes held his.

A sense of fierce protection swelled through his chest. "I'm gonna find him."

"I hope you do."

"And until we do, I'll make sure you're covered."

"What does that mean?"

"That means I'm not leaving Manning Grove until I know you're safe."

"Hunter," she began, but he cut her off.

"For as long as it takes," he assured her.

"You don't need to disrupt your life like that."

A temporary disruption in his life was better than a permanent one in hers. "I'm on a job. You'll just happen to benefit from that job."

He didn't mention the other benefit to that job, getting to know Frankie better both in and out of her bedroom.

And because of that, he wasn't going to stay at The Dumpster Inn. "You're still not done paying me for my Rover."

"I don't have any money." She snagged her bottom lip with her teeth. Again, a telling sign her finances were a struggle.

Using his thumb, he pulled her lip free. "I don't want your money."

Her relief was apparent. She could never play poker since she wore her emotions on her sleeve. "Then what do you want?"

You. "A place to stay while I'm in town and some kick-ass meals."

"That's it? Nothing else?"

"I want more but not for payment. What else I want from you, I want you to give willingly."

"Leo..."

"Yeah, I get that you wouldn't want some man just moving in temporarily. It might confuse him. But we'll think up an excuse." At three, he wasn't going to understand that Hunter was interested in his mother for more than a meal and conversation.

"And you can't sleep in my bed. He joins me most mornings. I know he's only three but..."

"Yeah, I get that, too. I can stay on the couch." Though, that would really fucking suck.

"Or in Leo's room and I can move him in with me."

Well, that just put a whole new kink in his plan. "What size is his bed?"

She smirked. "A twin. It has a waterproof mattress pad, in case you wet the bed." Her expression turned serious. "I appreciate what you're doing, Hunter, but you don't have to do this."

He knew he didn't have to, but he couldn't just walk away. Not yet. Not now. "I want to. I can't in good faith leave you to your own defenses."

"I can take care of us."

"I know you can, *loquilla*. But you don't have to do this alone."

"The police department is good around here."

"I'm sure they are. I met two members of them when you fucked up my Rover, remember? But how fast can they respond if Taz breaks into your house with the intent to do you harm?"

Her lip got caught between her teeth again as he watched her wheels spinning. Yep, she'd never be able to play poker with the Shadows or even Rissa, who was a fucking card shark.

Finally, she said after releasing the lip he wanted to

nibble on himself, "Well, hell. You know how to scare a girl."

"Think before you act," he reminded her. "Before you refuse my help, think about it."

"I'm not refusing your help, Hunter. I'm stubborn but I'm not stupid."

He didn't realize how tense he was until just then. Her accepting his help, her acceptance of him moving in temporarily shoved a huge weight off his shoulders.

He thought it would be a fight. He was surprised it wasn't. "It wasn't meant to scare you."

"Oh yes it was. You knew you'd get me to agree by reminding me how ugly Taz could be. I never want to be in that situation again. I don't want my son growing up with that kind of male influence in his life. You said Leo's my everything and you're right. But I want to give him everything, too. I may not be able to afford to give him all I'd like to, but I can raise him right. That's the best gift I could ever give him."

"You're a good mom, Frankie."

"I was raised by a great mom who I learned from."

Which reminded him... "We still need to have that discussion."

"But not now."

"Not tonight," Hunter agreed.

"Steel's probably wondering what happened to us," she murmured, staring at his mouth.

A mouth he wanted to touch all over her body. He wanted to relearn her taste all over again. "He can wonder for a little while longer."

"It's hard to find a babysitter," she said, now sounding distracted.

Hunter grinned. "Right now, he doesn't have a choice."

"Which means we should take advantage of that."

"I'm glad you're in agreement. I like when you're

agreeable."

"Don't get used to it."

He snorted lightly. "I won't."

"So..."

"So..." he repeated, dropping his head until his lips were right above hers, sliding his hand into her hair again to hold her still.

"Are you going to kiss me?" Her warm breath mingled with his.

"I'm thinking about it," he murmured.

"Thinking before acting," she teased softly.

"It's a good habit to have."

She leaned in until their lips were practically touching. "I can't promise it'll become a habit."

In one way, he hoped not. Especially when it came to things like tackling him in the kitchen the other day.

He closed the hairsbreadth gap between them, separating her soft lips with his, and before he could slip his tongue inside her mouth, hers slipped into his. She took control of the kiss and he let her. He liked it. It confirmed that she was kissing him because she wanted to, and not feeling as if she "owed" him.

She wanted him as much as he wanted her.

While he allowed her to take over the kiss, he drew his hands down her shoulders, over her arms, until he snagged her wrists, planting both palms on his chest. He knew she would feel how hard, how fast his heart was thumping but he didn't give a shit.

He also wanted her to feel he was solid, he was there for her. She didn't need to worry. Not while he was in town. For however long that would be.

He pulled back a little bit. "Frankie."

Her eyelids were heavy and her lips parted when her eyes met his. "Yes?"

"Backseat of your car." At least that was parked inside

her garage and there wouldn't be any witnesses. Especially her young son.

They could make this quick.

But not *too* quick. "It's unlocked?"

She nodded. "Condom?"

He returned the nod. "Wallet."

"Then why are we standing here?"

"I'm waiting on you, sweet cheeks." He stepped back, pulled her away from the garage and smacked her ass hard enough it had to sting.

She glared at him over her shoulder. "*Sweet cheeks?*"

"Well, you must've been complaining to Steel about me calling you *loquilla.*"

"I did no such thing," she huffed as she moved to the rear garage door and slipped into the dark interior.

"Uh huh," he answered, following her inside, his cock already twitching with anticipation.

"We have to make this quick."

He brushed a hand over his denim-clad erection. "Don't worry, this will be quick."

He heard a snort in the dark and just as his eyes were adjusting, she flipped on the bare bulb that hung from the ceiling.

"Atmosphere," she announced, yanking the rear driver's side door open and climbing in. "God, I feel like a teenager again!"

So did he as he stood back and watched her ass wiggle and shift as she removed the car seat, shoved it in his direction, crawled over the rear seat, flopped onto that tempting ass and turned her head to look at him. "Let's go!"

He set the car seat down on the floor. "We're gonna have to open both back doors," he said, trying not to let the thought of the two of them being jammed into the back of her old Nissan Altima bother him. He needed to concentrate on her, not his surroundings.

"Why?"

"Because we'll need air. It's hot enough in this garage as it is." And while that was true, it wasn't the only reason.

She shrugged and pushed open the rear passenger side door. "Wallet out. Pants off. Condom on. Let's go." Then she snapped her fucking fingers.

"Damn, woman," he muttered under his breath. He'd do what she wanted because he wanted it, too. Not because she demanded it. And, anyway, who was stupid enough to ignore a woman who demanded, "Pants off. Condom on. Let's go?"

Not him.

Especially with a woman like Frankie.

That meant he did exactly that. Once he was settled in the back seat, she climbed onto his lap, her shorts—and panties, if she had been wearing any—tossed to the floorboard and she planted her hands on his shoulders.

"Do you need—"

Before he could finish asking her if she needed any foreplay, she said, "Just need this," and circled her fist around his throbbing cock and sank down onto his lap.

"Fuck," he breathed. His brain was still functioning enough to unclip the back of her bikini, grab one of her tits, and suck her nipple into his mouth.

Yeah, he remembered correctly. Perfect size for *his* mouth.

"This is all I've thought about since you left the other night," she breathed into his ear as her arms encircled his head and held him against her breasts.

It was all he could think of, too, when he wasn't busy hunting Taz. Hell, sometimes even when he was.

Her wet silky heat surrounded him as she rose and fell in a slow, steady pace. While he was all for slow and steady to start, he wanted to yell, "Let's go," just like she had.

He didn't.

Instead, he grabbed two handfuls of her ass and guided her to a stop with him deep inside her. She didn't become completely still, instead she circled her hips, grinding him even deeper. His balls were already screaming for release, and while he said they needed to be quick, he didn't want it to be that quick. He wasn't sure how many chances they'd get to do this in the upcoming days, which made him want to savor the moment.

"You're so fucking wet, Frankie."

"You make me this way."

Fuck. His chest squeezed at that admission. What man didn't want to hear that?

He released her ass and grabbed her face, pulling her to him, capturing her mouth, swallowing her groan. This time, it was all him in control.

Her nails dug into his shoulders, even through the cotton of his T-shirt. He didn't give a fuck, she could shred it for all he cared right now.

As their tongues tangled, she ground against him even harder, her soft tits pressed to his chest.

If there was a fucking heaven, he couldn't imagine that moment wasn't it. She was everything he liked in a woman, minus the short temper. But that made her who she was, so as long as he could brace knowing it was coming, he could handle it.

Even though she was stubborn, she was smart enough to accept help. She was a survivor and so was he. He liked that about her. She wasn't one to curl up in a corner and give up.

The love of a mother could be fierce. Could be a driving force. But to have Frankie direct that same intense desire at him...

Yeah, he'd eat that shit right up.

But it could be addicting.

And that was one habit he needed to avoid. His skill was to hunt people, which meant D sent him wherever he was needed. Which also meant he kept a bag packed at all times.

The woman in his lap, who was now rising and falling again on his cock, needed steady in her life. So did her son.

That wasn't him.

That meant this was temporary. The "right now" in this back seat. And whatever stolen moments they'd be able to find while he was in her house.

Not just in bed, either. Sitting across from her at her kitchen table, eating her food, having conversation. Teasing her, like calling her sweet cheeks, just to see the spark in her eyes.

He was there for a job, but that didn't mean he couldn't enjoy a few parts of his day with her. Not only getting to know her, but her son.

She didn't need to tell him she was going to come, because her nails digging into his flesh like a tiger's claw told him.

Her low groan pulled one from him as she got even wetter and she tensed around him, squeezing, pulsating, riding him harder and faster.

"Mouth," he managed to say, and she understood what he wanted.

Their lips sealed together, and he swallowed every gasp, every ragged breath, as she rode that peak to the very top. Then let herself fall back down.

He followed quickly behind, driving up with a grunt as she drove down to meet him.

And then his ass landed on the seat, all her weight on him, and he didn't even care. Their mouths had separated just barely when he came and they were both breathing hard, neither moving, neither saying anything, just enjoying that blood rush, that high that came from a satisfying orgasm.

He slowly opened his eyes and was surprised to find hers already open, staring at him. "Wow," she breathed.

He smiled.

"That *was* quick."

His smile fell.

Her lips twitched and she added, "Sweet cheeks."

"It was supposed to be quick. That's why it's a *quickie,*" he explained needlessly. "And don't act like you didn't get what you needed."

She shoved her face into his neck and smiled against his damp skin.

He wrapped his arms tighter around her. "You're just trying to be a pain in my ass." For fuck's sake, she felt good in his arms. Like she belonged there. Pain in the ass or not.

Even in the back of her piece of shit vehicle in a closed-up, boiling hot garage, he was in no rush to move. Until suddenly his chest got tight and his fingers flexed against her as their surroundings began to close in on him.

Normally he didn't have a problem being in a vehicle. Not when it was moving, and his mind was concentrating on traffic and the like. But in the shadowed interior of a small car in a badly lit, tiny garage, he found himself in that tunnel. That familiar tunnel which grew narrower and darker. Then began to spin.

Which happened right before he would go into a full-blown panic attack.

He needed air, light and freedom.

Now.

"*Loquilla,*" he pushed out of his constricted throat. "Need to get rid of this condom."

She didn't lift her head, in fact, she snuggled closer. "I like where I'm at."

"Gotta check on your son. Don't need the condom leaking. Need to get out of this heat." Those were all valid excuses for her to move off his lap and let him up.

With hands on her hips, he pulled her up. Her arms fell from around his neck and she reluctantly moved off him.

"We'll find time to do this again in a better place," he told her. Because that was a given.

Right now, he needed to free himself of this impending darkness, before he saw nothing but black.

His pulse began to rush, and his heart raced faster as he scrambled from the car, ripping off the condom as he went.

He gulped air as he kept himself from collapsing to the concrete floor. He concentrated on finding a trash can with his narrowed vision, to rid himself of the evidence of his release.

He snagged his clothes where they lay in a pile and as soon as he was dressed enough not to flash the neighbors, he yanked up the garage door and let the humid night air in. The street light two houses down helped him see a little better and he took long, soothing breaths in through the nose and out through the mouth.

As he faced the street, he squeezed his eyes shut, then opened them, repeating that until his vision was restored.

Then he finally breathed with relief.

Crisis averted.

He heard and felt her behind him, and her warm hand touched his lower back right above his holster, which made his muscles involuntarily tense once again.

"You okay?"

"Yeah," he murmured. "Fine." He pulled away from her and stepped out into the driveway. "Let's get in the house so Steel can head out."

As he headed in that direction, he heard her close the garage door behind her.

He should've done it for her because it was old and heavy. But, right now, he was just thankful to be upright and functioning.

Chapter Ten

FRANKIE HAD no idea why Hunter suddenly acted like that. Every muscle had gone tight in his body and he'd begun to sweat more than during their "quickie." His tone had also become wooden. Had she done something wrong?

No, he should be able to take a little ribbing about sex. She had done it several times when they had spent the day in bed a few days ago. During those hours, he had laughed when she teased him and seemed to have a sense of humor.

She reminded herself if a man had a problem with something, it was *his* problem, not hers.

She shouldn't have to temper her words for anyone. She was who she was. Either he accepted her that way, or he could go the hell home.

If it was only her, she'd tell him to do just that. But it wasn't and she worried about Leo.

Hunter was right, if Taz was determined to find and get to her, the local PD might not be able to respond in a timely fashion. Manning Grove Police Department was small, but covered a large area. She couldn't ask them to post a patrol car outside her home for who knew how long.

Max Bryson, the Chief of Police, probably wouldn't

agree to that anyway. He'd advise her to move in with her mom temporarily. But her mom lived in an over fifty-five community and they'd frown on a three-year-old staying long-term in the development. Not only that, she suffered from a lot of migraines, as well as other health issues, which was why she couldn't watch Leo regularly while Frankie worked.

So, whatever she had said or done that he didn't like, he could just get over it.

She followed him through the dark into the house and when they stepped into the light of the kitchen, she noticed small tears in the back of his threadbare T-shirt, as well as red stains from the blood she had drawn.

Damn.

Unfortunately, she wasn't the only one who spotted them.

Steel and Leo were still at the table, only now Lego pieces were strewn all over the top and they were building something. Not that Frankie could figure out what.

Steel's gaze had hesitated on her then landed on Hunter's shoulders as he opened the fridge and pulled out a couple beers. As Hunter straightened, he twisted off a cap with a flick of his wrist.

When Steel's eyes narrowed and his mouth opened, Frankie cut him off. "There was a feral cat outside."

The lines crinkled around his eyes as Steel said, "I'll just bet there was."

Before Hunter could say anything, Leo greeted him with a loud "hi" again.

"Hi," Hunter responded.

"I'm Leo," her son announced.

Her son was a social butterfly, that was for sure. "Baby, he knows who you are. You told him the other day."

"I'm three."

"He knows that, too," Frankie reminded him.

"I don't know him," Leo crowed to the ceiling.

Frankie let her eyes roll, only because she knew her son wasn't watching. "You met him the other day, he's going to be staying here for a little while."

She didn't miss Steel's eyebrows shoot up as he shot a frown at Hunter.

"I don't know him," Leo repeated, this time a touch more quietly while turning eyes that mirrored Frankie's toward her. "He play with *Legooooos?*"

"His name is Hunter, baby. And he told me he can't wait to play Legos with you."

Frankie ignored the look Hunter sent her way.

"Hun... Hund...der." Sometimes he struggled with pronouncing a hard "T."

"Hunter," the man repeated more slowly.

"Hunder," Leo tried again, wrinkling up his face in frustration.

"Close, baby," Frankie said, accepting the second open beer from Hunter with a nod of thanks.

He moved closer to the table and ruffled Leo's hair. "Tell you what, little man. You can call me something no one else does. It'll be special just for you."

Leo's eyes lit up and he bounced a bit in his chair. "What?" he asked in his outside voice.

"You can call me Danny. Is that easier?"

Leo nodded.

Danny. She had sex with the man and didn't know his real name? Was it Daniel Hunter? Hell, his name might be on his dog tags and she never even thought to look the other day when that was all he was wearing, besides his expansive tattoo, in her bed.

"Why don't you try it, Leo?" she encouraged him after clearing her throat so she wouldn't sound breathless from that memory.

Leo shrugged and turned his attention back to his Legos. "Danny."

"There you go," Hunter said in a low voice, then leaned over, picked up a Lego and snapped it into place.

That deep, masculine voice talking to her son, Hunter ruffling Leo's hair, it all sent tingles to places it shouldn't. Like her nipples. And her ovaries.

In fact, an egg might have just shot down her fallopian tube at the speed of sound.

Frankie squeezed her thighs together. *Down, hormones, down.*

Her reaction also didn't go unnoticed by Steel. That man missed nothing.

Which took her back to what Hunter said about her wearing a bikini top around him. He was right, she needed to change. She'd do so as soon as she took Leo up to bed.

She glanced up at the clock on the wall above the table. Soon. Because right now, she couldn't pull her son away to do just that. Not while Leo had two men willing to play Legos with him.

He didn't have a father, so any good male influence around him she'd accept.

Even if only temporary.

But, unfortunately, it didn't last once Hunter told Steel, "We need to talk."

Steel immediately jerked his chin up and unfolded his bulky body from his chair. "Keep building, little buddy."

Leo only nodded, not lifting his gaze from the two pieces he was connecting. His little tongue was sticking out and that pulled a smile from her.

"Don't you want to eat something?" Frankie called to Hunter, as he stalked from the kitchen with Steel on his heels.

"In a bit," he called back from the front of the house, then she heard the door close.

"Okay, little man. I think it's time you get ready for bed."

Leo didn't answer, just shook his head and grabbed another plastic piece.

"Yes, it's getting late and I don't need a cranky little boy on my hands."

"Not cranky," he announced.

"Not yet, but you will be. You had a long day and Steel kept you busy. You're probably tuckered out."

"No."

"Yes."

"No."

There was no doubt where her son got his stubbornness. "It's not an option, Leo."

"No."

Frankie pinned her lips together as she began to gather the pieces and throw them back in the container.

"No! Not done, Momma!" he screamed and slammed his hand on the table, the remaining loose pieces jumping from its surface.

Okay, then. Somebody was certainly over-tired. Hopefully that meant Leo would sleep all night and not wake her up at the crack of dawn.

She glanced in the direction the men went. They never decided whether Hunter was taking the couch or Leo's bed.

She'd just make the decision for him. She'd tuck Leo in with her tonight wearing a pair of his pull-ups, hoping they'd hold up so she didn't wake up in a wet spot.

"Leo," she murmured, bracing for a too-familiar fight.

"Mom-*maaaaa!*"

"You don't need to yell, I'm standing right next to you."

"You don't *liiiiiisten!*"

Frankie blinked. "Wow, mister. I'll pretend I didn't hear that." She took a breath, then started again, "You're going to sleep in my bed tonight."

His dark brown eyes lifted to her and the crease on his forehead smoothed out. "I am?"

"Yes, but you have to promise not to kick your momma during the night, okay?"

Leo released a loud, dramatic sigh. "*Ooookay*."

Frankie smiled at his acceptance, but expected to wake up with bruises anyway. "I'm going to put you to bed now and come up later and we can snuggle."

"'Kay."

She helped him out of his booster seat and prepared for part two of the fight to get Leo to bed.

But he was more tired than she realized because it wasn't fifteen minutes later when she was heading back downstairs, her bikini top thrown into the hamper, her cleavage now tucked into a bra and a loose V-neck tee, and Leo already passed out in her bed wearing only a pair of Toy Story pull-ups.

She stopped at the foot of the steps when she heard male voices still out front. She pressed her back against the wall next to the door, knowing she shouldn't listen in, but telling herself it may concern their safety and well-being.

Though, mostly, she was just plain nosy.

"After all that fucking bullshit, you didn't find any trace of him in Lancaster."

"I'm not sure where the fucker is, but he needs to be found." Hunter was pacing the length of the porch restlessly and kept passing by the front door.

"No shit. You've already spent too much time on this. D's going to have a fucking fit. We need to flush him out somehow and end this."

"Yeah, but how?"

"Dangle a carrot," Steel said. Frankie peeked through the crack of the curtain that covered the narrow window next to the front door. The man's arms were crossed over his insanely broad chest as he perched on the porch railing in that tight white tank, worn, holey jeans and scuffed up cowboy boots.

Given the state of the railing and his muscular bulk, Steel was taking his life into his own hands by doing so.

"Okay, but we need a carrot."

Steel jerked his chin toward the house. "Got two right in there."

Hunter's pacing screeched to a halt and he spun on Steel. "No."

Steel shrugged. "I've been here three days, brother. Three. You were here, what, two? I know her better than you."

"No, you don't," Hunter growled.

"Not in the biblical sense, but I've been around her longer. And what I see is a woman who can be fierce when protecting her child. I think she'd go for it. She'd agree to us using herself or Leo as bait."

Frankie could no longer breathe. Her stomach twisted at the thought of putting her son in danger on purpose.

"We're not using a three-year-old as *bait*," Hunter said in a low, dangerous tone.

"There's six of us. One of him. We also got D and I'm sure Slade, if we need him and once he knows the truth. Hell, I'm sure D could get some of his club brothers involved if we need more hands on deck. But we won't. This Taz is only one fucking turd. We don't need a bunch of people to flush one turd."

Hunter shook his head. "No. We'll find another way."

"It's been fucking months, brother. *Months*. And when D loses his patience and pulls the plug on this job, then what? You're back in Shadow Valley and Frankie's up here unprotected with that shitbag on the loose. Maybe he's long gone and couldn't give a rat's ass about her since he has no idea about Leo. Or maybe he'll want to finish what he started. We don't know how that motherfucker thinks."

"He's slick to stay off our radar, that's for sure. I'm hoping it's because he's not only under our radar, but six feet under."

"But we don't know that."

No, they didn't. Frankie didn't know where Taz was. Worse, the men out front didn't know where Taz was. He could be anywhere.

"We've got the manpower, we just need to be smart about it."

"She'd have to be willing and even if she is, I'm not sure I agree with any of this," Hunter grumbled low.

"Not your kid, man. Also, not your woman."

Steel was right. She wasn't Hunter's woman and Leo wasn't his kid. His job was to find Taz for a whole different reason than to keep her and Leo safe. Hunter had no good reason to care about them.

They could walk away, and she'd be left swinging in the breeze, vulnerable to anything Taz pulled. Her only saving grace would be if Taz couldn't give a shit about her.

She couldn't be so lucky.

Frankie chewed on her bottom lip as she considered her limited options.

Move out of the country.

Keep changing her and Leo's name and move to another state. But she'd never be able to settle for too long in any one place, which was not good for Leo. He needed stability. Family. Even if it was only his grandmother and her.

The last option would be to let them be bait, get this whole thing over with in a controlled environment. She assumed if he popped up, he'd be thrown back in jail for breaking his parole. But then...

Once he did his time, he'd be free once more.

Shit. Frankie scrubbed her hands down her face and bit back a frustrated scream.

Then she thought back to something Steel said. Well, didn't actually say out loud, but Frankie had read between the lines.

They were hired to find Taz by his half-brother. However, it didn't seem as though it would be a happy family reunion due to Taz being a part of a rival motorcycle club. From what Steel said, it sounded like very bad blood existed between the Dirty Angels—the club Leo's uncle belonged to—and these Warriors.

Not only bad blood, but toxic.

Steel admitted the two clubs had clashed for decades. And the Warriors had done things or planned to do things to the Angels' members, women and children. That's when Hunter and his coworkers, or team, or whatever they were —which she wasn't sure what yet—had stepped in, tracking them down.

What Steel hadn't said was what they did to these Warriors once they found them. If her guess was right, they weren't asked to play nice, or even incarcerated. Instead, the Warriors' life took a dark turn. Like a permanent sleep type of dark.

She considered the two men out front. Both prior military, both working for a business called In the Shadows Security, but was what they did actually security? Or was that a small part of the truth?

Were they hired killers?

She closed her eyes and leaned her head back against the wall. Had she slept with some cold-blooded executioner? Was one going to be sleeping under the same roof as her son?

Fuck. Frankie was between a rock and a hard place with this whole thing.

Hunter could be no better than Taz, who most likely felt no remorse about what he did to Frankie. His goal was to seriously injure her, make her miscarry, even kill her.

Was Hunter the kind of man who could take another person's life without remorse?

He kept a gun and a knife on him at all times, which was not a habit of an average person. Most of the MGPD didn't even carry a weapon off-duty, and they were law enforcement.

But Hunter wanted to protect her and Leo, right? That was what he said.

Taz wanted the opposite.

Fuck, she had misjudged Taz big time. She couldn't do that again, not with the men on her front porch. Not when someone so valuable was asleep in her bed upstairs.

Even so, she couldn't sit back and do nothing if Taz was out there. She needed closure.

However that came about.

She would choose Leo's life over anyone's. Even her own.

So, whatever Hunter, Steel and the rest of his "team" needed to do, she'd agree to. If it put her at risk, so be it.

As long as her baby was safe, that was all that mattered.

HUNTER GLANCED over his shoulder as the front door opened and Frankie slipped out, closing it softly behind her.

"He settle?" he asked her, then realized what he asked.

Steel grinned at him and Hunter shot him a scowl, which pretty much implied he should keep his fucking trap shut.

Not that Steel ever listened.

"Yes, he was exhausted and fell asleep right away."

Hunter let his gaze roam down her body. Her tits were now covered, *thank fuck*, but the V of her snug shirt still showed an ample amount of cleavage. He was certain Steel noticed that, too.

As soon as she stepped within reach, he reached out and

snagged her wrist, pulling her closer. She tugged her arm from his grasp but remained at his side.

His gaze slid to Steel who was concentrating on his boots, wearing an unmistakable grin.

"Are you two talking about Taz?" she asked, making him wonder how much she heard.

"Yeah," Steel said, lifting his head, his grin wiped away, his expression back to being all business.

"Still nothing?"

Hunter wasn't sure how much he should tell her. He shook his head. "We think he went underground. Came up with nothing in Lancaster."

"He might come out for me."

She said it so softly, Hunter thought he misheard her.

"What?" Steel asked, his eyes meeting Hunter's. He wondered if he looked as surprised as Steel.

"He might come out of hiding for me," Frankie repeated, louder this time. "Especially if he finds out about Leo."

"Frankie—" Hunter started.

She lifted a hand and turned to face him. "No. Don't shut that idea down. I want this whole thing over. I wanted this whole thing over with him before I found out I was pregnant. I worry every damn day, Hunter. Every day. I don't want to live like this anymore. I know having a PFA is a joke. It won't stop someone determined to cause me or Leo harm. Especially someone who isn't afraid of doing time. If this is the only way to flush him out, then we need to do this. I'll say it again..." She took a deep breath, then said slowly, "I want this over."

Hunter wanted this whole thing over, too. But not at the risk of putting Frankie and her son in harm's way.

"I think it could work," Steel said. "I know you don't like it, brother, but maybe if we get the local cops involved, it'll help. You said they know the background, right?"

"They know everything that happened," Frankie said before Hunter could. "I trust them and would feel better if they were involved, too. Because..." She looked from Steel to Hunter. "No offense, but besides you both wearing dog tags, I know nothing about your backgrounds. All I know is what you've told me, the name of the business you both work for. But I don't know what you actually do. Are you even capable of handling a man like Taz? And if you find him, then what? You turn him over to the police? I need more than what you've given me. But, even with that said, I'm willing to be used to draw him out so Max and his officers can take him into custody."

"Frankie, if they take him into custody, he won't be there long. Eventually he'll be free again and you'll be back to where you are now," Hunter admitted.

"Then what's the solution?"

It was a valid question. One Hunter didn't want to answer. And by judging the look on Steel's face, he didn't either.

Because what they planned to do could land any of them in the cell next to Rocky. Just that thought made Hunter's heart beat more rapidly. The last thing he wanted to do was follow in his own father's footsteps by finding a way out of a cell on a gurney with a sheet knotted around his neck.

"We could see if the local PD is willing to partner with us to draw him out. Let them think we're helping them take him into custody."

"And then what?" she asked.

"We do what we do best."

"Which is?"

Hunter could push her off, not tell her the truth, or he could be completely upfront about it.

"What do you want to see happen to the father of your child, Frankie?" Before she could answer, he continued so she knew the magnitude of any decision she made. "Think carefully, this is a decision you'll have to live with the rest of your life if it comes to fruition. This is something you may have to lie to your son about each and every time he asks about his biological father."

He grabbed her arm again and drew her to him, turning her to face him. Her face was tipped up and even in the dim light he could see she was actually thinking first before acting. Before making a very important decision.

"I want this over. How ever that has to happen, needs to happen."

Hunter had no doubt with her cold, flat tone she was serious about what she just said. This woman was no wilting flower. Steel was right, she would defend her son like a ferocious lioness.

Even if it meant her son's father had to die.

Chapter Eleven

HUNTER'S EYELIDS lifted and he had no clue where the fuck he was. His heart was racing, his skin covered in sweat, every muscle in his body had turned to stone. He blinked and blinked again. He couldn't see shit. Nothing but darkness.

A heavy weight crushed his chest. His lungs wouldn't expand to let in any oxygen, his mouth wouldn't open to suck in air.

He was suffocating. Dying.

And when that final and permanent sleep came, he'd do it alone.

Not only from bleeding from his gunshot wounds, but from slowly being crushed to death by what seemed like tons of rubble.

He'd never escape. He'd never be found. He'd never be rescued. Because no one knew where the fuck he was. No one but the insurgent who shot him, if that motherfucker was even still alive.

Most likely he wasn't. Not after an airstrike ripped through that part of Baghdad. After being shot, Hunter took cover in the remains of a bombed-out apartment building. The best place he could hide ended up being the worst.

When he heard the aircraft's engines coming closer, he ducked into a corner, hunkered down, covered his head, and kissed his ass goodbye, not expecting to ever see the light of day again.

He did. But during those hours, the two days afterward, until the time he was found and unburied, starving and dehydrated, completely out of his mind, there had been many times he wished he hadn't.

Being buried alive could break even the strongest man.

Hunter was no exception.

He wanted to think he was invincible. That short window of time in his life proved him wrong. It humbled him when he discovered he was breakable.

He survived, yes. But left undamaged? No.

Operation Enduring Freedom.

Fuck him.

That operation trapped him and a lot of his military brothers for the rest of their lives. They'd never truly be "free" again. They paid the price. Sometimes the ultimate one. Either while still over there or after they returned home.

Nobody escaped that "operation" unscathed.

He slid his hand down his sweat-drenched body, and, without needing to look, he found the circular, puckered scar near his hip. He slid it lower, finding the one on his thigh.

He was one of the lucky ones. He managed to come home with all his limbs, and also on his two feet.

He only came home with scars.

And a bad case of claustrophobia due to being buried for two days under the crumpled remains of a building.

Later, he'd been taught what to do when everything collapsed around him, dragging him unwilling back to those days. He was supposed to picture a place that made him feel "safe." Or count backward from ten. Or work on his breathing.

But, for fuck's sake, it was hard to picture a safe place when he was in a room not much bigger than a closet. He closed his eyes again and pictured Frankie in a bikini on the beach with him in the Caribbean. Surrounded by endless blue sky and vast turquoise water. The soft, white sand between her toes. The lapping of the surf against the shore. And her throaty laughter as she turned her head toward him, her smile bigger than life, her eyes holding a gleam and a promise.

Then her smile disappeared as she glanced up, shaded her eyes from the sun with her hand, and he heard it.

The droning of the plane's engine, the dropping of a bomb, the blasts that made his ears ring and cause a pressure so strong in his head he thought it would explode like a melon struck with a sledgehammer.

He jackknifed up and out of bed, then fell to his knees on the floor with a pained grunt. With his tunneled vision, he still couldn't see shit. He reached out and worked his way across the small expanse of floor by touch alone until he found the door, turning the knob and yanking it open.

The cooler air from the hallway finally filled his lungs and he wheezed in relief. After crawling his way down the few feet to the bathroom, he used the door jamb to pull himself to his feet, felt around blindly until he found the switch and flipped it. The room flooded with light, but his thoughts were still clouded, so he tried to focus his narrowed vision on one thing... the shower.

He stumbled the couple feet to the tub, ripped open the curtain and turned the faucet all the way to the right. He climbed in, not even bothering to remove his boxers first, pressed both palms to the shower wall and let the frigid water run over him as he dropped his head forward and closed his eyes.

The cold seeped into his skin, shaking memories loose, washing away the sweat, the proof of his weakness. Goosebumps rose and shivers swept through him, validation he was still alive.

He was going to stay under that cold water until he couldn't endure any more, until those memories were washed down the drain. At least for now, until they returned once more. Because they *would* return. They always did.

He could never escape.

He'd always be trapped.

But he could do his best not to let it win, let it rule his life.

He opened his eyes and turned his head as he heard a noise above the shower. With the curtain wide open, water fell over the edge of the tub onto the floor, soaking the little oval rug Frankie kept in front of the shower, which also sat in front of the toilet because the bathroom was so small.

But it was Frankie he now focused on, standing in the doorway.

Her long dark hair fell around bare shoulders, her pink tank top was loose but hid none of her curves, but it was the concern in her eyes that caught his attention.

He didn't mean to wake her. And he cursed silently that she witnessed him in the state he was currently in.

Vulnerable and weak.

How could he protect her from Taz when he couldn't even protect himself from his own past?

Without a word, she moved to the shower and shut off the water. He could do nothing but stare at her, his teeth chattering and his body shaking from the cold.

She lifted her hand and, after a few moments, he took it, letting her guide him out of the tub until they stood toe to toe, water pooling at his feet.

She remained silent as she grabbed a towel off the rack and wiped the water from his face and his eyes.

Suddenly he could see more clearly. The darkness that ringed his vision was gone. His thoughts were quiet.

His memories tucked back where they belonged.

He was there in the now. The present. In a bathroom in a town called Manning Grove. With a woman who was beautiful inside and out. One with spirit and a temper to match. One who could be his everything.

If he allowed it.

Which he wouldn't.

He knew better than to even try.

He loved his freedom, and the knowledge he could just pick up and go helped keep him sane.

The woman pushing his soaked boxers down and toweling the beads of water off him, rubbing the circulation back into his skin needed roots. She needed steady.

He was far from that.

He had struggled to sign the mortgage papers on his condo. He had struggled to commit to Diesel. But he did it and now he had his team and, luckily, D gave him a lot of freedom, as if the man knew what Hunter needed.

Hunter would never be able to work in a cubicle or a nine-to-five, so he was happy to find his place in Shadow Valley. But hunting, his preference, kept him on the move.

It was what he needed. He was more like a potted Ficus tree rather than a rooted oak. He could be moved anywhere.

And knowing that helped keep him on an even path.

It wasn't until Frankie hung the towel back on the rack, did he realize she had finished drying him off. That he still stood in the center of her tiny bathroom unmoving.

She'd asked nothing of him.

He'd provided nothing in return.

Then he moved, grasping her face with both of his hands, crushing their lips together, backing her out of the bathroom, into the hallway to the top of the steps. There were only two bedrooms upstairs, Leo's and hers. Leo's was too small and hers was occupied.

They not only needed to be quiet, he also needed a

condom. He released her mouth and pressed their foreheads together.

"I need to listen for Leo," she whispered.

Right. He wasn't sure how scarred a three-year-old would end up if he climbed out of bed and found his mother being fucked against a wall in the hallway.

He'd like to avoid being the reason for the boy's future nightmares.

"Yeah. And I need to grab a condom." He pulled away but kept a grip on her face, holding her gaze. "How often does he wake up in the middle of the night?"

"He doesn't unless he's sick."

"What time does he normally climb into bed with you in the morning?"

"Depends. No earlier than five usually."

"What time is it now?"

"Almost three."

"If I move him back to his bed, will I wake him?"

Frankie shook her head. "No, he's a heavy sleeper. But—"

"I'll be out of your bed before five."

Her eyes widened and then she nodded.

"I can't stay in that room, Frankie. It's like a coffin."

As she opened her mouth, he cut her off. "Not now. Let's get him back in his room and I can grab my duffel."

Within minutes, Frankie had Leo tucked back into his bed and was coming back into her own room, where Hunter waited while she had gotten her son settled. He had placed a strip of condoms on the nightstand and he let his gaze rake over her as she closed the door softly behind her. She leaned back against the door as she regarded him in her bed, waiting.

"You okay?" she asked.

"Yeah." He was now. Some panic attacks lasted longer

than others, but once they passed, he was fine. Until the next time.

"What happened?"

"We only have a couple hours. I don't want those hours to be about me. I want them to be about you." And that was true. Any stolen moments he had with Frankie while he was up here, he was going to take advantage of them. "Time's wasting, *loquilla*, the longer you stand there dressed."

With a smile, she pushed off the door and approached the bed. "Must be in a rush."

"The point is, I don't want to rush this time. We've got two hours, let's use our time wisely. You lock the door?"

She went back and turned the lock on the knob, then approached the nightstand, pulling open the drawer, grabbing a baby monitor, turning it on and setting it next to the condoms.

She placed a knee on the bed, and he shook his head. "Clothes off before you get on this bed, Frankie. And take your time doing it."

She put her foot back on the floor, stared at him for a second, tilted her head, shot him a smile and grabbed the bottom of her tank top. Slowly, oh so fucking slowly, as if she had music playing in her head, she worked that top up her body, over her tits, and pulled it off her head. Once she was free of it, her hair spilled back around her shoulders and she shook it out.

Fuck yeah, that just made her tits shake and her nipples bead tight.

"I want my dick between them."

Her eyelids lowered and her lips parted as she cupped her tits and pushed them together. Her voice caught when she asked, "Now?"

He shook his head. "No, show isn't over yet."

She slid her hands from her tits down her stomach and

then hooked her thumbs in the elastic waistband of her pajama shorts.

"Slow, Frankie. Really fucking slow," he whispered.

Her head was dropped forward, but she tipped her dark eyes up to his. "Shorts and panties together?"

"Fuck no. Separate."

She took her time shimmying out of the pajama shorts until they dropped to her feet and she stood there in only a pair of panties. Pink, like her pussy.

"You wet?" His question came out rough and raw.

"Maybe."

Now she was just teasing him. "Check."

She slipped one hand into her panties and he watched her hand move under the fabric as she slipped a finger, maybe even two, between her plump lips.

Fuck.

He could taste her already. He could feel that wet heat squeezing his dick and milking him dry.

His cock twitched against his hip, catching her attention. A puff of breath escaped her parted lips and a flush rose up her chest.

"Well?"

Her fingers were still moving. He knew damn well it didn't take that long to tell.

She nodded.

"Lick your fingers clean," he ordered, even knowing that might be the death of him.

He stopped breathing as she slipped her hand from her panties, tucked two fingers in her mouth, circled her lips around them and closed her eyes as if she was savoring an expensive gourmet meal.

A string of precum dripped off the tip of his cock and landed on his hip. He captured it with the pad of his thumb, moved on his knees to the edge of the bed and offered it to her.

She leaned forward, took his thumb into her mouth, the tip of her tongue running along his digit and, *fuck*, if he didn't almost blow his load right there and then.

Her unfocused eyes, her soft expression, her tits, her wet pussy, that ass... Everything about her turned him on.

He pulled his thumb from her mouth and struggled to say, "Panties off slow, Frankie. Turn around while you do it. Show me your ass."

She turned until her back was to him, hooking her fingers in her cotton panties and wiggling her hips back and forth as she worked them down over her ass that he wanted to lose himself in, to eat, to slap, to fuck.

When the pink fabric was gathered at the top of her thighs, he demanded, "Bend over as you take them the rest of the way off."

He realized right then and there, as she did as she was told, the woman, during sex, always did anything he asked or demanded. Not once had she argued.

During sex, she'd give up control. Other times, not so much.

Note taken.

While she was bent over, stepping out of her panties, he said, "Grab your ankles and stay there until I tell you otherwise."

Her body jerked in response, but she did it, not saying a word.

"Spread your legs a little bit, baby. That's it. Show me what you have for me." His voice sounded thick even to his own ears.

Her plump flesh was shiny, tempting. He drew a finger through her slick folds. *Fuck*, this woman was responsive.

He sucked his finger clean, then grabbed her hips and buried his face against her, his tongue now following his finger's previous path. He sucked each fold, flicked her clit hard enough to make her twitch, ran his tongue back up and then even higher until he circled her puckered hole with the tip. She lurched forward and made a noise.

A noise of complaint or encouragement?

He didn't waste time trying to figure it out, instead he slipped two fingers inside her heat and used them to fuck her as he swept his tongue over her ass, teasing her.

Seconds later, her legs were shaking and whimpers, sounding as if she were fighting them, escaped her.

She liked it. No, she more than liked it.

He sped up the pace of his fingers, added a third and pushed his thumb against her clit as he tried to dip his tongue inside her, but she clenched down, shutting him out.

"Hunter," she breathed.

"Let me in, Frankie."

He hadn't stopped plunging his fingers in and out of her with one hand, with the other he smacked her ass hard, making her gasp and jerk forward slightly. He realized he wouldn't be able to do that again, it was too loud and he worried about waking up Leo.

"Let me in, Frankie," he growled softly instead.

"Okay." Her whisper held a shake, but he could feel her relax around his fingers, against the hand he had back on her hip, holding her in place.

This time he was able to dip his tongue inside her. With his tongue fucking her ass, and his fingers fucking her pussy, she began to shake so violently, he thought she might fall to the floor.

But she remained on her feet long enough for the orgasm to rip through her. The other day in her bed, she hadn't tempered her screams, her responses. Tonight, she managed to muffle her cry.

Before he could back away, she began to crumble, and he grabbed her quickly to pull her toward him so she'd land on the bed. Within seconds, he had her on her back and beneath him, his hips cushioned by her soft thighs as he stared down into her face, her expression lax and satisfied.

"That was..." she began.

"Yeah," he answered. His cock was throbbing and dripping, his balls pulled tight. He had no time to analyze her response.

He lifted up just enough to grab a condom, rip it open and roll it on. "Ready?"

She nodded, her eyelids still heavy, her eyes still unfocused.

Yes, this was how a woman should look in his bed. Sexy and satisfied. She could take care of the sexy part; he'd make sure to take care of the satisfied.

He settled back between her thighs, lined himself up and hesitated.

A trickle of something he didn't recognize slid down his spine.

No, he knew what it was.

Fear.

Every time he fucked Frankie, it was as though a net wrapped around him, trying to tie him down, pulling him under, trapping him.

It wasn't her doing it, she hadn't asked for anything from him. They hadn't known each other long enough for that to even happen.

And it made no sense. He could only assume his mind was playing games with him. Making him think this was something permanent. Unescapable.

He needed to remind himself that was far from the truth.

Her softly calling his name snapped his attention back to her. She was who he should be concentrating on, not his unreasonable fears.

"Yeah, baby," he whispered.

"You disappearing into your head is not concentrating on me."

He fought back a grin. "I'll make up for it."

"You better," she said with her own grin.

"Let's not get carried away," he warned her.

"No, let's *get* carried away. I said I'm ready, you're the one taking your sweet ol' ti—" A rush of breath replaced her words when he tilted his hips and took her hard.

"Thought you were ready?" he teased.

Her answer was tilting her hips and wrapping her thighs around his. Every time he powered deep, she met him half-way, taking everything he gave her and giving it back to him twofold.

Hot.

Wet.

Silk.

Heaven.

Her breathy mews drove him on as he trapped one nipple in his mouth and sucked it hard, giving it no mercy. Her back arched, her head tilted back, and he released her nipple quickly because she was drawing a deep breath, preparing to wail.

He covered her mouth with his, smothering her cry, capturing the proof of her orgasm as she rocked against him, not slowing down, encouraging him to take her faster and harder. Her nails dug into his ass as she held on tightly. And in turn, he used her mouth to smother his own groans.

But in the end, he broke away to bury his face in her neck as he powered deep one last time, coming inside her with a grunt.

He stilled. Not wanting to move. Liking where he was at even though he was disappointed his plans to take their time flew out the window.

Her rapid breath swept along his cheek as he lifted his

head just long enough to glance at the clock. They had plenty of time to make the second round last longer.

As long as the monitor stayed quiet.

And they did, too.

They managed it and he also managed to bring Frankie to orgasm two more times before he flopped onto his back, wrapped the used condom in a tissue, then hauled Frankie against him.

He ended up staring up at the ceiling with her curled into his side, one hand planted on his chest, her palm covering his dog tags, one of her thighs thrown over his, her breathing slow and steady.

Forty-five minutes later, still unable to sleep, he carefully freed himself, slipping from the bed, finding his bag, getting dressed and heading downstairs to make a strong pot of coffee.

He was going to need it.

Chapter Twelve

HE MADE one more round through the quiet house. He had a difficult time falling asleep on her couch tonight even though the living room was larger than Leo's bedroom. But moving downstairs didn't help, so he gave up.

He walked down the short hallway at the top of the steps, opened Frankie's door and peered through the dark. His night vision was decent when he wasn't in the middle of a panic attack, so he could see Frankie's shadowed figure curled around Leo. He'd tell her in the morning she could move him back into his room. He wasn't going to be able to use the boy's bed. He also needed to explain why.

However, he wasn't sure if he was ready to share that info with her.

It was one thing to have a weakness, it was another to expose it.

None of the Shadows knew the extent of his panic attacks, they just knew he didn't like tight spaces.

He let his gaze slide over the bed. The top sheet was kicked onto the floor since Frankie complained Leo made her too hot.

But it tugged at him, seeing mother and son. That dedication and deep love she had for Leo, even though he was a result from a bad situation.

He closed his eyes as another memory pushed forward. One he hadn't thought about in a long time. His mother trying to encircle him in her arms after the news of his father's suicide in prison.

But Hunter didn't need to be comforted. He didn't need his tears wiped away. Because they were non-existent. He felt nothing. If anything, he felt a strange sense of relief the man would never hurt a soul again.

Not one more person would be his victim.

And the same needed to be true for Taz.

It was up to Hunter to make it so. Especially for the two in that bed. And he'd do his best to give them the safety and security they deserved.

He pulled the door until it was only open a crack and moved to the stairway, then settled halfway down the steps where he could keep one eye on the front entryway and one ear towards Frankie's room.

He dropped his head in his hands and drew his palms over his face, thinking about everything that went on only that morning at Manning Grove PD.

Steel had met him there, having already given Chief Max Bryson a heads up that they were coming.

"Not sure if this will work," Hunter grumbled out in the parking lot of the police station.

Steel shrugged. "Can't hurt to try, if they're willing."

"But they need a reason to be willing," Hunter reminded him.

"The fucker skipped out on parole. He's got a warrant, and they know Frankie personally since they all grew up in the same town. It probably won't be hard to convince them that we're looking out for her. At least in a roundabout way, but they don't need to know that."

"But if the cops flush him out, that means he'll either be

on their radar or, worse, end up in their custody. If he ends up in custody, it's going to make it harder for us to step in and take care of business." Hunter kept his voice down since they were standing in cop central. They might not take too kindly to the Shadows' type of "taking care of business."

"We just need to be ready for him. Grab him before they do. He disappears and no one's the wiser. Cops will think he didn't take the bait."

"Just don't like getting the cops involved."

"Neither do any of us. But we're not having any luck finding the slippery fucker. It's a good plan if we stay in control of it, use the cops as our puppets."

Hunter's gaze swept the lot. "Jesus, not the best place to be calling cops puppets." He blew out a breath and scraped a hand over his hair. "Another option would be to bring her and Leo back to Shadow Valley. Lock her down tight and have Mitch or Axel Jamison put out some sort of press release in hopes Taz sees or hears it."

Steel gave him an impatient look. "If you were a Shadow Warrior, would you show up in the Valley? Fuck no. It would be suicide. He's more likely to surface in Manning Grove, especially if he doesn't know we're here waiting for him."

"Putting out a press release with her former name, her photo and Leo's info is going to out Frankie and Leo." *Fuck,* this whole idea made his stomach churn.

"No shit. That's the point. They're bait."

Hunter's jaw got tight. "I know they're fucking bait. But I don't fucking like it."

Steel arched a brow at him. "And like I said before, beside you tapping that a few times, why else would you care? We're doing her a solid by ridding her of the reason she had to change her name in the first place. She can breathe easy after we take care of the one person she fears and who has any claim to her son."

He fucking hated all of this. It pissed him the fuck off that he couldn't find Taz on his own. He'd never failed at any job. And this felt like a big fat fucking failure. Using a woman and child as bait to bring out some psycho was making him itch, and not just because it was Frankie and Leo. Because he didn't want to do that with any woman or child.

It was risky.

But at this point, they were out of options to flush the fucker out. "If the cops agree to this, we need to time it just right. We need everyone up here and in place before the press release."

"And that'll happen, but I'm not sure D's gonna want everyone's ass up here for any length of time."

Steel was probably right. "He'll need to give us a week. Then after that, if the asshole doesn't pop his head up, I'll remain and everyone else can split. Like you said, he's one fucking turd. If I can't handle one fucking piece of shit, then I need to get a job as a cashier at a dollar store."

"Don't think D's gonna want your ass up here that long, either, Danny. He's been griping already. Every time Jewel is pregnant, he gets crankier than normal. You'd think he was the one having to squeeze the kid out."

"Well, he's going to have to deal with whatever time is needed to get the job done."

"You tell him that." Steel jerked his chin toward the brick building. "First, we need the cops to agree."

"If they do, then I'll deal with D. Slade paid us to find his brother. Thinking if he knew the truth, he'd still want us to find him. Just for a different reason."

Steel nodded. "And I'm thinking D needs to tell him what we've found so far, so he's prepared that this isn't going to be some happy family reunion."

It turned out, the chief did agree. And after they left the station, Hunter had a long talk with his boss, who grunted his reluctant agreement. He also said he would catch Slade up to speed.

Everybody but Diesel was heading north first thing in the morning. At noon, the chief would issue a press release. That statement would announce Sucely Hernandez was searching for her missing son... Brandon Bussard, Jr. And a half hour later, Chief Bryson would get in front of the cameras again to announce Brandon Jr. was found just wandering in a nearby park, he was safe and no reason to form search parties, which was one of Bryson's fears. That the town would be overwhelmed with good citizens wanting to help find Leo when he wasn't even lost.

Even so, if two national news announcements didn't flush the fucker out, nothing would. He only hoped Taz had access to a TV or radio wherever he'd gone to ground. Because if he didn't, they were doing this all for nothing.

In the morning, Hunter was going to tell Frankie not to take Leo to daycare, that he'd watch him instead when she went to work. She'd have Steel and Ryder stake out the restaurant where she waitressed. Mercy and Brick would take turns driving around town, keeping an eye out for Bussard. Walker would be staked out in front of the house. Hunter would be inside the house with Leo, keeping watch.

The plan was set, it just needed to be put into motion.

Problem was, the whole thing left a bad taste in his mouth.

He'd sat Frankie down after he returned from the police station and explained what had been decided. She tried to hide she was nervous about the whole thing, too, but she agreed. Then she emailed Max Bryson current pictures of her and Leo for the press release.

When she dropped Leo off at daycare and went to work earlier, Hunter went for a long fucking run to clear his head and try to rid himself of the bad feeling that permeated every cell in his body. He came back, showered and crashed in Frankie's bed for a few hours.

Unfortunately, he woke up in a sweat again, this time because he had a nightmare where Taz took Frankie hostage and when Hunter finally found her, she was lying in a pool of blood, her throat slit and there was evidence of rape.

Just like Buzz Bussard had done to Crow's mother.

Like father, like son.

Fucking motherfucker.

That was not going to happen this time, Hunter would make sure of it. This was one mission he could not fail at. *They* could not fail at.

He had good men helping him. He trusted his "brothers." Frankie just needed to trust Hunter to do right by her.

His attention came back to the present when he heard her bare feet padding along the worn wood floor of the hallway, even though he could tell she was trying to be quiet. He didn't have to look to figure out she hesitated at the top of the steps.

He doubted she was searching for him, more like taking a bathroom break. Or maybe she couldn't sleep, either, with what was pending.

He couldn't blame her if she couldn't.

"Frankie," he murmured, still not turning around.

"Be right back," she whispered.

A couple minutes later, he heard the toilet flush and her feet moving along the hall again and then down the steps until she stood on the step behind him. She was close enough he could feel her heat and if he leaned back, he'd rest against her shins. He lifted a hand and waited.

Her fingers met his and he clasped them tightly. He guided her around him carefully and to a seat on the step in front of him. Spreading his knees wider, he made room for her to settle against him, but it was still a tight fit since the stairway was narrow.

"Thought you were asleep."

She shook her head. "I heard you open the door."

"Didn't mean to wake you."

"I can't stop thinking about tomorrow. Or later today, I should say."

"You worried?" Of course, she was fucking worried.

She turned to look over her shoulder at him. "Aren't you?"

Of course he was also fucking worried, but he couldn't tell her that. He didn't want to worry her further. "We'll get it handled and you'll be able to breathe easy after that."

"Until he gets released from jail again."

Hunter pursed his lips. "*Loquilla...*"

"The cops won't be arresting him, will they?"

"Not if we can help it." There was no point in lying. They could make it appear to the cops Taz didn't take the bait if his team grabbed him first, but they couldn't lie to Frankie and still set her mind at ease. And he wanted to give her that. Erase that worry once Taz was dealt with permanently.

She studied his face in the dim light and he kept his expression blank.

"Good."

Good? His lips parted and he slowly released the breath he held. "You okay with that?"

Her face got hard and she whispered fiercely, "I will do *anything* for my son."

Luckily, she wouldn't have to do anything. He didn't want her to be forced to live with that. Taking a man's life should never come easy.

Even for him and D's crew.

It was easier to live with if the person deserved it. But still, by taking someone's life, it meant they were acting as judge and jury, which was nothing to take lightly.

"I told you, you're a great mom..." Maybe he could take

her mind off of what would be happening later. "Tell me about yours."

THEY HADN'T TALKED about it yet and it wasn't like it was a secret, but she wasn't sure why he wanted to know. He was only in Manning Grove until the issue with Taz was "handled." Then he'd go back to wherever he came from, probably never to be heard from again. So, her personal life— the part not affected directly by Leo's father—couldn't be that important to him.

"You tell me about your parents first." If he wanted her to share, he should be willing, too.

His chin jerked back at her request. He clearly wasn't expecting it.

"That won't take long. My father was a bad fucking drunk. He hit my mother when he was wasted. He drove truck cross-country. Mix alcohol and an eighteen-wheeler and that can do a lot of damage."

Oh, good Lord, she wasn't prepared for that answer. "And did he?"

"Ran his truck through a group of young kids on a school field trip. Killing, maiming, injuring a number of them."

Frankie smothered her gasp with her hand.

"Right," he muttered because he heard her anyway. He sucked in a sharp breath. "Left a path of destruction. Probably mentally scarring the ones who survived for life."

"Oh my God," Frankie whispered.

"No god involved in that, Frankie, just the devil himself."

"I'm sorry."

"Nothing to be sorry about. My mother should've left him. She didn't. The end. Now your turn." She could taste the bitterness in his words.

Her turn? No, now she had questions. "Is he still in prison?"

"Didn't want to do the time he deserved, so he hung himself in his cell." Now his voice held nothing. Zero. No emotion at all.

"What about your mother?"

"Living with her sister in Florida. I call once a month and visit her at Christmas. That's it."

She'd give anything to talk to her real mother just once. "Hunter..."

"Frankie, it's the way shit is. Not all people are meant to be parents. The second I was old enough to enlist, I did. Not sure if alcoholism is genetic, but figured I needed a purpose in life to fight it if it is. Now, I'm done talking about it. Tell me about the woman you call your mother."

It had to affect him more than he let on, but he was "done talking about it" and wanted to hear more about her. She was certain any other questions she asked about his parents or childhood would be ignored, so she asked, "Why are you interested?" instead.

His body surged against her and there was a long pause before he answered. "Because I'm interested."

This time his voice didn't sound lifeless and cold. This time his words held some depth to them. She found that curious. This caring tone made warmth swirl through her belly, which she found a little worrisome. She should be avoiding any kind of emotional attachment to this man.

Even so, Frankie leaned back against him and he crossed his arms around her chest, holding her tightly. His cheek rested in her hair as she began to tell him about her adopted mother. He already knew Diane wasn't her birth mother, but she wasn't sure how much more he knew.

"You know my birth mother's name was Camila Hernandez. She came to the States from Guatemala when she was eight months pregnant with me for a couple of reasons. The first was to see if she could find my father. To this day, I have no idea who or where he is. She never found him before I was born, and then... Well, I'm getting ahead of myself. My father was in the Air Force and stationed in Honduras when they met."

"Soto Cano Air Base."

She had no idea where the man was stationed, but maybe Hunter knew the area. "If you say so. Anyway, I don't know if he knew my mother was pregnant when he transferred back to the States. But from what Diane—"

"Diane?"

"My adopted mom. From what she was told, it wasn't a love affair, it was only a short 'fling,'" she air-quoted that last word, "so he might never have known. At least, I want to hope that's true, otherwise, he abandoned a woman he got pregnant." Or "helped" get pregnant. Frankie's mother played a part in that, too.

"And you."

"And me," she echoed. She took a breath. "Anyway, he was only one reason. The other was the area she lived in was overrun by violent gangs. Women were raped and killed all the time. She worried not only about herself, but me, as well."

"As she should."

"I'm not sure how she ended up in Manning Grove, I'm not sure if Diane knows that, either, but for whatever reason she settled here, they became close friends. Diane was a Spanish teacher at the high school and the only person my mother would communicate with because her English was so limited."

"Diane taught you Spanish."

"Yes. She wanted me to be bilingual and we're teaching Leo, too. Anyway, after I was born, while my mother was still in the hospital, she was arrested and eventually deported. Being born here automatically made me a citizen and she begged Diane to take me so I could have the better life my mother was so desperate for. Diane, not having any family of her own, agreed. She raised me from an infant and she's the only mother I've ever known."

"You never went to Guatemala?"

Frankie shook her head. "No point. I was Leo's age when my mother was murdered, just like she feared. She was walking home from work and was shot, robbed, and left in an alley to die." Maybe raped, too. Frankie wasn't sure, and there was no way of knowing. The rape and murder of women was so common there and the police so corrupt, no investigation was done. No one cared enough to give her mother justice.

"Fuck," Hunter whispered into her hair, his arms tightening even more around her. She rested her hands on his forearms that crossed her chest and she squeezed them slightly.

"She was determined to give us a better life, a safer one. Then when she was detained, she found a way to at least save me. Only..." She squeezed her eyes shut for a moment and took a breath. "I fucked that up by making a stupid decision by being with Taz. I put myself in the path of danger and almost lost Leo. My mother did everything she could to save me. And this is why I'll do anything I can to save Leo."

"You didn't know he was dangerous, Frankie. You can't blame yourself for that."

She turned her head enough to see his face. "No? You just said your mother should've left your father. I should've walked away from Taz the first time he hit me. I should've refused to accept his excuse or apology."

"Maybe you wanted to see the good in him."

Wasn't that human nature? "Maybe your mother wanted to see the good in your father."

"Right," Hunter murmured.

"Your father couldn't have been all that bad. I'm sure your mother loved him and... he made you." And Hunter was there with her, helping her when he didn't have to be. "So, I thank him for that."

"Frankie," he whispered.

"However, a real man doesn't hit a woman *ever*. Have you ever hit a woman? Out of anger? When you were drunk? Or just... just because?"

"No. But that doesn't mean I wouldn't. If my life was threatened. If one of my teammates' life was threatened. Or someone I cared about was at risk. You're damn right I would strike a woman. I would take out that threat without hesitation. Women aren't helpless, Frankie. They can kill or hurt you as fast as any man. A man who underestimates a woman is making a big fucking mistake."

She squeezed his forearms again, noticing how tense his muscles had become. "That's different. How about striking a woman because she tripped and spilled your beer?"

Hunter's growl was low when he asked, "He did that?"

"I spilled it on him." Normally, she'd never accept that type of behavior from anyone. Why she let that go, she'd never know. The man could pull the charm out of his ass at the drop of a hat. And he'd immediately apologized and begged her forgiveness, saying he'd had a rotten day and a headache, and every other excuse in the book. Even though a red flag had been raised that day, she also believed in giving people second chances. She shouldn't have with Taz.

She should've kicked his ass out that minute. But she'd been lonely. And he had worked hard at bringing her around after he first asked her out and she'd said no. Not once during those weeks had she seen even a glimpse of his temper.

Bait and switch.

He had baited her and once he caught her, the real Taz came out.

Now they would bait him. And finally, justice would be served.

She had always been strong, but having Leo only made her stronger.

When she saw those double lines on her pregnancy test, she had panicked. She didn't want to be tied to Taz and she didn't want him to be the father to her child. She hadn't even decided on how she was going to handle her unexpected pregnancy until she woke up in the hospital and was told that her baby had survived the trauma.

Then she knew exactly what she was going to do. And she did it.

"I will never, ever let that happen to me again."

"Which is why my Rover is sitting in pieces right now."

She turned in his arms and leaned back against his right thigh so she could face him better. "And this is why I'm allowing you to use us as bait. I want this over. Like you said, I want to breathe easy. I don't want to be worried and suspicious if someone is pulled over in front of the house just checking their GPS."

"Your swing impressed me."

She had been scared out of her gourd that day, then, once the fear passed, anger had taken over. She had totally lost control and acted on impulse. "I'm sorry I trashed your SUV. I still owe you for that. And now I'll owe you for taking care of Taz." She had no idea how she'd ever repay him.

"We need to get him first."

We. His "team." He hadn't talked much about them. And she was putting her and Leo's safety in their hands, along with the local police force. "Are you all former military?"

"Yes."

"Same branch?"

"No. Steel was a Marine. A Raider, in fact. And you haven't met the rest yet, but you will when we meet here in the morning. Brick was a Navy SEAL. Mercy, Delta Force. Ryder, Army Ranger. Walker, Night Stalker."

He forgot someone. "And you?"

It took him a few seconds to answer, but he finally murmured, "Green Beret."

She didn't know much about all those titles, but she knew enough to be impressed. "I'm feeling a little better now about this 'operation.' You're all special forces, right?"

"Yeah."

"What about your boss... This Diesel?"

Hunter snorted softly. "He's from a different kind of 'army.' He's the Sergeant at Arms for the Dirty Angels MC."

She knew nothing about special forces, but she also knew nothing about motorcycle clubs, especially since Taz never talked about the tattoos on his back. He'd said it was in his past, Frankie had believed him and left it there. "The rival club of those Shadow Warriors."

"Yeah. We thought the Warriors were all gone. We missed Taz somehow."

We missed Taz somehow.

Missed... Which made it sound as if they had been searching for the members of that club.

"What does a Sergeant at Arms do?"

"The dirty work."

"For his club?"

"Yeah, his club, his family. Pretty much one and the same."

"And he hired you and the others to help with that dirty work?"

"We take all kinds of jobs. We protect people...."

"Like bodyguards."

"We track people..."

"Like those Warriors. Like Taz."

"We do stake-outs, investigations, things like that."

166

Things like that. Like exterminating a rival MC.

We missed Taz somehow.

Could the man who had his arms wrapped around her right now, the man she'd allowed into her house with her three-year-old, be just as ruthless as Taz? Or worse, was he a killer? Had Taz even ever killed anyone?

"As a Green Beret, did you have to take anyone's life?"

"We had a job, we did it."

Not even a hesitation this time. Frankie chewed on her bottom lip. "You're on a job now."

"Yep."

"So, you'll do what you need to do," she stated.

"Right."

"No matter what it is." Again, she made it a statement, not a question.

He didn't answer.

"Do you think Taz ever killed anyone?"

"Don't know, *loquilla*. He tried to kill you. And Leo."

That was true.

"Frankie," he murmured, "you lifted that bat to hit me and if I wouldn't have stopped you, I'd most likely be dead. You would've done what you *thought* you needed to do to protect yourself and your child. Think about that."

That was true, too.

He wasn't done. "I haven't hidden the fact that when we find Taz, he will no longer be a threat to you or Leo."

Again, true.

"How do you think that will happen?"

"Apparently, not by asking him nicely," she answered with all seriousness.

Hunter chuckled softly. Frankie was tired of this heaviness and worry, so to hear him laugh made her lips curve up.

"No, we won't be asking him anything."

"You're not doing this only for me, though. You

mentioned 'missing' Taz. You were hunting all of these Warriors down."

"We were."

She was surprised when he didn't deny it. But then, he hadn't lied to her yet. Or she didn't think he had. But she'd misjudged someone before. "Why?"

"Because they hurt a lot of people. They were a constant threat to Diesel's family and club. We're talking serious shit here. It was an ongoing war that lasted decades. Diesel, as their club's enforcer and protector, decided to end the war once and for all."

End the war once and for all. And what better men to use than former special forces operators? Men who had most likely seen war themselves. Survivors. Men who could do a job and do it right. "And you and your team helped him."

"We saw some pretty ugly stuff, Frankie. Stuff you don't just scrape off. Especially when it happens to innocent people. We're talking women and children, not just men fighting amongst themselves."

"And you protect women and children."

"Especially these women and children." He snagged her chin in his fingers and lifted her face until their eyes locked. "Especially you. And Leo."

Frankie swallowed because his eyes had become intense, heated. "Why especially me? Or is it because you know Leo's uncle? You're doing it for him?"

"Even without Leo, I'd do it for you."

Frankie inhaled a breath and her heart began to race. Again, she reminded herself not to get emotionally attached to a man who was only temporary. So she said, "I like having sex with you." Then cringed internally at that idiotic statement.

But he grinned, his brown eyes crinkling at the corners, the ones she knew had gold flecks throughout, even though she couldn't see them in the low light. "I like having sex with you, too, *loquilla*."

She dug into the tiny pocket of her PJ shorts and lifted the condom she had snagged from his bag before coming down the stairs.

His eyes moved from her face to the condom and back. His grin was gone and something else replaced it. Something that made her toes want to curl. "Leo's in your bed."

"You're getting good at moving him without him waking up."

"You can move him back in there permanently. I can't find sleep in that room."

She wanted to know more about that, too. Why he had been crawling on the floor. Why he took a freezing cold shower. Why he couldn't sleep in Leo's bedroom. There was so much more she wanted to know about him. "Is the bed too small?"

"The room itself." He lifted a hand to stop her next question. "I'll explain, but not now. Right now, we have the little man to move and other business to attend to."

She smiled at his use of "little man." Leo loved it and so did she. "I'm glad I won't be standing in front of the cameras tomorrow with Max, since I'm sure I'll have bags under my eyes from lack of sleep."

"Sleep is overrated. You only grab one?"

She dug into her pocket again and lifted a second one.

His grin returned. "You thought before you acted. Proud of you," he teased.

She snorted softly and shoved at his chest.

He snagged her wrist and tugged her against him, then captured her lips, sweeping his tongue through her mouth once, twice, before letting her go. "Let's get him moved since I need to be out of your bed by five."

Hunter helped her rise to her feet. They went up the

stairs and got Leo settled back into his room. Luckily, without waking him.

Frankie hung back for a few minutes to study her son while he slept, hoping this whole thing with Hunter, his fellow teammates and the police went smoothly. Then she closed the door and headed to her own room where Hunter waited, the monitor already turned on next to the bed. Just in case.

But she looked forward to spending a little time forgetting about what would happen later that day. And letting the man naked in her bed wash away the worry. Even if, like him, it was only temporary.

Chapter Thirteen

FRANKIE GASPED as Hunter sucked her nipple deeper into his mouth. It wasn't gentle, but it was glorious. Her back arched and her head rolled back on the pillow. He had one hand covering her mouth to smother her cries and the other was where they were connected as he powered up and into her over and over. His thumb was doing all kinds of things to make her hips jump.

She was pretty sure he kept his mouth on her nipples to mute his own reactions. But she didn't care, she encouraged it. This man knew how to use his tongue, his fingers and his cock. And, *fuck*, Frankie loved it all.

And wanted it all, since her vagina would go back to growing cobwebs once he left town due to the limited selection of single men in Manning Grove. Plus, having Leo, she worried about who she brought home and introduced into his life. Not to mention, she was a little gun shy after Taz.

But here she was with a man she'd only known for days in her bed, who was *rocking* her world. She nipped his palm and his fingers jerked against her face. She smiled, but it was quickly lost when he removed his hand, demanded, "Quiet," from her in a shiver-worthy growl, shoved an arm under her hips and yanked them up to a different angle to pound her even harder.

He pressed his cheek against hers and said in a ragged voice, "Keep it together, Frankie. It'll really suck if we get interrupted."

It would most definitely suck. He had given her an orgasm once while he ate her like he was in a pie-eating contest with his hands tied behind his back.

And, yes, did he win that blue ribbon.

"Frankie," came his ragged whisper in her ear.

"Yeah?"

"Gonna come soon?"

"Depends on you," she answered.

When he suddenly pulled out, it was like he had drawn the breath from her along with him. She bit back a squeak as he twisted her onto her belly, yanked her hips up and shoved her head down, plunging inside of her all the way to the root.

Again, not gentle, but *definitely* glorious.

She twisted her face into the pillow and muffled her gasp. But his low grunts that accompanied each thrust made her clench around him. If it wasn't so noisy, she could imagine him smacking her ass hard as he fucked her.

Oh yes, that would be glorious and welcome, too. That first day they'd had sex, she discovered he knew how to do it just right, making it hot and not hurt. And she was surprised to find out how much it turned her on.

She was learning he liked to push her boundaries and also discovering she liked things she never expected.

His fingers weaved into her hair and he fisted his hand, holding on tightly, tugging slightly, just enough for her to feel a sweet burn against her scalp.

Shoving a hand beneath herself, she ground her fingers against her swollen and sensitive clit as he drove even deeper and harder.

"Feel you rippling 'round me, *loquilla*. Keep that shit up and I'm gonna come before you."

No, he wasn't. She was right there. Just at that point where it wouldn't take much to topple her over.

As if he could read her mind—or her body—he knew just what it would take. A wet digit pressed against her tight anus and she clenched harder.

"Let me in." His voice was tight, labored, the pull against her scalp became sharper. Then he jerked the fistful of hair he had prisoner, demanding, "Let me in."

She closed her eyes, struggled to suck in air, as she concentrated on "letting him in."

This time it was gentle *and* glorious.

"Hunter," she whimpered softly. Then she tensed and everything exploded within her. Her climax radiated from her center outward, taking him along with her as he planted himself deep and stayed there, his own orgasm so strong, she could feel his cock throbbing, even through the condom. She could only imagine if he wasn't wearing one, he'd be filling her, marking her from the inside, claiming her as his.

But those thoughts were foolish.

Today, Max was doing the press release. Hopefully, in the next couple of days Taz would surface. Then, once Hunter and his crew did their thing, the man currently giving her his weight would be gone.

His forehead pressed against her back, his fingers loosened in her hair, but he remained buried to the root inside her, his breath beating a rhythm against her heated skin. After a few moments, he nudged her, telling her without words to drop her hips to the bed and she did so, until she was flat on her stomach. His weight still covered her, his face tucked against the side of her head, his hands planted on the mattress, probably so he wouldn't crush her.

She cherished that moment as long as she could. With him above her, she felt secure. And though she could take care of herself and Leo on her own, and had been doing so for more than the past three years, it was nice to have someone else looking out for them for a change.

He was beginning to soften inside her so she knew he would be moving soon, sliding off of her and heading down the hall to dispose of the condom and clean up. She got a glimpse of the clock next to the portable monitor on the nightstand. They still had an hour before he needed to slip from her bed, so he'd be back after his trip to the bathroom. He always came back, he always pulled her into his side and she liked that, too.

She wondered what it would be like to have a man like Hunter in her bed every night and also stepping in as a father to her son.

She felt awful she couldn't give that to Leo. A balanced home with both a feminine and masculine influence.

One day, maybe.

However, today was not that day. And those thoughts were not only foolish, but dangerous. She had been hurt badly once. She should know better than to allow that to happen again.

Think before you act, Frankie.

With a groan, he moved, sliding out and off her. He removed the condom, slipped into his boxers and headed down the hall without a word. She rolled onto her back because every time he returned, he was a sight to see and she didn't want to miss it. Especially when he dropped his boxers to his feet before climbing back into bed.

Which he did this time, too.

He brushed his knuckle over her cheek, sweeping away a stray lock of hair. "Go do your thing and hurry back," he told her in a low rumble.

He didn't have to tell her twice. And when it was her turn to climb back into bed, he wrapped one of those muscular arms around her and tucked her into his side, like he always did. Using his shoulder as a pillow, she let her fingers drift over his warm, smooth skin, his pebbled nipple, then over his defined abs.

She never saw abs like that on a man in real life—definitely not in her bed—and had wondered if they really existed. Now she knew they did and were a result of hard, dedicated work. As she explored the distinct ridges and valleys, his muscles danced under her fingers.

She glanced down at her own stomach which was far from flat, had stretch marks from carrying Leo, and even a touch of cellulite.

She nuzzled her face into his neck and told it, "I need to lose some weight. Do some crunches or something."

"Says who?" came the deep grumble, his question vibrating against her ear.

"Says me. I don't have an excuse any more. Leo is three."

He snagged her hand and stilled the motion, giving her fingers a light squeeze. "You're fine. You look great in those bikini tops you love to wear."

He liked them because they obviously emphasized her breasts. But the rest... Most of her faults she kept hidden by wearing high-waisted shorts. "You don't have an ounce of fat on you. I have your share."

He lifted their clasped hands to his lips and brushed them over her knuckles. "You keep it."

"I don't want it."

Suddenly, she found herself flat on her back again, his weight pressing her into the mattress, his forehead to hers, his light brown and gold eyes serious. "*Loquilla*, I want you to have it. It's yours. It's you. I've got no complaints."

But it won't always be you in my bed.

"I'd look better thin."

He huffed out a breath. "Frankie, you look smokin' hot thick."

"Thick?" she whispered.

His face was too close to focus on it. She tried to roll her head away, but he grabbed her face between his hands and held her still. "It's a compliment. Don't get bent about it."

"How can I not? We live in a world where beauty is everything—"

"Everything about you is beautiful, Frankie."

She heard the words but didn't believe them. "I'm far from perfect. My actions have been far from perfect, too."

"Nobody is perfect, baby. Nobody. Stop beating yourself up about things that aren't important."

"I should try harder," she insisted.

"At what?"

"Working out, getting in shape."

"A man wants something worth holding onto in his bed. In his life. Any man would be lucky to have you."

How about you?

But before she could ask him, he rolled onto his back again and tucked her against him, his fingers lightly gliding up and down her spine.

"I like a woman who eats. Like a woman who cooks. Like a woman who's confident. Surprised to hear you say everything you just did."

Even the most confident of women still have moments of doubt. She said out loud, "Strong women still have weaknesses."

"As do strong men."

"Well, I told you my weakness. What about yours?"

His lips flattened, he tucked his chin to his chest and met her eyes. "Slick, *loquilla*. Real fucking slick."

She trailed her fingers down his bearded cheek and over his lips, her eyes following the same path. "You said you were going to tell me. Why does Leo's room feel like a coffin? Why can't you sleep?"

He didn't say anything for the longest time, then he took

her hand, pulled it from his face and slid it down his stomach, pausing it over his gunshot wound above his hip. "This," was all he said before guiding her hand lower, to his thigh and he stopped it over his wound there, covering her hand with his and holding it there. "This."

She was confused. "Because you got shot?"

"Because I got shot, I took cover from enemy fire."

A shiver threatened to sweep through her at the words "enemy fire." She couldn't even imagine being in the type of situation where you could die at any moment. You were fighting for not only other's lives, but your own.

He continued, "I took cover in the closest place I could find. I thought it was a safe place until I heard what was coming."

"What was coming?" she whispered, not sure she wanted to hear it. Dread crawled up her throat, even though she *knew* he survived whatever it was. But again, she couldn't imagine hiding somewhere to avoid dying and then hearing something worse coming.

"A plane. One of ours. Dropping bombs, flushing out the insurgents. They had no clue I was in the area, or any of my unit, in fact. One hit the building I was in, demolishing it."

"But you got out," she breathed.

"Eventually. But I couldn't get myself out. I was buried."

"You got out," she repeated, unable to stop it. Of course he got out, he was in her bed.

"Yeah. I got out, *loquilla*."

"How long? How long where you trapped?"

"A couple days."

A couple days buried under debris, shot and bleeding, not knowing whether you were going to live or die. Sounded like a nightmare. Which was why he probably couldn't sleep.

"I admit Leo's room is small, but small enough to affect you?"

"Truth is, I struggle with your whole house. The rooms are all small, the hallway and stairway narrow. It constantly feels like the walls are closing in on me. That the floor is rising and the ceiling is lowering. Though, I know in reality it isn't happening, it's a fear I can't shake. I was diagnosed with PTSD-induced claustrophobia."

"Was that what happened last night?" She'd never forget seeing him like that, on his hands and knees, feeling his way through the bathroom, and then following him in to see him standing under water as cold as it could get. Her stomach had risen into her throat and began to choke her, while her heart had squeezed painfully at the look on his face.

"A panic attack."

Yes, that was what that look was. Complete panic. "Have you tried to get help for them?"

"I did. Once I realized what was happening. Not much I can do about it but avoid certain situations. And recognize some of the triggers."

"Like small, dark rooms." Her house was small, but her mom had handed it down to her when she moved into her retirement community. And Frankie would be forever grateful for the chance to give Leo a roof over his head, but his room was smaller than a lot of walk-in closets in expensive homes.

"Yeah."

"Is your team aware of it?"

"No, no one knows but you. And the doctors who diagnosed me."

He shared something with her that he hadn't with his own team? The men who supposedly had his back? "You haven't told anyone?"

"No reason to. But you witnessed me during an episode, so I needed to explain it. I also wanted to let you know why I couldn't sleep in Leo's room."

"You knew it could possibly trigger you, but you tried anyway." All so he could stay close and protect them.

"Yeah, *loquilla*, it was there or the couch since I can't be in your bed."

"You can. Once Leo goes to sleep and before he wakes up."

"Right. I can sneak in here after he falls asleep and leave before he discovers me in the morning sleeping with his mother."

The way he said that shot a pain through Frankie's chest. Her heart squeezed and she studied his face. "I don't want him to get the wrong idea."

"He's three, Frankie."

"You're only here for a few days. I don't want him to think..."

"The wrong idea," he finished for her, turning his head until he was staring at the ceiling.

She studied his strong profile. The few strands of gray at his temples, his jawline covered in a tightly trimmed beard, his cheekbones, his nose, his lips she'd gotten to know oh so very well.

"He's impressionable," she whispered.

"Frankie, he's three," Hunter repeated.

"And how many three-year-olds have you had?" His head jerked as if he'd been slapped, but his expression remained blank, which made her feel bad for asking that question. But she felt the need to defend her reasoning. "He doesn't have a father and he's aware he's different from some of the other kids. Other kids in daycare mention theirs. I'm just waiting for the day he asks me where his is. Why didn't he have one? Do you know how much that'll break my heart?" Her voice caught and she quickly cleared her throat.

Hunter's chest rose sharply again as he continued to stare at the ceiling.

Now she felt the need to fill the awkward silence. "I can't just tell him his father didn't want him to exist. That the man whose blood runs through his veins is a piece of shit. That I'm all he'll ever have." *Damn*, something kept getting caught in her throat and her eyes began to burn.

His head turned toward her. "You're not all he'll ever have."

She raised her brows. "No?"

"He has his grandmother."

An ache began deep in her chest.

"And it's not like you'll never meet another man. Like I said, any man would be lucky to have you, Frankie."

That ache intensified. "I don't want just any man."

Hunter's nostrils flared and he turned his face back to the ceiling. "You shouldn't accept just any, either."

"And that's why I need to be careful about who's in my bed. I don't want to give Leo the wrong idea. Or the false hope that the man I'm having sex with is anything more than just that... A man I'm having sex with."

"Fuck," Hunter muttered. A muscle twitched in his cheek. It took him a few moments for him to explain his reaction, but she waited him out. "Claustrophobia doesn't just apply to closed spaces, Frankie. It applies to other things, as well."

Things like relationships.

But she hadn't fooled herself into believing that was where this was going between them. She knew better.

"I'm asking nothing from you, Hunter. It is what it is. I expect nothing more. I've appreciated the time you've spent in my bed and I hope it continues while you're here in town. Once your job's finished, I know you'll leave. I'm not a clingy woman, I'm not needy. I never have been, so you don't have to worry about that."

He rolled to his side and cupped her cheek. "If there was ever a woman I'd want to give anything more to,

Frankie, it would be you. But that's not me, it's not how I live my life. I struggled to put down roots in Shadow Valley, I still struggle with it every day. The deeper those roots grow, the harder it is on me. Some days I want to take a chainsaw and cut myself free just so I can breathe. Diesel needs me, my team needs me and even though I'm doing my best to overcome that issue, I'm not sure if I ever will. Being trapped is a true fear I carry around with me every damn day. And, trust me, I've never told anyone that, either. I'm giving you more of me right now than I've ever given anyone."

Holy shit. She moved until she was on top, straddling his waist and pressing her chest into his. She combed her fingers through the sides of his hair and pressed her lips to his, but only briefly. When she lifted her head, she whispered, "Thank you for letting me in. I'm sure it's not easy for men like you to reveal your weaknesses. You're expected to be strong one hundred percent of the time, but that has to be exhausting. I can't tell you how much it means to me you've shared what you did."

"Frankie."

"Yes?" She held her breath.

"You tell anyone, I'll have to kill you."

She blinked. Then the breath rushed out of her, she dropped her forehead onto his shoulder and laughed. His arms wrapped around her, holding her tight.

"Frankie," he said again.

She lifted her head. "Yes?"

He smoothed her hair away from her face and whispered, "If it was going to be anyone, it would be you."

Her laughter died and she swallowed hard when her throat tightened and the sting in her eyes returned. What should be a compliment of sorts was more like a sword jammed into her chest.

If it was going to be anyone, it would be you.

She couldn't dwell on that remark. She couldn't expect anything more than what he just handed her. She should be grateful for what he did give her.

He cared about her. Even though it had only been days, he did.

She cared about him, too.

Think before you act, Frankie.

She was afraid that "act" would be feeling more than just caring. She could very easily fall in love with the man beneath her in her bed. It might not be smart because he admitted he struggled with putting down roots and Frankie needed roots. If not for her, then for Leo.

If things had been different—

No, things were what they were. She needed to accept that. To keep that at the forefront of her mind.

A saying she once heard years ago popped into her thoughts: *We can imprison ourselves with our wants, wishes, and false dreams.*

She couldn't remember who said it, but it was true.

Wanting something that might never happen can weigh down a person, destroy any appreciation for everything they did have, no matter how small or insignificant it seemed.

She had discovered this when her dream had been to attend culinary school. Her mom couldn't afford to cover the tuition on a teacher's salary, so Frankie had done the next best thing she could think of. Working in restaurants. Stalking the cooks and the chefs in the kitchen, learning what she could, when she could. But waitressing brought in more money than a line cook, and that was where she'd have to start. At the bottom. She just never rose to the top.

Even so, she had to appreciate what she did have. She didn't have a large house, but it was hers. She might not make a lot of money, but she was employed. Even though her son didn't have a father to love him, he had a mother who loved him enough for two. She might not have more with Hunter than the moments together in her bed, but those moments would be remembered for a lifetime.

Not a "what if," but a "what is."

And what she had was a man like Hunter currently in her bed and she needed to appreciate the time they had together.

She didn't know if he was waiting for a response from her, but even so, she couldn't vocalize one and not let the disappointment she was fighting become evident.

Instead, she brushed her lips against the soft, warm skin of his shoulder. He let her slip from his arms as she moved lower, sliding her mouth across his chest and down, her tongue tracing each ridge until she got to his navel where she circled it, then followed the trail of dark hair for a few inches only to veer to his left. She kissed the scar on his hip and whispered, "Thank you for your service," then she moved on, pressing light kisses diagonally across his body until she reached his right thigh and kissed the scar there, too. "Thank you for helping us."

His hands slid into her hair, his fingers curling as he took hold, but he didn't restrict her movement. She settled between his thighs and took him semi-soft into her mouth. But as his body arched beneath her, he grew to a point where she could no longer take all of him.

Instead of words, she'd let her actions tell him how much she appreciated him, appreciated their limited time together. Her tongue swept along his length, flicked a pearl of precum off the tip and then took him as far as she could. His fingers flexed against her scalp and she tipped her eyes up to find him watching her with his eyes dark and hooded, his lips parted.

"Frankie, you don't have to." His whispered words sounded raw, strained.

She released him only long enough to say, "I know, but I

want to. You've done so much for others, I want to do something for you."

She circled the tip with her tongue and his cock flexed in her hand. She tightened her fist, slowly working it up and down his length as she took her time teasing and sucking the head. Dipping the tip of her tongue in the slit, savoring his salty taste.

His hips bucked against her. "Frankie."

"Hmm?" she hummed around his cock.

"*Fuuuuuck*," he moaned as she scraped her teeth lightly over the crown before swallowing him as far as she could.

Then she took him just a little bit deeper.

"Frankie," he panted, his abdominal muscles dancing, his hips twitching, his fingers tightening almost painfully in her hair.

She lifted her head. "Relax."

His brown eyes widened, he slammed his head back onto the pillow and barked out a laugh. "Right!"

"Quiet." She gave the same command he did earlier, then went back to town, with much more enthusiasm.

"Oh fuck, baby." He almost sounded in pain, but that couldn't be right. So, she tried harder. "Damn... I... Fuck. *Frankie*."

She lifted her head again. "When's the last time you got head?"

He dipped his chin to look at her in surprise. "What?"

"When's the last time you got head?"

"I think the question should be, when was the last time I got head *like this*?"

She grinned, squeezing her fingers around his root even tighter. "I'm doing okay then?" she teased.

His head shot off the pillow and he stared at her. Frankie bit back a giggle. "Are you fucking serious?" His head flopped back down. "Why are we having a conversation?"

"Because you kept calling my name. I figured you'd

rather talk. You keep telling me to think before I act, so I'm thinking."

His mouth dropped open, then he laughed so loudly, Frankie worried he'd wake Leo. He was still laughing when he said, "This time act, don't think."

"Sure?"

"Yeah, baby, I'm sure."

She was soaked again just from giving him head, but the warmth that landed in her center just then wasn't from that. It was from him simply calling her "baby." She liked it so much better than "*loquilla.*"

Not "what if," Frankie, "what is." What is. What is.

What was happening was what they had. No more, no less. She needed to avoid thinking any differently.

"Ah, *fuck*, baby. Keep doing that and... Fuck it... Just keep doing that."

Frankie smiled around his cock and did just that.

And not a minute later, his hips surged up, she took everything he gave her, and waited until his muscles became loose once more before crawling back to his side and tangling herself around him. With a kiss to her forehead, he intertwined their legs, and the two of them remained quiet until he slipped from her bed forty-five minutes later.

Chapter Fourteen

HUNTER PEERED AROUND THE THREADBARE, sun-faded curtain next to the front door. His eyes immediately landed on the nondescript sedan parked two houses down, just outside the glow of the street light. Walker, wearing a baseball cap, sat low behind the wheel, and anyone seeing him might think he was taking a nap. He wasn't. The man was on high alert.

Mercy and Brick were in two other nondescript rentals, making rounds through town.

Ryder was parked at the corner of Frankie's block. Steel planted himself in front of Frankie's place of employment. Even though Hunter had her call off work, Taz might still show up there looking for her.

Hunter kept her home since Max Bryson had done the first press release at noon and it would be strange for Frankie to show up at work even though her son was "found" not a half hour later. The announcements went flawlessly.

But that didn't mean the rest of the mission would.

All of them knew better than to expect that. It was when

things went smoothly all the hairs on the backs of their necks stood. They were more comfortable when shit hit the fan. But for this mission, Hunter hoped like hell it went smoothly.

He did one more check around the house. Scoped out the backyard for any movement, eyed the garage, made sure the shitty lock on the back kitchen door was engaged, then headed up the steps.

Leo was already asleep in his own room, Frankie trying to read in hers. Even though she tried to hide how nervous she was, he saw it. And he doubted she was getting any reading done.

He hit the head in preparation of a long night since he planned on keeping watch.

They doubted Taz would show up this soon—if he was going to show up at all—but no one wanted to take a chance.

As he stood in front of the toilet, the bathroom door opened, and he expected it to be Frankie.

It wasn't.

It was her son.

Leo was wiping his eyes with his fists. "Whatcha doin', Danny?"

Hunter looked down at his dick in his hand and then back at the kid, who was also staring at Hunter's dick in his hand. "Taking a piss."

He shook his dick and tucked it back in his cargo pants, zipping them shut as Leo approached.

"You didn't sit."

"Only sit when I—" *Shit*, he couldn't say that. "I stand to pee, little man."

"Momma makes me sit when I pee in da poddy."

"She probably has a good reason for that."

"I wanna try standin'."

Fuck. He needed to call Frankie in. Teaching a kid to "pee in the potty" was out of his wheelhouse. "Let me get your momma."

"No! Want you!" Leo screamed which made Hunter wince since the room was so small.

"I... uh..." *Fuck.* "Do you even need to pee?"

Leo nodded, his head flopping back and forth like it was too heavy to nod.

Fuck.

"Uh. Okay..." Hunter stepped back from the toilet and pointed. "Stand there, little man." Leo scrambled into place. "Now, drop your drawers and point your..." What the fuck did kids call their dick?

"Pee pee."

That sounded about right. "Point your pee pee into the center, then do your thing."

Leo blinked his large brown eyes up at him. And, *Jesus,* something tugged at Hunter he didn't recognize.

But Leo not only dropped his pull-up a little, he dropped them all the way to the floor, so everything was hanging out.

Fuck. He lifted his head and was about to yell for Frankie when Leo said, "'Kay."

He could do this. He didn't need Frankie. The boy didn't have a man in his life, and he needed to learn to be a man. Even if only when taking a piss.

But the kid was three. He could hardly reach the toilet. "I'm going to hold you up. Okay?"

Leo's head bobbed back and forth again like he had no spine. "'Kay."

Hunter hooked him under the armpits and lifted him above the rim and tilted him forward just a bit. "Okay, grab your..." *Fuck.* "Pee pee, aim and shoot."

Leo giggled. Was the kid setting him up?

He was three, Hunter reminded himself.

"Grab it and go," Hunter encouraged him.

Leo grabbed it and, unfortunately, his aim game was not on point. Hunter watched the yellow stream arc up and then hit the rim of the toilet, splashing them both.

"F—" Hunter bit back his curse, took a breath and glanced down at both of them.

"I shot it!" Leo crowed, laughing.

"Yeah, you did. And this is why your momma makes you sit."

"Wanna do it again."

Yeah, that wasn't going to happen. Now, they both needed to clean up.

Hunter heard a noise to his right and saw Frankie leaning in the doorway with a huge grin and her dark eyes full of amusement.

"Just in time to clean up your little man."

"I'll give you an A for good effort," she said, fighting back a laugh.

Hunter set Leo down away from the puddle on the floor and when Leo bent over to pull up his diaper, Hunter stopped him with, "No, Momma's got to clean you up first."

"Danny's going to grab a wet washcloth and clean you up, while Momma gets something to clean up the spill." She turned and walked away.

"I don't want you going downstairs alone, Frankie," he called.

She appeared in the doorway, her eyes wide. "Really?"

Hunter's eyes dropped to Leo, then hit hers again. "Really. Stay upstairs. I'll go grab some paper towels. You clean up your boy and put him back in bed."

"Momma, read me 'nother story," Leo interjected, still standing there with his pull-up around his ankles and his little T-shirt yanked up his rounded belly.

"I already read you two when I put you to bed earlier."

"Wanna 'nother one."

"Oh, well, since when do you always get what you want?" Frankie asked with a frown.

"Since forever."

Frankie rolled her eyes and pinned her lips together. "You got that wrong. The correct answer was 'since never.' You don't get to demand things. You can ask, but if I say no, then you have to accept that."

"An' if I say no, you hafta 'cept that."

Frankie's head jerked back, and her eyes narrowed on her son. As her mouth opened, Hunter pushed past Leo and stepped in front of Frankie. He tucked a finger under her chin, closed her mouth and stared down into her eyes. "Baby, get him cleaned up. I'll grab the paper towels and take care of this mess. Then I'll read him a story."

And, fuck him, if Frankie's face didn't go soft and her lips part, an audible breath escaping. "Okay," she whispered. "I think I just dropped like a dozen eggs, so you might have to double up on the condoms tonight to be safe. I'm not responsible for my fertility right now."

Hunter grinned and dropped his mouth to her ear. "We'll use your mouth. And there's another option, too. Shouldn't be an issue."

Her mouth dropped open even farther as he pushed past her and headed downstairs.

———

THREE DAYS. Three fucking days after the press release and nothing. Not one peep from the asshole whose sperm tagged her egg.

Frankie was about to lose her mind. She knew the Shadows Security *hot-as-fuck* men were out there, watching and waiting. Following her to and from work. Sitting outside the restaurant while she busted her ass inside to make tips. Staking out her house. Roaming around Manning Grove. And doing whatever other secret squirrel shit they did.

Hunter was on edge. Which made her on edge even worse. He was on his cell phone constantly communicating with his "team." She tried to keep busy when she wasn't at work by cooking up a storm, making meals and trying out new recipes that the chef at The Carriage House taught her. Somehow, Hunter would get those meals out to his guys and the feedback she'd get was positive. Full containers went out, empty containers were returned with requests for bigger servings next time.

She gladly obliged but her groceries were getting low and her garden picked thin. That was when Hunter even allowed her to go out and work in her garden. He usually stood somewhere where he couldn't be seen, but where he could keep an eye on her and Leo.

Then there was Leo... Her son followed Hunter around emulating him a lot. Too much so. He was getting way too attached to the man who wouldn't be sticking around much longer.

Her son no longer wanted Frankie to read him a bedtime story. Instead, he demanded Hunter do it. And, despite Frankie's annoyance at Leo's demands, Hunter did it. He tolerated the short time in Leo's tiny room to read her son a story in his deep, deep, pussy-clenching voice.

Though as soon as Leo nodded off, Hunter didn't linger. He'd bolt from Leo's room, head downstairs and step out back into the shadows for some air.

Frankie told him to stop giving into Leo's demands, otherwise, her son would turn into an intolerable monster. Even at three, he had a strong personality that needed a firm hand. Hunter was going to spoil the shit out of him, then leave that mess behind for her to deal with when he was finished in Manning Grove.

He ignored her. Which was why when two nights ago after they had a whole one-sided conversation about just that, she went to her bedroom by herself and locked the door. He could sleep on the damn couch or sit up all night on watch. She didn't give a flying fuck.

That was until he picked her bedroom door lock and secured it behind him, his expression not showing any kind of happy.

"You lock me out of your room and bed again, I'm going to get one of my brothers to take him to the park, so I can teach his mother a lesson and we won't have to worry about how loud she gets when I have her across my knee."

Frankie had to admit—reluctantly—that warning made her toes curl, her pussy pulse and every cell in her body quiver.

And then he did teach her a lesson, but quietly and, while it was definitely not gentle, it was once again *glorious*. So glorious she swore she heard angels singing and cherubs flitting around playing harps afterward.

After that was over, she had no energy to argue anything.

At least for a good fifteen minutes.

But now, as she trudged up the steps after her long shift, her feet sore from being on them for hours, her face aching from smiling at her customers, and sporting a huge tension headache, she was ready for all of this to be over.

Taz needed to expose himself so Hunter and his fellow Shadows could "take care of business."

As she hit the top couple of steps, she heard murmuring coming through the open bathroom door. Then she heard Leo giggle and chatter something she didn't catch. Sometimes when he got really excited his words blended together and she had to make him slow down and repeat it.

Which was what Leo was doing when Frankie moved in

that direction, expecting déjà vu and a puddle of urine on the floor.

That wasn't what she found.

She stopped short just outside the bathroom, seeing Leo sitting on the edge of the sink, wearing only The Incredible Hulk pull-ups, and Hunter, only wearing black cargo pants, standing in front of the sink, leaning toward the mirror, a razor in his hand, shaving cream on his face.

The stroke of the razor was smooth and slow as he explained to Leo how to shave.

He was three!

And, more importantly, why was Hunter shaving off his beard?

"Momma!" Leo yelled, but didn't leap off the sink, coming running to her, hug her tightly and tell her how much he missed her. Hell no. He remained where he was near his new manly mentor.

Great.

She was losing her own kid. The one she carried for nine months, who kicked the shit out of her insides, and then gave her permanent stretch marks. That kid.

"Don't shave your beard," she said quickly, but Hunter ignored her, stretched out his skin and made another pass with the razor on his neck.

"I'm not. Just cleaning up the edges and giving the little man a lesson."

"He won't remember that lesson by the time he has enough hair to shave."

Hunter dropped his hand and turned to look at Frankie. "He might."

"I doubt it. Someone else will have to teach him that lesson when it's closer to that time."

Hunter carefully put the razor down on the opposite side of the sink, grabbed Leo by the armpits and put him onto his feet. "Give your momma a hug. Apparently, she had a long day." He shot Frankie a frown.

"You done?" Leo asked him, her son blinking up at the man with eyes full of worship.

Damn it.

Hunter ruffled his dark brown hair, which was already standing on end, most likely from the bits of blue Playdoh she spotted in it. "Yeah, bud, I'm done for now. Say hello to your momma. I'm sure she missed you."

Hunter reached for a hand towel and began to wipe away the remaining shaving cream as he stared into the mirror and while he did it, Frankie couldn't miss his jaw working.

She had said something he didn't like. But they weren't going to pretend he was sticking around to teach Leo things when he was ready to learn them.

He wasn't.

So, there was no point in pretending.

"Danny put shavin' cream on my face!" Leo spouted loudly.

Frankie's eyebrows rose but she kept her attention on her son. "He did?"

Leo's head bounced back and forth in a sloppy nod. "Yeah! An' then he shaved my face!"

Frankie lifted her gaze to see Hunter watching her in the mirror. He shook his head slightly. She dropped her attention back to Leo. "How cool! You're getting to be such a big boy. Peeing in the potty and shaving," she muttered. "Next, he'll take you driving."

Hunter's hands gripped the edge of the counter and he dropped his head, shaking it again.

Leo darted past her and screamed down the hallway, driving an invisible car. "Yeah, drivin'! Vroom vroom."

"No," was all Frankie said, then turned to follow her son.

"You two do not go downstairs without me," came the low warning.

She stopped in her tracks, backed up a couple of steps, leaned into the bathroom and announced, "We need to talk." Then she followed Leo into his room, snagged him by the waist and carried him downstairs giggling so they could watch a half hour of cartoons together before putting him to bed.

———

"I TOLD you not to go downstairs without me, *loquilla*," came the growl near her ear. Her hands were submerged in soapy water as she washed the dishes. His heat seared her back as he caged her in by planting his palms on the counter on either side of her. "You disobeyed me, and disobeying comes with consequences."

"Can't wait," she said, trying her best to sound bored. She was anything but. Though, she was disappointed he was back to using "*loquilla*" instead of "baby."

"This isn't a game, Frankie. You gotta keep on your toes and you need to listen."

She went back to scrubbing the dish with the sponge. "I can't take much more of this."

"What?"

"All of it. My nerves are shot."

"As soon as he surfaces, we'll be out of your hair. Your life can go back to how it was, and you won't have to worry about him showing up and messing with you."

That was the problem. She didn't want her life to go back to how it was. Things had changed in the last couple of weeks.

But, she reminded herself for the millionth time, this was fantasy, not reality. Temporary, not permanent. Leo was Taz's son, not Hunter's.

She dropped her head and closed her eyes. She only wanted the best for Leo, and she couldn't give him that.

She could barely get by with what she made at the restaurant, her home was small, old and in need of repairs, her car on its last legs. Their future was bleak. She couldn't start a college fund for Leo, she couldn't buy him new clothes, and she certainly couldn't provide him with a good male influence.

"Frankie, you wanted to talk. So, talk."

She dropped the sponge into the water and turned in his arms, leaning back against the edge of the sink.

She couldn't let being so close to him change her mind. "I think you need to switch with one of the other guys." It came out in a rush, but she knew he heard her because his chin jerked back, and his eyes narrowed.

Also, because he asked, "What?"

Not "What?" like "I didn't hear you," but "What?" like "What the fuck?"

And she knew he heard her clearly because that "What?" was very growly.

She pushed onward by nodding and saying, "I think Steel or one of the other guys needs to guard the house, while you—"

"I'm watching over the kid and I'm watching over you. The fuck if I'm letting Steel or Brick... or any of them... in here to take over that job."

"Why? Are they not as capable as you?"

His mouth opened, closed, then opened once more. "Our team is the best in the business."

"So then, it shouldn't be an issue."

His nostrils flared, and a muscle pulsed in his cheek. "It's an issue."

"I'm worried Leo's getting attached to you. You'll up and leave when this is all over, Hunter. Then what? This was why I wasn't eager to go out and start dating again. I didn't want to disappoint him by having a man come into his life and then split."

"It's no more than if an uncle came to visit."

Her eyes bugged out. "Oh no. I'm not playing that game where I have my kid call the men I'm dating 'Uncle.'" She shuddered. "It's creepy and wrong."

Chapter Fifteen

FIRST OF ALL, Frankie needed to not use the word "men" when it came to dating. That meant multiples. She needed to find one man. A good one.

Second of all...

He pushed away from both the counter and her, and turned his back to her, scrubbing a hand over his hair and down his cheek, trying not to bellow his frustration.

Second of all, she shouldn't be looking for *any* man.

Fuck him.

Fuck him.

Fuck him with a fucking goddamn red-hot poker.

Jam it up his ass and in his eye. *Fuck.*

"Frankie," he murmured, still facing away from her.

"What, Hunter?" She sounded annoyed, but he didn't give a fuck.

"You're stuck with me." When she didn't say anything, he continued, trying not to lose his shit about her wanting him out of her house. "We have our mission set, we have our positions, we're not switching it up. If you don't like it, too fucking bad."

He turned in time to watch her chest rise and fall and

her eyes change when she whispered, "It's not just Leo I'm worried about."

He did a slow blink and ignored her deeper implication, hoping he misunderstood. "We're here to keep you safe. We know what we're doing, Frankie."

"But what are *we* doing, Hunter?"

Fuck, he hadn't misunderstood. A prickle of unease slithered down his spine. "Frankie, you yourself said 'it is what it is.' You expected nothing more than what I was giving you. Are you telling me now, that's not true?"

Fuck, that wasn't true.

"You're not only burrowing into my son's life, but mine, too. Problem is, I like it... too much. I don't want to get used to this, because when you walk out the door," she flung her hand out toward the front of the house, "it's going to hurt. And you *will* walk out that door."

"I had no idea you were feeling differently." He had no fucking clue. If he had, he would have parked his ass on the couch, not in her bed.

She planted her hands on her hips, tilted her head to the side and huffed, "Really?"

He took a step closer to her. "Yeah, really. I can't be tied down, Frankie."

She closed her eyes and whispered, "I know."

"Then I'm not getting where you're going."

Her eyes opened and she gave him a hard look. "Then you're not listening. I said you need to switch out with one of your crew."

He stared at the reason his blood pressure was spiking. "And you didn't listen when I said that ain't happening."

"I need some separation from you. And you from Leo."

He took another step closer until they were only a couple feet apart. "Again, not happening."

She spun away from him. "I can't do this."

"It'll be over soon, Frankie." His patience was at its limit.

"I know!" she hissed. "That's the problem. I'm falling in love with you and so is Leo."

The words on Hunter's tongue dissolved and he stepped back, giving them some space.

"It is what it is," he said, unable to form any other response. He swallowed, trying to open his narrowing throat.

Frankie huffed out a bitter laugh. "It is what it is. You're right." She spun on him, her expression holding a whole lot of hurt. "It is what it is. You're here for a job, you're here to help me. And I'm grateful for that second part, believe me. I expected nothing more from you because I wasn't looking for that myself. But shit happens. Things I can't control. Having you in my bed night after night... Seeing how you are with Leo... Watching you fix things around my house... I didn't mean for it to happen, it just did. It caught me unprepared."

He opened his mouth to proclaim, "It's just sex," but he snapped it shut, because that was a fucking lie. It wasn't just sex. It was way more than fucking sex.

So much more.

His heart began to thunder in his chest and his breath became shallow.

He had stepped in it.

He stuck his fucking foot right in it.

He wasn't even aware of it until just now. Seeing Frankie's face, hearing her words, feeling her ache.

He got it.

He did. He just didn't like it.

He wasn't sure if he could live with it.

But if him being in her home was going to cause her and Leo pain, then he had to do something about that. He needed to switch out. Put Mercy or Ryder in the house. They were safe since each of them had no interest in any other woman than the one they already had.

They wouldn't put the moves on Frankie, so that possibility wouldn't be eating at him.

But he didn't want to fucking leave.

He wanted to be in this house, be in her bed.

But he also didn't want to cause her pain.

Because he couldn't stay. He couldn't settle.

His roots were still shallow in Shadow Valley, and she needed more than that. She and her son needed deep and solid.

She didn't need a man who took off at a moment's notice to head across country when required. She needed a man who was stable.

He wasn't it.

He wasn't looking for a relationship.

He wasn't looking for a family.

It wasn't them. It was him.

Because if it could be him, it would be them.

He needed his freedom. He needed his space.

He had looked death directly in the face the last time that had been taken away from him. He never wanted to be in a situation where he felt trapped again. He might not survive it a second time.

He realized she was still talking but he couldn't hear anything except a roar in his ears.

His vision unclouded and he didn't see anger or sadness but instead fear on her face. Was she worried about him?

He mentally shook himself and she was whispering his name, her hand squeezing his arm.

"What's wrong?"

"Didn't you hear that noise?"

His spine snapped straight, and his mind cleared as the last of the fog shook free. He listened carefully. "What noise?"

"Outside."

He heard nothing, but he was taking no chances. "Get upstairs. Get in Leo's room and lock the door."

"Hun—"

"Now, Frankie, no back-talk."

Her mouth opened, but she closed it quickly, nodded and headed out of the kitchen.

"Do not leave his room until I come get you."

She didn't respond but he heard her running up the steps.

He had removed his gun from the small of his back when he was shaving since he didn't want Leo asking him about it. But he'd secured it again once he tossed a T-shirt over his head before searching out Frankie in the kitchen.

He was glad he did.

He pulled his weapon from the holster and his cell phone from the side pocket of his cargo pants.

He texted the team. *Noise. House. Rear. Eyes?*

Walker quickly texted back. *Nothing.*

Various times of ETA were texted back to him. Steel was only two minutes out, but Walker was closer.

He texted back quickly. *Don't come in hot.*

Copy came back from all of them, except Walker, who Hunter expected to come in on foot and under cover since he was so close.

Hunter turned off the overhead kitchen light and put his back to the wall next to the door that led to the backyard. He held his breath and listened carefully but still heard nothing.

He double checked the lock and as he was doing so, heard a scratching noise and a clunk on the small overhang above the door and stoop. How that raggedy roof would hold anyone's weight, he had no fucking clue, but he wasn't waiting for it to come crashing down and deposit Taz at his feet.

Fuck no. He was taking that fucker out.

He moved through the house—for once glad it was small—and out the front door, grabbing a key as he went and locking it behind him. Then he slipped around to the side of the house nearest the garage and spotted Walker in the shadows.

When Walker gave him a hand signal, Hunter shook his head and pointed to his ear.

Walker nodded and disappeared around the back of the garage and before he could move, Steel was next to him.

Jesus. Good thing it was Steel and not Taz. Hunter's game was off. He needed to focus and stop thinking about everything Frankie had said.

"You shit yourself?" Steel asked under his breath.

Hunter shot him a "fuck you" look and began to move, gun out, ears open, eyes focused.

Steel moved with him, his back practically touching Hunter's, his weapon out and his eyes peeled.

As they reached the back corner of the house, they spotted Walker at the rear corner of the garage closest to the house. He was visually sweeping the yard. When his eyes landed on Hunter, he shook his head.

Fuck.

Hunter pointed up at the roof over the back door and Walker again shook his head.

Then they heard it.

A loud yowl and a thump. A fucking cat streaked past them, the tail curled high and puffed out.

Walker dropped his head and shook it. Hunter could see his body shaking from where he stood.

Hunter lifted one finger and they listened for a few more minutes. Nothing.

Just a fucking neighborhood cat.

All three holstered their handguns. Then met halfway.

Steel snorted. "There's that fucking wild pussy you said scratched your back, Danny-boy."

"And that's the only type of pussy that'll let you touch it, asshole," Hunter growled back.

Walker pulled his phone out and said quietly, "Gonna text the other three, tell them to stand-down and not blow their cover in case Taz is in the area."

"Well, if the fucker's watching, he now knows we're waiting for him," Hunter said, his gaze sliding through the dark backyard one more time.

Steel whacked him on the back. "Three days already, dude. Time's ticking. D's gonna give us two more, then we're being recalled. So... whataya gonna do when that happens?"

Hunter stared at the house. "She wants me to switch out."

He sensed rather than saw Steel jerk next to him. "What?"

"She wants me out, someone else in." Hunter turned toward Steel to see his grin. "Not you. You're not getting in there." He meant that in more ways than one.

"Must be you ain't giving her the dick good enough."

"She isn't in charge of this mission, brother," Walker said as he stepped shoulder to shoulder with Hunter. "You are. She doesn't make the rules, you do. You wanna remain in there, you remain in there. She likes it, she doesn't like it. Doesn't fucking matter. Not her call. She's benefitting from someone else's job. She should be happy that she's not only getting one of her problems taken care of but getting some dick while that's happening."

Hunter's lips flattened out and did something smart, he waited to respond.

Gotta think before you act, loquilla.

She wasn't the only one.

"So, who are you gonna swap out with? Mercy or Ryder?" Steel asked. "Apparently, you'll only choose someone who already has their dick in a cock cage."

Mercy or Ryder.

Neither.

Walker was right. "Not her say how this is run," Hunter told him. "I'm staying in that house and I'm staying longer than two days if that shit stain doesn't show up. I'm staying until D loses his fucking mind and then, and only then, if Taz hasn't come up for air, I'll head back."

Steel's lips twitched. "Must be one sweet cunt."

"Brother," Walker murmured the warning low.

Hunter leaned dangerously close to Steel and growled, "You stayed three days with her, what do you think?"

Steel's jaw worked a couple times before he spit out, "Thinking she's worth staying until the boss man loses his fucking mind."

Hunter straightened and nodded once. "Just a clarification. She isn't sweet, she's fucking hot and spicy and will scorch you with that first bite."

"Just your type." Walker chuckled next to him and Steel grinned.

That would be true if he had a type.

He glanced back at the house. Apparently, he had one.

"Keep to the shadows and get back where you need to be," Hunter said. "I'm gonna go get where I need to be, too. Whether she likes it or not."

"Fuck. To be a fly on the wall," Walker said as he disappeared behind the garage.

"Guess you're going to be kicking that spice up a notch. Careful you're not permanently scarred, Danny."

When Steel turned to go, Hunter stopped him with a soft, "Brother."

Steel turned back around, his brows raised. Hunter held out his hand and they clasped arms, Hunter's hand by Steel's elbow, Steel's by his. "Gotta thank you for stepping into my place for three days when I headed to Lancaster. Gotta thank you for showing up so quickly just now."

Steel stared at him for a second, squeezing Hunter's

forearm. "Always got your back, just like you got mine. And that place I stepped into wasn't yours at the time. Seems it is now." Steel grinned and released his arm. "You're fucked. Gonna go get on Adam & Eve's website and order you a cock cage. Extra small, right?" He spun on his heels as he laughed, then disappeared around the side of the house.

Hunter dropped his head and stared at his boots for a long moment. Sucking in a deep breath, he set his jaw and headed into the house.

Chapter Sixteen

"IF YOU THINK I'm leaving this house, you are fucking crazy, woman. I'm staying. Deal with it. I'll sleep on the fucking couch if you can't handle us spending time together. That's fine. It'll be all business from here on out." He gripped the back of his neck with his hand and twisted it back and forth. "Fuck!" he growled, then left her room, probably wanting to slam the door, but didn't since Leo was sleeping.

That was what he said. That was what he did.

That being three nights ago after they had found a cat on the roof and not Taz.

She let him stomp out and grabbed her tablet, attempting to read until she fell asleep, but she couldn't do either.

Because she wanted him in her bed. But she wasn't going to invite him back.

No fucking sir.

She was already in deep and didn't need to fall down that hole any further.

This morning the rest of his team was heading back to Shadow Valley. She only knew that because last night over a late dinner, he mentioned it. But that was all he said. Instead of them having a conversation, he had one with Leo the rest of the meal.

If he'd rather have a conversation with her three-year-old that was fine with her.

Though, in truth, it wasn't.

Watching Leo's face as he did his best to have a conversation with the man across the table from him, not only warmed her heart, it broke it.

Leo would be devastated when Hunter left.

Who was she kidding? So would she.

And as tempted as she was to call him upstairs back to her bed for the nights he'd remain in Manning Grove, she resisted.

But now it was a little after two a.m. and she lay in her bed wide awake, parts of her aching which shouldn't be. Aching for a man she shouldn't, either. She had two choices. Take matters into her own hands or succumb to her weakness and go downstairs.

They had hardly said more than a few words to each other the last three days but what she wanted from him didn't take words.

She rolled over and yanked open her nightstand drawer.

No, it took condoms.

Condom. Singular. She only needed one.

Afterward, she could come back upstairs sated and hopefully sleep until Leo woke her up.

She grabbed a condom, slipped out of bed, tucked her wayward boobs back into her tank top but skipped her PJ shorts, which she had dropped to the floor before climbing in. And, after peeking in on Leo to make sure he was sleeping solidly, hoofed it down the steps in the dark in just her loose, sleeveless tank and panties.

As she hit the bottom of the steps, she turned her head toward her living room and came to a stop.

Hunter was sitting on the couch, not appearing to be sleeping.

Oh no, because not only were his bare feet planted on the floor, but his knees were spread, his head tilted back resting on the back of the couch, and quite possibly his eyes were closed but she couldn't tell because of the dark and distance.

She held her breath as she took one step into her small living room, staring at why, even though his eyes were closed, she knew he wasn't sleeping.

His hand was wrapped around his erection, his boxers pushed halfway down his thighs. And he was pumping that hand at a rapid, but steady pace.

Frankie released the breath she'd been holding, and the ragged rush of air sounded deafening in the otherwise quiet room.

His hand stilled, his head turned, and his eyes opened.

Frankie found herself frozen where she stood, her eyes holding his.

She half expected him to release himself and yank up his boxers since he'd been caught.

He didn't.

Instead, he stared at her and began to stroke again.

And if that sight didn't make her pussy throb, her nipples bead and her core heat up, nothing would.

He tracked her as she moved deeper into the room, a trickle of wet slipping from her and dampening her panties even further. He kept sliding his fist up and down his cock as she stopped directly in front of him, not sure where to look first. His face with his eyelids heavy and mouth parted. The corded muscles bulging in his neck. The rise and fall of his tattooed bare chest, the gleam from his dog tags still visible in the limited light. The heavy muscles of his thighs contracting with each pull of his hand.

Or his thick cock, circled by long fingers. Both of which

she knew intimately and had done very wicked, glorious things to almost every part of her body.

Which she hoped he was willing to use on her again.

She stepped between his knees and licked her lips, wanting to taste the shiny crown of his cock, but thinking she might only have one shot at him, so she needed to go big or go home. Or, at least, back upstairs.

She didn't want to waste this time with him losing himself in her mouth instead of where she wanted him. She also didn't want to watch him come with his fist, so she needed to act.

But as she went to climb onto his lap, he stopped her with a palm between her breasts. "You don't want me in your house or your bed, but you want to use me for your own pleasure."

He had released his cock and it bobbed between them. "Yes." She didn't care if that sounded selfish, because for once, she wanted to be selfish. She needed to be selfish.

She needed the man on that couch. She needed him to do those wicked, glorious things to her.

She just somehow had to coat her heart in Teflon, so her emotions remained detached from her desires. She didn't know how that would work, but it needed to. Otherwise, coming downstairs was going to be a bigger mistake than letting him into her bed in the first place. She already had enough regrets in her life and she didn't need more.

But what happened next, she would not regret.

At all.

His hand that had been stroking his cock, tangled in her hair, fisted it, and yanked her head back so sharply she gasped. The fingers pressed to her chest curled into the worn cotton and he yanked her tank top so hard, her body shot forward, but the shirt still gave way with a tear, exposing her breasts.

Keeping her neck arched sharply by using his grip in her

hair, he leaned forward and bit the flesh right above her right nipple and she whimpered.

Not gentle, but glorious.

"Condom. Now."

Her fingers trembled as she tried to open the wrapper, making it take three attempts, but she got it open, then reached out blindly to find his twitching cock and roll it on.

Her strained neck was starting to ache, her pussy was throbbing, and she could feel the slickness between her upper thighs. He sucked her left nipple into his mouth, his tongue circled the nub and flicking it.

She tried to move forward, to mount him, but he held her in place with her hair.

She whispered a throaty, "Hunter." But he ignored her, instead switching nipples, sucking the one, tweaking the other with his fingers.

Not gentle, not tender. Rough and raw like her whisper.

He let her breast go and wrapped his arm around her waist, pulling her off balance, her hands finding his shoulders to keep from falling. She scrambled to straddle him, her knees digging into the couch cushions on both sides of his spread thighs. Her legs were not nearly as long as his, so this position planted her soaked pussy along the hard line of his cock. Rocking his hips, he slid himself between her slick labia, his length brushing against her sensitive clit.

Every one of her nerve endings was popping and hissing like a cut electric line, so she could come simply by what he was doing. He continued to thrust up, but not inside her, letting her ride his hard length. She ground against him, now chasing that orgasm. She wanted it.

She needed it.

And when she found it, he pressed his face into her arched neck, his teeth skimming along her stretched skin. She rode that climax to completion, still sliding him back and forth between her folds, her body twitching every time his cock brushed against her swollen clit.

As soon as the last wave had waned, he hooked her under her thighs and lifted her, grunting, "Position me."

Grabbing his cock, she lined him up and when he let her thighs go, she settled on his lap, his cock filling her, stretching her, unable to go any deeper.

A sigh escaped her. They hadn't had sex for the last two nights and she never knew she'd miss it so damn much.

Not sex in general. Sex with Hunter.

His tongue followed the line of her throat and he sucked at the hollow, released her hair, dug his fingers into both of her ass cheeks and began to guide her up and down. He held tightly to her flesh, separating her cheeks, exposing her vulnerable spot. A spot he had touched, licked and teased but had gone no further with her.

Would she let him if he tried tonight?

She was afraid she was falling so deeply she'd say yes to anything.

That wasn't her. That wasn't Frankie. She was not a woman who let a man control her. Not even Taz. If that man hadn't caught her that day making arrangements to disappear, she would have been gone.

But this wasn't Taz, this wasn't any other man. This was Hunter.

This was a man who was sacrificing his time to help her and her son. This was a man who remained in a house which triggered his claustrophobia to help them.

While she wanted to use him for her own needs, she wanted him to use her, too.

Mutual satisfaction.

So, if he wanted to go there, she'd do her best not to stop him.

When his lips touched the spot where her neck met her shoulder, she braced for him to bite her. He didn't, instead his breath puffed warmly against her heated skin. She held her own as his hands slid lower on her ass, his fingers finding where they were connected, one dipping in alongside his cock, an odd, but exhilarating, feeling. She ground down against his cock and finger, her forehead landing hard on his shoulder as she muffled a groan against his skin.

He slid his finger back out and up along her crease until he stopped exactly where she knew he would, then without hesitation or even preparation, he thrust it inside.

She sucked in a shaky breath as he plunged it in and out of her, in the opposite rhythm of his cock. Adding a second finger, he fucked both her pussy and her ass at the same time.

Any and all thoughts dissipated like a chef throwing a handful of flour in the air.

The sensations he was causing destroyed all rational thoughts.

The tip of his tongue traced up her neck again, along her jaw and when he put his mouth to her ear and growled, "That pussy is mine, that ass is mine," another orgasm ripped through her, causing her to clench down on his cock and fingers, causing her to lose her mind and hiss out a, "Yes."

Because if she had been in her right mind, she never would agree with his claiming of her. She was falling in love with him, but he would never own her.

No man ever would.

But for this moment, she allowed it. Allowed him to think what was hers was his.

Because soon he would leave what he just claimed behind. For that reason, she let him have his fantasy. She also let herself have her own.

And that fantasy included one more climax before he got his.

The hand gripping her ass slid up her back and into her

hair again, taking hold and moving her until they were eye to eye, nose to nose. Lips close, their breaths meeting, merging.

"Baby," he breathed.

Not *loquilla*, not Frankie. Baby.

The way he said it chipped the Teflon she'd coated her heart with.

She struggled to patch that missing piece as their rhythm slowed, their lips touched, and he breathed the word "baby" again, this time into her mouth where she tasted it.

Then she tasted him as he claimed not only her pussy and her ass, but her mouth. It began soft but became more frantic, his tongue taking control of hers.

A groan bubbled up her throat when he didn't let up, his hips driving up, his fingers gliding in and out of her, his lips plundering hers.

She stopped breathing, but only for a moment as he grunted and his hips shot up and he spilled himself deep inside her. She came again as she rocked back and forth, grinding her clit against him, her beaded nipples brushing along his hot, damp skin.

Then he broke the kiss, pinned their foreheads together and breathed, "Baby," one final time.

She closed her eyes, let that swirl through her mind before tucking it away where she'd keep it as a memory.

Nothing was said between them until the sweat on their skin was almost dry and their labored breathing smoothed out.

After the few moments she allowed herself to stay connected, she pulled away and he didn't fight it. He let her go without a word as she nabbed her panties and went back upstairs to clean up.

Back in her room, in her bed, she once again stared through the dark, but this time her eyes were glued to the knob on her bedroom door, waiting for it to turn.

It didn't.

And the sleep she was hoping for never came, either.

———

"'Nough time wasted," came the bark through the phone. "Been a month since the pigs made that announcement. The fucker's hopefully dead."

"If he isn't?"

"Then he isn't," Diesel answered. "Pigs can deal with 'im if he shows up in their territory."

"D—"

"Pussy worth losin' your job over? Slade ain't payin' for you to take a fuckin' vacation full of gettin' some snatch. Him payin' for you to get a rub an' tug would be fuckin' cheaper."

"We all want to find Taz."

"Yeah, started out for one reason, turned into another. Now you're ridin' the third reason. She wanna pay for personal protection, she can fuckin' pay. She don't, then I need your ass back here. Got payin' jobs here waitin'."

"She can't afford to pay for protection. She's barely making it as it is."

"So's most Americans. Ain't gettin' a hand-out from us even if she squirted out Slade's nephew. If you're so fuckin' worried 'bout 'er, bring 'er back here. Set 'er up in your place. You get the snatch, she gets protection from the club, the Shadows. Hell, the sisterhood. An' Slade gets to help raise his blood to keep 'im from becomin' a fuckwad like the rest of his family. If the bitch don't wanna move, then it's on her."

Pussy. Snatch. Bitch. Hunter dropped his head, his phone held away from his ear as he did his best not to snap out on his boss.

The last three weeks had been difficult with keeping his

hands off Frankie. He had left it her choice whether to sneak down the stairs and join him. She hadn't. Only that one night and then that was it.

They were civil with each other. He watched Leo and the house when she went to work. He stuck close, but not in her personal space when she was home. Her days off, he went with her to her mom's to visit. Her mom still wasn't sure what to think about him, but the older woman uttered more words to him than Frankie did. If it wasn't for Leo being a chatty kid, the silence would have made him lose his shit.

He'd watch her when she wasn't looking. And he caught her many a time watching him when she didn't realize he was paying attention. But he was. That was his job, to pay attention.

And it was so fucking hard not to pay attention to the woman he wanted to shove against the wall and fuck from behind until she squirted all over his cock when she came.

Jesus. He shouldn't be getting a half-chub while his boss was on the other end of the phone. He pressed the phone back to his ear.

"Time is money, brother," Diesel was saying. "If she don't got it, then we don't got it. Got me?"

"D—"

"Ass back here today. With or without 'er. You wanna keep searchin' for that motherfucker, then do it on your own fuckin' time. Got me?"

Hunter pressed his lips together to stem the flow of words which would only piss off the big man. Instead he forced out, "Got you."

"Today," D barked and the call cut off.

Hunter's gaze lifted from the dark phone to Leo, who was running around the backyard chasing a blue inflatable ball. He'd almost catch it, accidentally kick it, scream non-sensical things, then chase it some more on his stubby legs.

Hunter sucked in a breath when the kid face-planted into the grass, his momentum almost tumbling him end over end.

Fuck! Hunter raced over to him, hooking him by the underarms and putting him back on his feet before searching his body to make sure there was no blood or injuries. "You okay?" His heart dropped from his throat back into his chest as the kid looked unharmed.

Leo smiled big and screamed, "'Kay!" Then flopped to the ground and started rolling around in the grass, belly to back, belly to back, rolling toward the ball, giggling all the way.

Hunter sighed and shook his head, wondering if Frankie's kid was normal.

He pulled his cell phone back out of his back pocket, where he had shoved it when he saw Leo eat it, took a short video and sent it to Frankie along with the text: *Ur boy's whacked.*

She sent back a laughing emoji and the text: *He's perfect.*

Hunter had to admit, he was. She was raising him right. He was a happy kid even though he didn't have a lot of material things. But what he did have was good enough. Clean clothes, good homemade food, and a roof over his head.

And, most importantly, a mother who loved him without letting the bitterness of who his father was affect that love.

Leo was Frankie's and no one else's.

He would grow up into a well-adjusted man whether Frankie found a father-figure for him or not. Plenty of mothers raised their kids single-handedly. Plenty of fathers, too. It wasn't impossible. It just took a little more effort, which Frankie was willing to give.

Hunter continued to watch Leo being a goof, screaming and laughing, entertaining himself.

Unexpectedly, it hit him how he never thought about having this. It never crossed his mind he *could* have it.

He had held Diesel's daughters, both Indigo and Violet, on more than one occasion, usually when D wasn't around and Jewel shoved one of them in his direction because she needed extra hands.

While he had accepted the girls without complaint and felt a protectiveness for them, that was all he felt. Nothing tugged at him, pushing him toward ever wanting a family.

He was fine on his own. He was his own man, did his own thing. The only people he needed to answer to was Diesel and his team. And even that wasn't like having a wife and kid because, for the most part, he could tell them to fuck off or find a valid excuse to go do something else when the need arose.

He wouldn't be able to do that with a wife and kid. Or kids, plural. Fuck no, he'd be stuck dealing with them whether he wanted to or not. That was the responsibility of being a father and husband.

The band that would be slid onto his left ring finger could be like a noose, choking him until he panicked.

What kind of father and husband would he be when he would always be on the verge of spilling into the darkness?

A shitty one.

Hunter had a shitty father and he didn't want to inherit that title.

So, it was best to just remain the way he was. Free.

If he needed pussy, he could find pussy. That had never been a problem. If he ever had the urge to hold a kid, there were plenty to choose from in the DAMC family. *Plenty* to choose from. He swore the MC's church was turning into a fucking daycare. The brothers liked to fuck and knock up their ol' ladies, apparently.

Would Frankie and Leo fit right in? Fuck yeah. But not because of Hunter.

If Slade wanted to step up as a father-figure to his nephew, that was on him. But that would mean dragging Frankie's stubborn ass out of Manning Grove and setting her up in Shadow Valley.

Which could be beneficial to Hunter if Frankie wanted to keep it casual.

But her admitting she was falling in love with him was not keeping it casual. And he understood why she'd shut him out after that.

In truth, he was sort of relieved she had, because he was feeling shit about her he shouldn't.

He didn't blame her for protecting herself. He needed to do the same.

But with D insisting he come back to the Valley today, they were at a point where decisions had to be made. He wasn't comfortable with leaving Frankie and Leo up in the Grove with only local cops for protection.

Yeah, it had been a month since the press release and Max Bryson putting Frankie's name out to the world hoping the fucker would show himself. He hadn't. And D was right, Hunter couldn't wait forever.

With any luck, Taz was no longer breathing or couldn't give a fuck about Frankie or the fact she'd given birth to his son. It wasn't like she was going to ask for child support from the fucker. She'd continue to struggle on her own with her mom helping out whenever she could.

He'd hang with Leo until Frankie came home from her shift at the restaurant, sit her down and hope she'd listen to reason.

He wasn't holding out on that hope, though. She was stubborn like a mule and independent as fuck. Something that both turned him on and frustrated him at the same time.

Maybe he'd wait until she put Leo to bed since he went to bed about an hour after she got home and then take her outside just in case they ended up raising their voices. Leo didn't need to hear them arguing. Especially when it came to his safety. He might be only three, but he understood more than to be expected.

The kid was a sponge. And luckily smart as a whip, something he probably inherited from Frankie, *thank fuck*, and not his fuckstick DNA donor.

So, yeah, it was best that he and Frankie had their conversation out of the range of little ears.

Chapter Seventeen

FRANKIE HAD her back pressed to the hallway wall and her eyes closed as she listened to Hunter's deep timbre voice reading Leo his nightly bedtime story.

But she had a hard time making out the actual words over the blood rushing into her ears. Which it had been doing since she'd walked in the door and Hunter grumbled, "We gotta talk."

Hunter had fed Leo leftover veggie lasagna before she arrived home and she had grabbed a few bites in the kitchen at work. So, they hadn't even sat down to dinner together.

Though, even the nights they had, she'd kept herself distant from him. She had done her best to put up a wall, to lock away any feelings that had developed over the man who had taken over the care of her three-year-old like Leo was his own.

While she worried about Leo getting too attached to Hunter, she also was relieved Hunter was looking out for her son. If Taz decided to show up at her house, as least Hunter would protect him.

A rush of air had her opening her eyes as Hunter quickly strode out of Leo's room, like he normally did after reading to him, in his haste to get somewhere with more space. "Outside," he ordered without slowing down.

He turned the corner and she heard him jogging down the steps. She drew air into her lungs, not only to catch his familiar scent, but to bolster herself for their "talk."

She followed more slowly down the steps and heard the back door open but not close, so she headed in that direction.

He was waiting on the rear porch, his back to her when she stepped through the kitchen door and shut it behind her.

She stood inches from him, staring at his broad back, his black T-shirt pulled tightly over his shoulders but loose at the small of his back where she knew he kept his gun holstered.

She raised her hand to touch him, to feel his solidness and warmth, but let her fingers curl into her palm and dropped her hand before making contact.

Touching him wouldn't help either of them.

He'd been there a month and she expected him to move on at any time. She figured tonight was that time. She had mentally prepared herself for it and tried to create a plan on dealing with Leo once Hunter stepped back out of his life.

She had a feeling there would be a lot of tears. And not just Leo's. But she would keep her shit together while around her son and only let herself miss the man who stood in front of her when she was alone in bed at night.

"Frankie," he said softly.

She waited for him to turn around and face her, but he remained looking out over her backyard. It was getting darker earlier now that it was late summer, but there was still enough light to see everything clearly. Including the tension in those broad shoulders.

Again, she was tempted to touch him, but that would just make things messier than they already were.

"I gotta roll out of here tonight," he said, still not

looking at her. "I've been on this job too long. Time to move on to the next one."

This news shouldn't be surprising, but even so, it still was. "Are you giving up on finding Taz?"

That was when he turned, his face stony, his eyes even harder. "No. I'll do what I can to find him. It just won't be my main focus. Gave a heads up to the PD that I'm heading out and they need to keep vigil. But if he hasn't shown up by now, he most likely won't."

"Most likely," she repeated in a murmur.

"Can't stay here forever." Those words weren't harsh and she might have even detected a little bit of regret.

"That would be too much like putting down roots," Frankie said, trying not to sound bitter.

Hunter didn't answer, instead let his gaze sweep over her face, which she tried to keep neutral.

Damn it, she didn't want him to go.

In the past three weeks, she had convinced herself she couldn't wait for it all to be over. In reality, that was far from the truth. She wanted to be done with Taz, but not the man standing on her back porch who had ingrained himself into their life without meaning to.

He had only been doing his job.

His job was over.

Time for him to go.

"Frankie," Hunter whispered.

She realized she'd been staring at his chest. At the hint of dog tags hidden under his shirt. He never wore them out when he was dressed, they were always tucked away. She wondered why.

She lifted her gaze and met his. She swore he had a few more grays at his temples since showing up in front of her house over a month ago. Maybe she was only imagining it.

"I want you two to come with me." Her mouth opened and her eyes widened, until he continued, "We can get you and Leo set up somewhere temporarily. Get you out of this town and somewhere you could be watched over."

She snapped her mouth shut.

"I'm not comfortable with you remaining here until we have confirmation that Taz is no longer breathing."

"I have a job here. A house. My mom's here. Should that man have me running scared?"

"Yeah, *loquilla*, he should."

Loquilla. "Well, I'm not going to let him. It's been months since he was released from jail. I'm sure he has no interest in me or Leo, otherwise he would've been here by now." She sure hoped that was true. But Taz was unpredictable. She had learned that the hard way.

"We don't know that."

"You're right. We don't know if he'll ever show up. But me relocating to," she waved her hand around, "Shadow Valley, even temporarily, doesn't work for me. I can't lose my job, Hunter. And to try to find another one will be near impossible up here."

"Then move to the Valley permanently."

"What?" She raised her hand to stop his next words. "I'm not uprooting my family because you say so."

A muscle ticked in Hunter's cheek right above the line of his beard. "Why do you have to be so fucking stubborn?"

She planted her hands on her hips and stared up at him with her head tilted to the side. "Why do you?"

His chest rose and fell slowly, and his shoulders dropped at least an inch. He dropped his chin and his voice. "Baby."

And, *fuck*, if that didn't make her bare toes curl against the concrete. Just his fucking voice made her nipples tingle and her pussy clench.

She was so weak!

Nope, nope, nope. Don't let him past that barrier, Frankie.

Maybe she could... Maybe they could... Just one more time before he left. One for the road.

It has been three weeks and every damn night she forced herself to remain in her bed and not join him on the couch or invite him back upstairs.

She fought the good fight.

It was not the hardest thing she ever did in her life, but it was close.

However, she made it through. She hadn't succumbed to her desires and he was finally leaving. It needed to be a clean break. Having sex one more time would make it the opposite.

As soon as he left, she and Leo could begin healing the hole he would leave behind in their hearts.

Leo would go back to daycare; Frankie would go back to just... existing. Providing for her son. Getting through each day as they came.

Fuck. She needed to feel his skin against hers one more time.

Just once. And then she could move on.

She squeezed her eyes shut and pressed her fists to her outer thighs.

Who the hell was she kidding?

He moved closer, his heat now touching her, but she refused to open her eyes. Not yet.

Maybe he had his bag in the rental already and could just turn and walk away.

No goodbyes.

No watching him leave.

Not slow and painful, but quick, like ripping off a Band-Aid.

"Baby."

She shook her head. "Just go." She cursed the tremor in her voice. It revealed way too much. Hunter was sharp, he'd catch it.

"We need to set some rules."

Her eyes popped open. "What?"

"Rules. There needs to be some rules set. I can't leave without knowing you'll follow them."

She sighed. "What are these rules?" She'd have to hear them to determine whether she'd follow them.

"Call me every night, *loquilla*."

"Why?"

"Because I said so. Don't need another reason than that. Every night."

Because I said so.

"If I don't answer because I'm tied up or on a job, leave a message and your phone on. I'll call you back as soon as I can."

"Can I just text you?" She didn't know if she could bear to hear his voice every night.

"No. Anybody could take your phone and text. I want to hear your voice. That'll assure me you're okay."

Frankie pursed her lips and studied him. Maybe she and Leo wouldn't be the only ones feeling a loss. "That it?"

"No. Keep your phone on you at all times. Something happens, you hear something suspicious, you see someone suspicious, you lock yourself somewhere safe then call 911 first. Me second. Safety, 911, then me. In that order. You got me?"

Her heart began to thump furiously. He was not taking leaving lightly. She nodded.

"Bryson will have his officers do drive-bys when he can. That's his decision when those stop, not yours. You let the officers do their job. You do not interfere."

He reached out and cupped her jaw. He hadn't touched her in weeks. Not even an accidental brush and her worry at his rules quickly turned to something else.

He tipped her face to his and said, "Someone is sitting outside of your house, you follow that second rule. You secure yourself and Leo upstairs in a bedroom and you call. Frankie, you do *not* approach with your bat and bash the shit outta someone's vehicle. You get law enforcement here to take care of it. Think before you act, Frankie. Not only your life, but Leo's, could depend on it."

Think before you act, Frankie.

"Okay," she agreed softly.

He lifted one brow, his eyes no longer hard, the lines at the corners now soft. "Take what I'm saying seriously."

"I will."

"Promise?"

She nodded.

His fingers slid into her hair, his palm warm against her skin. "Your son is your everything."

You could be, too.

Twice in her life, she fell for the wrong man. The first time with Taz. Now she fell for a man who couldn't lay down roots. Who couldn't handle being in a relationship without feeling trapped.

Her heart hurt for herself, but hurt for him, too. He'd miss out on something that could be great and fulfilling.

She herself would miss out on that, too, because she stupidly fell in love with a man who couldn't feel the same. He never hid that fact. It wasn't his fault. He had said if he could, he would.

He couldn't.

So, he was leaving to get on with the life he could bear living.

And while she wished it could be different, she needed to bear living without him.

She promised to call him every night, but she wasn't sure if she could.

"Frankie."

She realized she'd been staring at his throat, so she tipped her eyes back to his. "Yes?"

"I want to kiss you goodbye. Will you let me?"

"No," she murmured, wrapping her hand around the

back of his head and tugging it lower. Their lips brushed as she said, "I'm going to kiss you goodbye, instead." She didn't miss his lips slightly curling at the ends before she crushed her mouth to his and he let her take control of the kiss, not fighting it, not encouraging it. Just letting her do what she needed.

She raked her nails down his back over the cotton of his T-shirt, the hand at the back of his head pressing him closer. His arm wrapped around her waist and pulled her tighter against him until she had no doubt how much he wanted her.

He groaned as she continued the sensual onslaught of his mouth, while she tugged his shirt out of his pants and burrowed her hand inside, this time raking her nails up his spine, so he could feel it against his skin. His fingers curled in her hair, once again making her feel that sting against her scalp that made certain parts of her quiver with need.

Fuck, she needed him.

She needed him.

If she could only have him one last time, she'd take it. She shouldn't, but she would. Any regrets she'd deal with later. She could throw them on top of the rest of the emotional heap she knew was building.

But for now, she had him. He wasn't pushing her away, thinking it was a bad idea. He was letting her run with it.

His cock was hard against her belly. His muscles flexed under her nails as she scraped them higher. He twisted his head to break their kiss but kept their lips close. His warm breath swept over her swollen lips as he said, "Wallet. Back pocket."

She dropped the hand which had taken purchase of his back, down to his pocket and pulled out his wallet. "Here?" she asked, her voice thick, dripping with want. She let her gaze shift through the backyard. Had it gotten dark enough? Could her neighbors see them? Did she even care?

Not if this was her last chance to get a piece of the man she wanted whole. A piece was better than nothing. And soon that's what she'd have.

Emptiness.

He must not have cared, either, his gruff voice demanded, "Hands to the wall, Frankie," and released her waist, turning her to face the side of the house next to the kitchen door.

He grabbed her wrists and bumped her forward with his chest, then planted her palms onto the siding stretched above her head and said in her ear, "Stay there. Don't move."

She shuddered and a rush of wetness soaked her panties under the knee-length black skirt she wore for work.

His hands came around her and he began to unbutton the white blouse she wore that emphasized her cleavage for maximum tips. When just her bra was exposed, he slipped his fingers into both cups and, capturing her nipples, twisted them hard. She dropped her head forward, her forehead pressing into the wood siding as she bit back her groan. He plucked at both hard tips, tweaked them again, then pulled his hands from her bra.

She wanted to complain but didn't when he shoved her skirt up to her hips and yanked down her damp panties. Once they were past her thighs, they dropped on their own to circle her ankles.

The warm night air swept along her bare ass, followed by his hand smoothing over her skin, one hand reaching around and finding how wet her pussy was. Evidence of how this man turned her on. Evidence of how he could talk her into anything. Including sex on her back porch where anyone could see them if they were looking hard enough.

She didn't care.

She only cared about what he was doing to her, which was sliding his fingers back and forth between her slick folds, teasing her clit, then dipping one finger inside of her, but only for a second. He did this same move again and again until she was going out of her mind. He was driving her to the brink already.

"Hunter," she whimpered.

Then his mouth was there, against her ear, his chest against her back, his thumb strumming her clit, making her hips twitch against him. "What do you want, baby?"

Baby.

That's what she wanted. She wanted for him to call her baby. She wanted to hear him call her that every morning when she woke up. Every night before she went to bed. She wanted to be his. She wanted him to be hers.

Instead, she said, "I want to come."

"Then come."

She was so wet, his two fingers slipped easily inside her while he ground his thumb against her. And within seconds, her knees begin to buckle as the waves of an orgasm swept through her.

"Is that all you want?" came his raw question directly into her ear. She shuddered again.

"No."

He shifted until his mouth was against her neck and he nibbled the length of it until he reached the now loose collar of her blouse. "Step out of your panties and spread your legs, baby."

She kicked her panties away and planted her bare feet wider on the concrete porch, the night air now tickling along her drenched pussy. His fingers, slick with her juices appeared in front of her face.

"I know how good you taste, baby, but do you? Tongue out."

Yes. Whatever he wanted from her, the answer was yes.

Opening her mouth wide, she stuck out her tongue and he drew his fingers over it.

"Fuck, Frankie," he groaned against her neck.

When he was done wiping his fingers clean, he said, "Now you know what I'll never forget. I'll always remember what you taste like, Frankie."

Holy shit. Her eyes rolled back at his words and her legs began to shake.

His body shifted against hers and she heard his buckle, his zipper, the whisper of fabric as he dropped his pants and boxers down. "Hips out, baby."

She pushed them out and he grabbed her hips and began to slide his erection along the crease of her ass. The skin of his cock felt like hot velvet, brushing across her anus, his sac soft as he pressed against her ass.

"What do you want, Frankie?"

"You."

"Where?"

"Anywhere you want to be." And that was true. She'd accept him anywhere. She just wanted him, however he wanted to give himself to her.

He plucked his wallet from her hand, which was still pressed to the wood siding, and after a few seconds, heard it drop to the ground. Her pussy clenched as the tearing of a condom wrapper was the only sound besides their rapid breathing.

He shifted, shifted again. Then the head of his cock was drawn with excruciating slowness from the top of her ass crack and down, down, down until it pressed her clit. Then he guided it back up, tucking the crown between her folds.

"What do you want, Frankie?"

Using her palms against the side of the house, she pushed back and impaled herself on him, her eyes fluttering closed as he filled her, taking his whole length. The backs of her thighs pressed against his, his fingers digging into the flesh at her hips. A long, ragged hiss slipped from him.

He kept his hips still as he grabbed both of her wrists,

stacked them together, and pinned them to the wall with one hand. With the other, he circled her throat, his thumb stroking her skin, then slid it down her chest, over her bra, down her belly over her shirt, over the gathered fabric of her skirt until he found her most sensitive area and pinched her gently.

She gasped and twitched against him as his cock flexed deep inside her. He slid almost all the way out and when he drove up, he pinched her again, harder this time.

She began to see spots behind her closed eyelids as he did the same thing again and again.

She wanted to beg him to stop because it was too much, but she also was afraid he *would* stop and she wanted more.

His cheek was pinned to the side of her head, his breathing harsh, each thrust accompanied with a low grunt that drove her mad.

When she climaxed, he cupped her mound, spread two fingers in a V and slid them until they bracketed his own cock and separated her swollen lips. His thumb circled her clit which was now so sensitive it was almost painful. But she didn't tell him to stop. She wanted more.

He was pounding her so hard, his hips slapped against her ass and she lost herself in the sound of it, along with his breath in her ear, and the sound of him sliding in and out of her wetness. Her juices were trickling down her inner thighs when he groaned, "So fucking wet, baby. So wet for me. You were made for me, Frankie."

Then stay whispered through her.

"Make me so fucking hard, baby. You're perfect."

Then don't go.

"Come for me one last time."

One last time...

She was a fool to have denied him these last three weeks. She shouldn't have denied herself the pleasure he brought her. All because she was falling in love with him.

Hell, too late.

She wasn't falling. She landed hard.

It was foolish, but true.

She could have had him every night. Gave herself more memories to hold onto.

But memories didn't keep one warm at night. They didn't keep one from being lonely. They did not ease the pain.

"Hunter," she whispered, her voice catching from both emotions and pleasure. A mix that made her heart ache.

"What do you need, baby?"

You. "I want to face you when I come."

He stilled and Frankie waited a few heartbeats. Did he not want to face her? Was there a reason he had her pinned to the side of the house, facing away from him? Was he worried she'd see something he was trying to hide?

Would he deny her request?

He released her wrists and he pulled out, turned her around, grabbed her ass and growled, "Arms around my neck."

She looped her arms around his neck and gasped in surprise when he lifted her weight, shoved her back into the siding, saying, "Legs around me, hold on."

She hooked her legs around his hips and in one thrust he was back inside her, his chest pinning her to the wall, his hands gripping her ass, and he drove up again, using his powerful thighs. He kissed her hard, grabbed her bottom lip between his teeth and tugged before pressing his forehead against hers.

Though it was hard to focus, their eyes remained open and locked, their mouths parted as he pounded the breath out of both of them.

Her ass would have bruises, her pussy would be sore and her heart would be broken tomorrow. But she was thankful to have this moment.

And when they came together, she told him *I love you* silently. Letting the words she didn't say out loud be expressed in her eyes instead.

Because she wanted him to know he meant something to her. Not just a protector. Much more than that.

He stilled and answered, "I'm sorry." Regret colored his apology. "I'm sorry I can't be who you want me to be. I told you before and I'll tell you again, if it could be anyone, it would be you, Frankie."

She buried her teeth into her bottom lip, hoping the pain would keep her from crying. She nodded because she didn't trust herself to answer.

He was beginning to soften inside her and soon they'd need to separate. But he made no move to do so.

He ran his nose along hers, kissed one eyelid, then the other, and brushed his lips lightly across hers. "I wish you hadn't shut me out these last three weeks."

She already regretted that decision. She couldn't fix that now.

One day she'd learn to make better decisions. Today was not that day when she whispered, "I love you, Hunter."

He slipped out of her, letting her feet reach the floor, then peeled her arms from around his neck, his eyes avoiding hers. He pulled the condom off, knotted the end and after hitching up his pants and boxers, dropped it in the large lidded trashcan sitting at the edge of the porch. He remained with his back to her as he finished fastening his pants and adjusting his clothes.

Then he said over his shoulder, "Bag's in the car already. It's late. I need to hit the road."

The thickness in his voice made her own throat tighten and her eyes burn.

She wished things could be different, she understood why they couldn't. But that didn't make this any easier.

Especially when he paused only to say, "Tell Leo

goodbye for me." Then he disappeared around the corner of the house into the dark.

———

SHE DIDN'T CALL him every night like he wanted. And he didn't call her, either.

Frankie thought that was for the best.

She figured Hunter did, too.

Chapter Eighteen

HUNTER SET his cigar in the ashtray by his barely-touched beer and studied how the smoke rose in a swirl. One overhead halogen bulb lit up the corner where they had set up the card table and folding metal chairs. Their voices echoed through the enormous, high-ceilinged warehouse which was home base for In the Shadows Security.

Where they worked. Sometimes where they played.

His head turned as he remembered Mercy "playing" with Squirrel, a fucknut former prospect of the Dirty Angels MC who had turned to the dark side and joined the Shadow Warriors. The squirrel dick also violated Crow's woman, Jazz, and injured Hawk's ol' lady, Kiki. So for that, he paid with his life.

But Mercy didn't make it easy for him. Squirrel suffered as much, if not more, than the women had.

Hunter stared at the spot for another moment, even though no evidence of that activity remained because Mercy, like the rest of them, knew how to dispatch a piece of shit like Squirrel and not leave a trace behind.

Unfortunately, one Shadow Warrior still remained at large that they knew of and his name was Taz.

Slade's half-brother. Leo's sperm donor.

Frankie's former lover.

Hunter was also in that last category.

Before he left Manning Grove, he had insisted she call him every night. She hadn't and he decided not to push it. Instead, he checked in with one of Manning Grove's finest every few days, just to make sure things were quiet and Frankie was doing okay.

They were and she was, Matt Bryson would tell him.

The cop seemed to get what Hunter was after. Almost as if he'd been through something similar. The man was a former Marine who saw action, so he probably had some of his own ghosts haunting him.

Hunter let his gaze slide around the table to the rest of his crew, who all carried ghosts of their own.

While they were each broken in some way, none of them talked about it. They just accepted the fact they were all fucked up in some manner and ignored it. Unless it affected a job or their safety. Which, *thank fuck*, it normally didn't.

All of them coped with one or more demons buried deep inside them.

However, Mercy and Ryder were two, out of the six of them, who had found women who fit them perfectly and could deal with the monkeys clinging to their backs. Parris aka Rissa, a professional therapist who could handle it, and Kelsea, who dealt with her own fucked up past. The women seemed to settle their men's souls in some way.

Out of all of them, they never figured Mercy would ever settle. He did. And though he'd never be completely whole, being with Rissa made him as solid as he'd ever be.

Kelsea and Ryder propped each other up. Two shaky halves which made a solid whole.

As Walker whipped cards around the table for their next hand of poker, Hunter wished for the millionth time things could be different.

That Frankie telling him she loved him hadn't almost sent him into a tail spin. When he saw it on her face, his vision had narrowed, his throat had closed, his blood had pumped furiously. Not from his orgasm, but from the fear of becoming trapped.

Though he knew she would never do that on purpose, he couldn't shake that panic.

Only now, he was tired of "if onlys." Because every night in his bed, the "if onlys" took over his thoughts.

If only. If only. If only.

He needed to stop dwelling on it. Because the longer he did, the more he wanted to pull up stakes and move on from Shadow Valley and his team. The earth that held his shallow roots was eroding fast.

He couldn't do that to his team, or to his boss, but mostly he had to resist doing it to himself.

For the most part, he was content where he was, with who he was. But those three powerful little words Frankie put out there between them had made him question everything.

He had wanted to reach out and grab her, hold her tight and never let go. But no matter how much his heart wanted it, his brain wouldn't allow it.

So, instead, he did what he did best, he moved. Away from her, out of Manning Grove and back to his steady.

What he had, which kept him grounded in Shadow Valley, circled the folding table.

With a curse, Brick slapped his cards onto the table, making it shake dangerously.

Ryder barked out a laugh and taunted, "See, asshole? Now you know what it's like when you deal shitty hands."

Brick picked up his shot glass, downed two fingers of whiskey, slapped it on the table and wiped the back of his hand across his mouth. "I'm a good dealer."

Steel snorted beside him. "Yeah, you deal a good hand to yourself and bullshit to the rest of us."

"I deal whatever's next in the pack," Brick grumbled.

Poker night would not be the same if they weren't riding each other's ass and riding them hard.

Hunter needed to push Frankie out of his head and concentrate on the game. He was already down a Benjamin. He needed to win that back.

"Tomorrow's a new day, new job, Hunter," Walker said around his cigar, which was tucked between his teeth. "You ready?"

Thank fuck he was starting a new job that would keep his mind occupied and his body on the move. He'd done a few small jobs locally since returning from Manning Grove a little over two weeks ago, but he was ready to see new sights.

While they all kept their ears to the ground in their hunt for Taz, it was no longer their main focus. They did what they could when they could since they were no longer being paid for it.

But they'd never give up the hunt, since it still stuck in all of their craws that Taz had slipped through their fingers.

At this point, the silence was so deafening, it had to be because Taz was sleeping six feet under. Maybe he beat the wrong woman and someone taught him a lesson he couldn't forget due to no longer having any brain function.

They could only be so fucking lucky.

But Hunter still wanted confirmation the man became a meal for maggots.

Walker smacked him on the back, making him jerk forward. "You need help with that job, you let me know. I've been itching for a challenge lately."

He was headed up to Maine in the morning to help hunt down a man who had taken some rich fucker's daughter. The police said all evidence pointed to the woman having gone willingly with the man, most likely a lover, so they dropped the case. The father didn't buy it. Said she'd never hook up with the guy.

She probably did. She probably liked the dick and was tired of Daddy running her life. So, what better revenge then to run off together on his dime?

Hunter hoped they'd bounced to some exotic locale, so he could spend some time on an island full of hot women in bikinis and plenty of booze.

That would be a welcome distraction.

Though, now he was picturing Frankie in her fucking tiny bikini top with her huge tits, the fabric straining to contain them.

Fuck.

"Earth to fucking Hunter," Mercy growled at the end of the table. "You with us?"

"Yeah," he mumbled, then tipped his Iron City beer bottle to his lips, the now room temperature brew sliding down his throat.

His gaze slid over Mercy, then Ryder. They said their women were at Brooke's baby shower tonight at Sophie's Sweet Treats in town. He wondered if Frankie would have fit in with the DAMC women.

He was pretty sure she would. The club sisterhood wasn't catty at all and the women all tended to support each other. During the month he spent in Manning Grove, Frankie never once talked about her friends or had one over. The only person she seemed to be close with was Diane, her "mom."

Between work and Leo, she was probably too busy to cultivate friendships. But she needed a support system. More than just her adopted mother.

Jesus fuck.

He needed to stop thinking and worrying about her. That was getting him nowhere fast.

As he curled his cards up to peek at his hand, his cell

phone vibrated on his hip. Anyone normally calling him was sitting at the table. Except for the boss man, who he assumed was home with his baby girls, while his pregnant ol' lady was also at the baby shower.

He unclipped the phone from the holder and glanced at the display.

His heart pounded when he saw the nickname *Loquilla* on the screen. She was finally doing what he had asked.

"Jesus," he muttered under his breath and on the second ring pushed from his chair and away from the small table.

He was not in the mood to be ridden hard and put away wet after speaking to Frankie in front of the rest of his team.

Ignoring the kissing noises coming from around the table, Hunter stepped into the shadows before sliding his finger across the screen.

He heard her before he could even put the phone to his ear.

"He's gone!"

The shriek on the other end of the phone made his blood turn to ice. That ice slithered down his spine and made the hair on his arms stand up.

"He's gone! He's gone! He's gone!" she screamed. A loud, broken sob then filled Hunter's ear.

"Frankie," he whispered, his heart no longer beating, instead it had seized in his chest.

"I went to pick him up at daycare after my shift and Patty said his father picked him up. *His father!*" she shrieked into the phone again. "You stirred up this shit and now he has Leo."

"I'm gonna call MGPD and get them to you. Get them on this ASAP. Then I'm heading up there."

"Too late," she cried.

Hunter's lungs emptied and his chest tightened at the desperation and pain in her voice. He spun on his heels and rushed back to the table, where all the men were now on their feet, eyes glued to him. Hunter hit the phone's speaker button so they could hear everything.

"I've lost him," came the cracked voice over the speaker.

She was losing her shit and he was struggling to hold onto his.

"No, baby, he's just... We'll get him back."

"What if he kills him?"

"He won't."

"How do you know?" she demanded in a scream.

He didn't. The man tried to kill his own child by pushing his mother down a flight of steps and kicking the shit out of her stomach. He was capable of anything. Just like his father Buzz was.

Fuck.

"Stay put. Call your Mom. Have her come to you. I'm getting a hold of Max Bryson and we're heading up there."

"Hunter..." Frankie's whisper was broken.

"Yeah, baby?"

"I'm scared."

"Yeah, baby."

So am I.

———

Hunter didn't wait for his team. He jumped on his bike and roared through the night. He made the three-hour trip in record time. The rest of them were following after they grabbed equipment and a couple of vehicles.

Being on his bike, he couldn't make phone calls, but he had Walker touch base with Manning Grove PD.

He almost dumped his bike in Frankie's driveway in his haste to get off it and get to her.

Two cruisers were parked haphazardly in her driveway. Her mom's car was on the street.

Before he could approach the house, Frankie was down

the front porch, across the yard, and her body hit him so hard, he was knocked back two steps. He finally caught his balance and wrapped his arms around her, squeezing her tight.

She was shaking so badly, if he didn't know better, he would have thought she had hypothermia.

He pressed his face into her hair and held on for dear fucking life. "Anything?"

"No," came the answer muffled into his chest. "No vehicle description. Nothing. He went into the daycare, claimed him and the one girl *let... him... go...* with that monster!" She was screaming again.

He wanted to scream, too. What fucking daycare just let a child go off with a stranger? It was unheard of.

"Was this a licensed daycare?"

"I couldn't afford a licensed daycare. And none of them would watch him the odd hours I worked, anyway. Patty watched kids out of her house, but she couldn't keep good help. Which is apparent since this newest idiot girl just let Taz take Leo! Patty never would've let him go if she'd been there. She knew better."

Jesus fuck! He had no clue some unlicensed hack was watching Leo. He would have put a stop to it before he left Manning Grove. Frankie didn't burden her mom with the responsibility of watching Leo on a daily basis because Diane had various health issues, like migraines, that put her in bed for sometimes days at a time.

But all that didn't matter right now. Taz had Leo and they needed to be found.

His gaze shifted to the house, where every light inside seemed to be lit. "Who's inside?"

"Max and Marc."

He had no idea who Marc was, but at least the chief was on scene. "Why aren't they out looking for him?"

"They said they have nothing to go on. They put out an

Amber Alert and have patrols cruising town but right now, until he contacts me, they have no starting point."

He could hear it in her voice, she was starting to shatter. She had done her best to hold herself together, but the longer this went, the more she was probably unraveling.

Hell, he had almost splintered on his ride up. He had kept his throttle pegged and rode recklessly all the way there, glad he didn't have cops chasing him. Because he wouldn't have stopped. Not until he reached his destination.

He gave her another squeeze and her arms tightened around his waist. "The guys are on their way up. I got a head start. I'm going to go in and talk to the chief. We need to get a bead on Taz before they do. Do you understand why?"

She nodded against him. "I just want Leo back."

"So do I, baby. And that's the primary focus. Leo's safety comes first. But to ensure that, we need Taz. Is that understood?"

She nodded again, still buried in his chest.

He dropped his head and said softly, just in case the cops could hear them, "That means if he contacts you, you tell me first. Not the cops. Me. The cops can only do so much. We can do what needs to be done."

He tried to keep the bite from his tone, but it was near impossible. While fear had gripped him at first with the thought of Leo being taken, now he had rage flowing through his veins.

Pure unadulterated rage and a taste for revenge.

And he wanted his face to be the last one Taz saw. Mercy wouldn't get a chance to play with Taz.

Taz belonged to Hunter. He owned the fucker.

He would not need his tactical knife or his gun to take the motherfucker out. He'd use his hands.

"Put your phone on silent, but keep an eye on it without

being obvious. If possible, I'm going to try to convince them to go out to search while I stay here with you."

"Hunter..." Her hands fisted at the back of his shirt.

He pressed his lips to the top of her head, wishing he could absorb her pain. "I know, baby, you don't have to say it. We need to stay strong, and keep the faith that Leo will come home to you very soon."

He dropped an arm around her shoulders and pulled her into his side, then guided her back to the house so he could take control of the situation without tipping off men who wore badges, carried registered weapons, and swore an oath to abide by the law.

Chapter Nineteen

FRANKIE PACED the small living room, phone in her hand, hoping like hell it would ring. She'd taken it off silent mode the second Max and Marc Bryson walked out the door to join the search. She was glad they trusted Hunter enough to remain behind with her while they did so. They called in every officer they had, even the ones off-duty and had the Pennsylvania State Police in the area, too.

But they still had nothing besides knowing who took Leo. And that wasn't enough.

Frankie had chewed every nail down to the quick as she'd restlessly walked from one end of the room to the other.

This was all her fault.

All of it.

She kept doing stupid things.

Giving into Taz's fake charm in the first place.

Then getting pregnant, despite using condoms.

Not getting out of Lancaster in time before Taz found out.

Not getting a gun to shoot his abusive ass when he first lifted a hand to her.

Not shooting his ass after he almost killed her.

Letting Hunter talk his way into her house.

Letting Hunter use them as bait.

Putting herself and Leo out there for Taz to find.

She thought she was doing right by her son. But she should've known better since everything she touched turned to shit.

Think before you act, Frankie.

And now, her very soul was missing.

Captured by that monster.

A monster she slept with.

A monster she got pregnant by.

A monster who could legally claim her son.

And if Leo survived this, Taz's chance to ever lay claim to her son again would be nil.

That was if Taz even survived it. Hunter assured her he wouldn't.

But Hunter had also assured her he'd keep her and Leo safe. Instead, he had left. And now it was too late.

Her son was out there with a dangerous stranger, probably scared, crying for his mother. Unable to figure out what was happening.

She stopped short in the middle of the living room, closed her eyes and fell to her knees. She jammed her fists into her eye sockets, lifted her face and screamed until there was nothing left inside her. Until she was nothing left but a shell. Her lungs ached, her throat was raw, her brain numb.

Strong arms encircled her, a wall of heat and muscle pressed against her back, words meant to be soothing whispered into her ear, but went unheard.

She was nothing without Leo.

He was her everything.

Her life. Her blood. Her purpose.

She was pulled into a lap and curled into a hard body, and Hunter rocked her back and forth.

But it didn't help. Nothing helped.

The only thing that would, would be finding the piece of her that was missing.

What seemed like endless moments later, her fingers were being peeled from the phone she clutched so hard, those fingers had seized.

Then she heard it. The ring. Hunter's voice ordering her to let go.

She didn't. She ripped it from his grasp and blinked her vision clear to read the display.

UNKNOWN CALLER.

Her heart skipped a beat, then began to race. She met Hunter's unreadable brown eyes and answered the call, pushing herself from his lap.

She caught movement from the corner of her eye and saw her mom come from the kitchen into the living room, her face pale, eyes large.

This could be it.

What she needed.

What they'd been waiting for.

A scratchy "Taz" escaped her.

Silence greeted her. One thumping heartbeat to the next.

Finally, "Used my son as bait to try an' catch me. Now I'm usin' my son to catch you, bitch."

She hadn't heard that voice in years. She had never planned on hearing it again.

But right now, even though it froze her blood, it was the best thing she'd ever heard. What he said might mean Leo was still alive.

She cleared the thickness from her throat. "He's okay? Please tell me he's okay."

"Put him on speaker," Hunter mouthed to her.

She ignored him and turned away. "Tell me he's okay." Her desperation bubbled up in her voice and she didn't bother to try and contain it.

"He's fine. Misses his momma. So, his momma needs to come see him one last time."

One last time.

"Don't hurt him," she whispered, grasping the phone with both hands, the only connection she had with her son.

"Don't plan on hurtin' him. Plan on hurtin' you. Tried to set me up. Those fuckin' asshole Shadows want me dead. They wanted us all dead. They're usin' you to get to me, the father of your child. You want the father of your child dead, Sussy. What kinda mother are you? A goddamn shitty one."

"Where do you want me to meet you? I'll meet you. Just don't hurt him."

Hunter reached for the phone, but she turned away again, keeping it out of his reach.

"I won't bring anyone with me but my mom. She can take Leo. You take me."

"Fuck that. No one's gettin' my boy, Sussy. I'm raisin' my boy. No one else. He needs his pop."

"If you're not letting him go, why would I come to you?"

"Because if you don't, he dies, Sussy. Can you live with that, you double-crossing bitch? Can you live with the guilt, your decision which killed your own flesh and blood?"

"You tried to kill him by pushing me down those steps, kicking me."

"Did a lot of thinkin' in the joint. Figured he was gone. Got no family, Bussard family name ends with me. He's my blood. He needs his pop to become a man."

Not a man like you. Not a man like his grandfather, either.

"Woulda left you alone, Sussy, if I hadn't heard that fuckin' pig mention Buzz's name, along with yours."

Her brows knitted in confusion. "Buzz?"

"Yeah. Callin' him Buzz. After his grandpap."

Why was the world tilting so sharply? She reached out

for balance and her palm landed on something hard. It wasn't the wall, it was Hunter's chest. He'd been sticking close. "His name is Leo," she whispered, though it fell on deaf ears.

"Took my boy from me, Sussy."

"You tried to take him from me four years ago!" she screamed into the phone. She squeezed her eyes shut and tried to slow her spinning thoughts. She needed to keep her head. "And now you have him. You didn't want him. You insisted I have an abortion."

"Glad you didn't. Spittin' image of his pop."

No, he wasn't. He looked nothing like Taz, thank fucking goodness.

"Where are you? I'll come right now." She spun away from Hunter and headed toward the front door, grabbing her car keys off the hook by the door. She was focusing on the phone, on Taz and once again hit a wall named Hunter as he blocked the door, his eyes intense, his gaze locked on her.

He shook his head but said nothing, probably not wanting Taz to hear his voice.

She raised her eyes to him, and he mouthed, "Location."

"Where, Taz? I can't come to you if I don't know where you are."

"Anyone comes with you, you're both dead. You got me?"

"I got you. I'm coming alone." Frankie tried to push past Hunter, but he didn't budge. She reached around him for the door handle, but he grabbed her wrist and pulled it to his chest in a firm hold, his mouth pressed in a thin line, his jaw hard.

A sob rose from deep within her chest as a tear she didn't know she had left slid down her cheek. Her voice broke as she said, "I don't know where you are."

"Deserted farm north off Route Six. Long dirt lane. Got a barn there. Be waitin' in that barn. Old sign out by the road says somethin' about fresh eggs for sale. Can't miss the sign. Me an' the boy will be waitin' for you. Got a good view of the lane, Sussy. Means that if I see anyone other than you comin' up it, I'm slicin' his fuckin' throat. Then you can come hug him one last time before he bleeds out and afterward, I'm finishin' teachin' you that lesson you never learned about not mindin' your man. You fuckin' got me?" The last came out in a roar and Frankie flinched.

She wobbled on her feet and strong hands gripped her elbows firmly to hold her up. "I got you, Taz. I'm coming alone. I promise."

"'Bout fuckin' time you listened." The phone went dead.

She stared at the blank screen, her knuckles white, no feeling left in her fingers. She lifted her head and said, "I'm going alone."

"The fuck you are. His ass is mine, Frankie. You'll stay here with your mom until the rest of my team gets here. They're not far out. One of them will stay with you. The others will follow me. Do you hear me?"

'Bout fuckin' time you listened.

He shook her. "Frankie, listen. This is important. I will handle this shit. Not you. Tell me where he is."

As if in a trance, she repeated the location word for word as Taz told her.

Then Hunter was in her face, holding her chin, making her meet his eyes. "You do *not* leave this house. You do *not* call the fucking cops. You stick with your mother. I got this. This is my mess. I'm cleaning it the fuck up."

This is my mess.

This was her mess, too. Leo was the flesh of her flesh. Blood of her blood. She needed to be there with him.

"Frankie!" Hunter barked in her face. "Tell me you're going to listen."

'Bout fuckin' time you listened.

Another tear slid down her cheek, followed quickly by another. And another. The tears seared her skin, burned her throat, ripped her heart in two.

She looked him in the eye and nodded.

The pad of his thumb broke the trail of tears as he swept it across her damp cheek, then he gave her a sharp nod back. "He calls you again, you say you're on your way. Don't give him an ETA. Just say you're struggling to find the farm. That's it. Nothing else, Frankie. Just keep him hanging. Keep him waiting."

She nodded again, unable to get words past her constricted throat.

He gently pulled her car keys from her fingers. "Need your car. My Harley's too loud, and he might think it's you in the car if he spots it. When I get there, I'm gonna ping the rest of the crew my location. Frankie..."

Frankie's gaze rose from her keys in his hand to his face. He tucked two fingers under her chin, pressed his lips to her forehead and whispered, "I will take care of this. Trust me. Leo will be home soon."

Her feet felt like they were made of lead as he released her, walked out the front door and closed it behind him.

———

"Funny how you needed to use my boy to get to me. Used him as bait. Couldn't get me any other way. Skills ain't what you thought they were, were they?"

"He's not your son." Hunter frowned and cursed his slip of the tongue.

"The fuck he ain't. He certainly ain't yours. I made him by laying between Sussy's sweet, soft thighs and pumping my dick in and out of her as she cried out my name, shooting my load deep. That boy's one hundred percent mine. Not yours. I got every right to have him. You don't."

"You have no right to have him. Never will."

"Got him now. That stupid bitch won't get him back, either. Told her that she'd lose him forever if she didn't show up alone."

"That was never gonna happen."

"Shame gotta kill my own boy because the bitch is so fuckin' selfish and doesn't listen for shit."

"That's never gonna happen, either."

"You talk big for not having control of the situation." Taz tilted his head and stared at him across the barn. "You stick your dick in that cunt? You have to teach her a few hard lessons, too, for not doin' what she's told? She got a temper on her. A wild spirit that needed to be broken. She was a tough one to break. Like a bitch who is pliable. Thought she was that, found out I was wrong. Didn't mean to plant my kid in her, didn't want to be stuck with a mouthy bitch who didn't know how to serve her man."

Hunter pressed his lips together to keep from snapping and his fingers curled at his sides. He had his knife on his calf, his Sig tucked in his waistband holster, but he didn't need those.

His hands were all he needed. He just needed to get close enough. Problem was, Taz had Leo tied to a chair, his mouth gagged. Frankie's son was crying, his face almost purple, his eyes swollen, probably from endless tears, snot was running down his chin.

It took everything Hunter had not to rush Taz and kill the motherfucker in front of the three-year-old. Rip the biker's throat right out of his neck and then shit down the cavity.

The other problem was, Taz stood behind Leo and was using him as a shield. The third problem was, Taz had a fucking knife in his hand. They stood about twenty feet apart so Taz could raise that blade before Hunter could get close enough. The wide blade held a razor sharp edge and would cut through skin like butter.

Hunter had to keep his head or things could go sideways fast.

He wished Brick was set up with his rifle and could take a head shot through one of the barn's broken windows. However, he had no way to get a message to Brick to see how far out he was.

Plus, Leo might end up wearing blood splatter. Three or not, that could be a memory which might never wash away. What the kid was dealing with now was bad enough.

Hunter needed to handle this carefully. Smartly.

But Leo's bloodshot eyes were focused on him and Hunter wasn't sure if he was imagining it or not, but he swore he heard a muffled "Danny" coming from behind the gag made from a bandana.

Fuck, little man, hang on. "Gonna make a deal with you."

Taz snorted.

Hunter continued, picking his words carefully, "Do right by your son. You take me, you tie me to that chair. Got Frankie's car outside with a car seat, strap Leo in it so he's safe, then come back and do what you want to me. I took out a lot of your MC members. It's me you want. Not Frankie, not Leo. I helped wipe your whole club out. I'm the one who's been looking for you. You want me. I won't try nothing funny. I'll do it willingly, just to see Leo be safe. I've lived a life, he hasn't. He should get that opportunity. Don't take that from him."

Offering himself to be tied up went against every grain in his body, his mind screamed at him it would shatter forever if he was ever restrained. But if Hunter was lucky, it wouldn't get that far. He had to fight the panic, the fear.

"Know you an' your fellow *Shadows,*" he sneered that last word, "hunted us down, took us out. You think I'm the only one left. That might not be fuckin' true. Ain't sayin' it is, ain't sayin' it ain't. You'll never know because I'm gonna take that deal. You wanna face your maker today, that's on you. It was gonna happen anyway, you'll just make it easier. I get you, I get my boy. I eventually get that bitch, too." He lifted the knife to Leo's throat, pressing it against the boy's skin.

Hunter held his breath. While it bothered him Leo was tied to the chair tightly, he was sort of relieved, too. The kid could be wiggly, and he didn't want Leo accidentally moving and cutting his own throat. It was bad enough he was sobbing loudly behind the gag.

"Gonna listen an' listen good. You got any weapons, you throw them over here."

Hunter lifted his hands up, palms out. "Got a gun at the small of my back. Gonna grab it and toss it your way. Got nothing else. Didn't prepare for this."

"Do it slowly," Taz warned.

Hunter nodded, pulled his Sig from the holster and tossed it toward Taz. It landed to the right of the chair and Taz pulled it closer to him with his foot.

"Now, fucker, you're gonna get on your knees. Fingers interlaced and to the back of your head. Ankles crossed. Just like the pigs had me do when they arrested me for tryin' to teach Sussy a lesson."

Hunter kept his eyes pinned to Taz as he lowered to his knees and did what Taz ordered.

"Don't move. You make the smallest move, this kid is done. You got me?"

"Got you," Hunter spat.

Taz leaned over and grabbed Hunter's gun, flipped off the safety and tucked his knife in his boot. He aimed the Sig at Hunter's forehead as he grabbed zip strips that were laying nearby. The shit he'd used to restrain Leo to the chair.

Fucking motherfucker.

Hunter felt a familiar burn in his chest, a tightening that was affecting his breathing. He tried to shake it off, but he could already feel those plastic ties tightening around his wrists and ankles. And that plain fucked with his head.

However, now was not the time for that.

He needed to think clearly and, if possible, two steps ahead of the asshole who was approaching him with those plastic ties.

Hunter jerked up his chin. "Once you got me restrained, you take him out of here, so he doesn't witness what you do to me."

"Needs to learn to be a badass."

"He's three, motherfucker."

"Know how fuckin' old he is. I fucked his mother and made him."

Hunter gritted his teeth, biting back everything he wanted to spew in his fury.

"You move, you eat it, and he gets to watch. That'll keep you cooperative."

Taz was right about that. He needed to get the fucker to take Leo out of the barn, so while he was gone, Hunter could work on getting free of the ties.

He wasn't sure he'd be able to do it in time, but he would as sure as fuck try.

If he failed at it, he failed Leo and Frankie, too.

Every muscle froze in Hunter's body as Taz cuffed his hands behind his back just like the cops did. The man had plenty of first-hand knowledge of being arrested and cuffed, his criminal record proved that.

He forced himself to keep breathing as the plastic ties tightened, cutting into his skin, pinning his wrists together. Taz gave the ties an extra jerk.

Hunter's heart pounded in his throat, his temples throbbed, the blood rushed into his ears. He struggled not to fight Taz looping the ties around his ankles and tightening them until he was hobbled. Then he used more zip strips to restrain Hunter's bound wrists to his tied ankles.

He was done.

Done.

Trapped.

Unable to breathe.

His vision was narrowing dangerously, and he fought it.

Keep your shit together, soldier, a voice screamed inside his head. *Failure is not an option.*

"Take him out," Hunter wheezed. "Take him out."

"Fuck you, asshole."

Despite the roar in his head, the darkness that circled his vision, he watched Taz cut Leo free from the chair, but kept him gagged as he carried Frankie's son out of the barn.

As soon as Taz's back was to him, Hunter reached for the knife strapped on his calf. But because Taz had bound his wrists to his ankles, he couldn't reach it. However, he could reach his boot and he used paracord as laces. If he could get one lace free of his boot in time, he could use it to saw through the zip tie.

Problem was, he knew he'd be cutting it close. Friction sawing wasn't quick, especially when he had all his limbs bound tight.

Fuck.

He couldn't give up. He needed to fight the panic and remain focused.

He pictured Frankie. He pictured Leo.

They were his motivation to keep his head on straight. To keep fighting.

But time was ticking, and he didn't have enough of it.

Which became evident when Taz walked back into the barn before Hunter could free the lace completely.

He slowed his motion but continued to work at it, hoping it didn't attract Taz's attention.

Hunter tracked Taz as the man pulled his knife from his boot, but left Hunter's .40 tucked into the front of his waistband.

Taz stopped about five feet in front of him, his feet planted wide, a smile on his bearded face and pure evil in his brown eyes. "Think you're a hero, sacrificin' yourself like that for my boy. For that bitch. Too stupid to realize I wasn't gonna hurt him. Gonna raise him. And I'm gonna make that bitch pay. Nothin' you can do about it since I got you trussed up like a pig and I'm ready to gut you. You took out my brothers, now it's time I take out you and yours." He spun his knife in his hand and his smile got even bigger. "Once I take you out, gonna wait for the rest. Sure they're ridin' in like the cavalry. Loyal as fuck, but stupid, too. Think you can best me, but, asshole, I'm one of the last ones standin'. There's a reason for that."

As Taz stood there, Hunter concentrated hard to keep the darkness at bay. He studied the piece of shit before him, wondering how in the hell Slade was so different from his brother before him.

Slade's life started just as shitty as Brandon Bussard's did. They had the same blood running through their veins.

Slade found the Marines, then boxing as an outlet, and eventually a good woman.

Taz was just...

Running footsteps coming from the back of the barn snapped both of their heads up.

Hunter breathed in relief when what Taz called the "cavalry" arrived but was surprised at their approach.

Until he saw who it was and what she carried.

Holy fuck!

At Frankie's blood-curdling scream, Taz spun to face her, his arms coming up in a defensive position, but he was too late. She already had her feet planted and put her whole body behind the swing of the wood bat. The strength of that impact splintered it when it made contact with Taz's head.

Frankie cried out in pain and dropped the shattered remains. A spray of warm liquid had splattered all over Hunter. He knew what it was immediately because Frankie wore it, too.

Taz was also losing it at a rapid rate as his body folded like an accordion and crashed to the floor, one side of his skull crushed in, leaking brain matter and blood. An eyeball hung from its crushed socket.

Holy fuck.

Frankie's chest was heaving, and she was gripping her hands together while wincing. Yeah, that impact had to hurt and not just Taz.

"Frankie," he barked, but she was staring at the crumpled remains of the father of her child.

The man she just took out with one fucking good swing.

"Frankie!" he yelled again. He needed her to listen, get her out of her own head and turn her attention to him.

She slowly lifted her sightless eyes to his.

"Get me the fuck out of these bindings."

She stared at him like he wasn't there, like he didn't exist. Then he could see it plain as day when she mentally shook herself free.

She reached for the knife Taz dropped.

"No!" he shouted. "Don't touch anything. Grab my knife on my right calf." When she didn't move fast enough, he yelled, "Now, Frankie!"

Her body jerked forward, then her face changed, and she rushed over to him, pushing up his pant leg and freeing his knife.

"Cut me free."

"I might cut you."

"Doesn't matter. Just cut me free."

He didn't care if he had to bleed, he just needed his freedom. And he needed it now.

He held himself still as she sawed at the bindings, only nicking him a few times.

He took a full breath of air as the last plastic tie fell free and he surged to his feet, grabbing her face in his hands.

Her beautiful face was splattered with that bastard's blood and she had put it there.

"I want you outside now. Go to Leo. He's in your car. Take my knife and carefully remove his gag and any bindings that remain. You keep your shit together, Frankie. Don't let him see you shatter. You got me?"

She nodded, her face already starting to morph.

He held her face firmly to keep her from looking at Taz. "Frankie, keep your shit together. For Leo. You can break down later when he's not watching. Not now. Your son needs you. He needs you in one solid piece, not in a million shards. Are you getting what I'm saying?"

She nodded.

"Say it."

"I get it." Her voice held a shake, but he had to trust she'd keep it together.

He shoved her face into his chest and her arms automatically circled his waist. He held her there with a hand to the back of her head, shuffling her around and toward the nearest barn door. One away from the carnage she created.

While he was proud of her for doing what needed to be done, he was disappointed she put herself in danger and was afraid she'd be scarred for life from her actions.

Things could've ended up differently.

She could've been dead.

Leo could've been dead.

And if that happened, Hunter might as well be dead because in that moment, in that sliver of time, he realized he couldn't live without either one of them.

His roots weren't grounded in the earth; they were grounded in Frankie. They were grounded in Leo.

He was rooted to them.

The only thing he now feared worse than being trapped, was losing the two best things that had come into his life. The two people who meant the most to him.

He could have lost them both today.

He needed to deal with the immediate problem, then he'd deal with that.

When he had her just outside the door, he stopped. "Soon as Steel gets here, he can drive you and Leo home. Get yourself cleaned up, get him settled as best you can. Keep your mom close. I'll be there when I can."

"I have my mom's car."

"We'll get it back to her. Got plenty of manpower on the way. You worry about you and Leo. I'll worry about the rest."

She went to step away, but she stopped and turned back to him. "Hunter..."

"Yeah, baby?" he asked softly.

"Thought I was going to lose you both tonight."

Same here.

He heard the hiccup and knew she was about to lose it. "Hunter..."

"Yeah," he breathed, struggling to keep his own shit in one piece.

"I love you."

Fuck, that didn't help. "I know, baby. Wait for Steel. Take care of your son," he said softly. "He needs you."

I need you. And I love you, too.

She stared at him through the dark for a second longer, then turned and walked away.

Hunter closed the barn door behind him and pulled out his phone. He dialed Mercy's cell, which was answered with a grunt.

"Clean up in aisle five."

"Made a mess?"

Hunter took a breath and stared at the splintered bat in a dark pool of blood. "Not me," Hunter muttered.

After an extended pause... "Who?"

"Frankie decided to try out for the big leagues."

"Fuck," Mercy grunted.

Hunter gripped the back of his neck and twisted. "Yeah."

"She hit a home run?"

"Out of the fucking park."

"Damn," the man mumbled. "We're not far out. Should be at your twenty in about five."

"Put Steel with Frankie and Leo. Leo knows him. Steel needs to get them home and squared away until I get there."

"Maybe you should take them. Leave Steel with us to clean up the mess."

"I need to stay because I'm thinking we should bring the cops in on this one."

"Why?" Mercy barked into the phone.

"They know Taz had Leo and put out an Amber Alert. They're out searching. Gonna be hard to explain that we just found him unharmed and Taz happen to slip away. Frankie did what she had to do to save me and her son. She'll get some hard questions, the DA will do a little digging, but in the end, that shit will roll right off her."

"Not sure that's smart. Media will get involved. Her name will be plastered all over the news as the woman who clubbed her baby's daddy to death."

That was fucking true. But Hunter was trying to figure out how to shield Frankie from dealing with the aftermath. She would get questioned by the cops either way. They would do an investigation since a felon kidnapped a child, even if it was his own son.

Mercy continued, "Let me think on it. We'll be there

265

shortly. We'll come up with a solid plan that keeps everyone out of cuffs. But the less attention on any of us, the better. And that includes your woman."

Your woman.

"And if you say she ain't your woman, I'm gonna club you with that fucking bat when I get there."

Hunter pinned his lips together. "Won't say it then."

"Good. Need to talk to Slade."

"And Diesel."

"Fuck," Mercy grunted. "We'll call D after we figure out what our plan is. No point in getting the boss man in an uproar."

"I'll call Slade."

Silence greeted him.

"I'll call him," Hunter repeated. It was the least he could do.

"Yeah," Mercy finally said. "Think we're here. Christ, if Walker hadn't pinged your fucking cell phone, it would've been near impossible to find this place. Sometimes he's worth keeping around."

Before Hunter could answer, the phone went dead.

He heard the powerful roar of Mercy's SUV on steroids. As well as another vehicle.

The fucking cavalry had arrived.

Chapter Twenty

HUNTER STEPPED OUTSIDE of Frankie's house and went to stand in the middle of the yard where no one would overhear him.

He wasn't sure if Slade's acceptance of what happened would come easy. The man knew his father was a monster, his brother was one, too. But still...

Blood was blood, even if it was toxic.

Slade had questioned himself in the past, worrying if he would end up like his father, Buzz, having the man's tainted blood running through his veins. He'd worried about it touching Diamond. He worried about it touching his son, Hudson, and any future sons. Hunter understood that worry too well.

But blood wasn't always family. Family wasn't always blood.

Slade's true brothers wore leather cuts, rode hogs and had Dirty Angels MC colors inked into their skin.

Hunter's true brothers wore dog tags, had each other's six, and worked hard shoulder to shoulder.

Even so...

"Brother," Hunter mumbled into the phone when Slade answered.

His "yeah" was quiet.

"It's done."

A long silence hung between them. Then the biker asked, "Kid okay?"

"Yeah."

"Mother okay?"

"Yep."

"That's all that matters." Slade's answer was flat, emotionless. Final. "He go quietly?"

Hunter told the truth. "Didn't know what hit him."

"Shame."

More silence.

Hunter broke it. "Sorry your family was full of fuck-ups."

"Which family isn't?"

Very true. But Slade's leaned toward the extreme.

"I got lucky," Slade said.

"Yeah."

"Good woman. Healthy son. And family that might not be blood, but just as good, if not better."

"Yeah, you're lucky you have that."

"Gonna be better when you bring my nephew home."

Hunter's head snapped up. "What?"

"Want him here. Needs to be raised right. Wanna see to it. Already talked to Diamond, she's on board."

This was news to Hunter. "He's got a mother. Grand-mother, too."

"Two women. Needs a man in his life, preferably more than one. Don't need them livin' with us, just close. Manning Grove ain't close enough."

Hunter agreed with that last part.

"Bring 'em home," Slade said more firmly. "Heard she's got financial issues. She won't have that here. She needs a place, we'll set her up in the compound. Want Hudson growin' up with my nephew. She needs a job, we'll get her one. Leo an' Frankie will be taken care of."

"Not sure she'll want to be taken care of, Slade. You haven't met her."

"Not her choice."

Oh fuck. "You know how stubborn your ol' lady is? That's about how stubborn Frankie is. You start barking orders, she's gonna dig in her heels and balk."

"Need Leo here. That means Frankie needs to be here, too. Do whatcha gotta do to convince her."

He had already been planning that, but not for the reason Slade wanted. "I'll do my best."

"Know it. Appreciate it. If she won't leave without the grandmother, then convince the grandmother, too."

Hunter stared at his boots and pressed the heel of his hand to his forehead. He wasn't sure he could convince Diane to move her daughter and grandson into a biker's compound.

Especially after dealing with a biker like Taz.

People had strong opinions about bikers and they usually weren't good ones if they didn't know any personally.

"Jesus, you're asking for miracles."

"Christmas ain't that far away."

Before Hunter could answer, his cell phone went dark.

Hunter tapped it against his thigh for a moment with his eyes squeezed shut.

He agreed Frankie and Leo needed to come to Shadow Valley. He also agreed Leo needed a male figure in the boy's life, and Slade would be a good one, biker or not.

But after tonight, after the possibility of losing them kicked him in the nuts, Hunter realized the male figure needed to be him.

Frankie loved him, so that was half the fight. The other

was getting her to leave her hometown and give up everything she knew.

That one wouldn't be so easy.

It might be easier if he admitted what he discovered tonight.

But Hunter wasn't sure if he was ready to say those words out loud.

He felt it. He knew it. But admitting it and taking steps to do something about it was a whole other story.

———

FRANKIE SWEPT the hair off Leo's forehead, leaned over and pressed her lips to his temple.

He had finally calmed down enough to sleep. He would sleep deeply because he was exhausted.

Leo wasn't the only one.

Steel and her mom had watched Leo while Frankie stood in the searing hot shower, watching the pink water circle down the drain.

She scrubbed herself raw to make sure every drop of Taz's blood was off her skin. And once it was, she got out and ran a bath for Leo.

Children were amazingly resilient. But even so, what happened to Leo might stick with him forever.

She could only hope it would eventually fade away.

As she pushed to her feet and stepped back from his bed, a large hand landed on her shoulder.

"He okay?"

"I don't know," she answered truthfully.

"Gonna talk to Mercy's woman. She's a therapist. She may have suggestions."

Frankie nodded. She couldn't afford to pay for a therapist for her own fucking kid who just went through a shitload of trauma.

Her throat tightened and she blinked back the sting.

She was a failure of a mother. She needed to do better. So, she'd take any free advice she could get and swallow her pride for her son.

"I hope he never remembers who that man was. If I have to lie, I will. He's young enough I hope he never remembers this."

"No guarantee," Hunter answered, his voice soft as he peered over Frankie's shoulder at a sleeping Leo.

She knew Hunter couldn't be in that room for any length of time, so she was surprised when he stepped around her to sit on the edge of Leo's bed. His weight dipped the mattress, shifting Leo enough to wake him.

Leo's sleepy brown eyes landed on Hunter. "Daddy?"

Was he asking about his father? Had Taz told Leo to call him Daddy? Or was he calling Hunter Daddy?

Frankie opened her mouth to correct him, but Hunter did it first. "Danny."

Leo blinked sleepily. "Daddy."

Hunter leaned over and scooped him up, pulling him into his lap. "No, little man, you know my name is Danny."

"No!" Leo shouted, suddenly very awake, his face getting flushed. "It's Daddy!"

Frankie closed her eyes, her heart cracking and breaking in two. She didn't think she had any emotions left after tonight. She was as wrung out as a sponge.

She couldn't tell her son Hunter was his father when he wasn't. Nor that his father was the one who had kidnapped him. Leo wouldn't understand it.

Hunter held Leo against his chest, rocking him back and forth. Leo had one hand curled tightly in Hunter's beard, his other gripping the metal chain that hung around the man's neck.

"Leo, you know my name is Danny. You're just tired," Hunter said, his face carefully blank.

"You're my daddy," Leo insisted.

Frankie pressed her fingertips to her mouth. Did Leo even realize what he was saying? He went through a major ordeal tonight, he could just be mixed up.

Hunter lifted his gaze to Frankie. While his face was unreadable, his eyes weren't. Her heart squeezed at what she saw in them.

But she could be wrong.

So many things happened tonight, and she was just as exhausted as Leo.

She stepped closer to the bed, close enough that her leg brushed Hunter's. Just that touch, that feeling of him being so solid, settled her nerves. "Baby, you need some sleep."

"Don't want 'im to go."

"Not going anywhere, little man," Hunter said, curling his fingers around the back of Frankie's knee, keeping her close, connected. "Will be here when you wake up."

"Promise?"

"Promise."

"Want waffles."

Hunter's lips twitched. "We'll make you a Belgian waffle with lots of syrup."

Leo's little brow furrowed. "Not Momma. You."

Hunter settled him back under the covers and said, "Me. I'll make us waffles. Promise. But morning won't come unless you go back to sleep."

Hunter pulled the covers up to Leo's neck and brushed the back of his knuckle down his cheek.

"'Kay."

Hunter hesitated one more minute, staring down at her son. Then he rose to his feet, snagged her hand and pulled her out of the tiny room and into the hallway.

He didn't stop there. He kept going until they were in her bedroom and the door was latched behind them.

When he released her, his back hit the closed door and

he slid down it until he landed hard on his ass, his knees bent, his hands covering his face, his head back against the door.

"Are you okay?" Was he having another panic attack?

What the hell was going on?

"Hunter!" She dropped to her knees between his feet and grabbed his wrists. "What's wrong?"

He dropped his hands. "Grateful to that motherfucker."

Frankie blinked. His words thick with emotion teared at her heart. But they made no sense.

"So fucking grateful. If I wasn't looking for him, I never would've found you. If I wasn't looking for him, I never would've found Leo. If I wasn't looking for him, never would have found my roots, Frankie."

What was he talking about, his roots? "In Manning Grove?"

He shook his head. "In you."

She sat on her heels and before she could say anything, she was flat on her back on her bedroom floor. His weight pressed her into the carpet, his hands were planted on either side of her head and he stared into her eyes.

A lump rose in her throat. She could feel those raw emotions coming off him in waves, like she could reach out and touch them. And as those waves washed over her she absorbed them, felt them, too.

This wasn't a panic attack by being in Leo's room, by Leo calling him Daddy. He wasn't feeling trapped.

This was something else.

Something deep, intense, unexpected.

"Never thought I'd want to be a father. Never thought I'd find a woman I'd want to build a family with. Or, hell, a woman I'd want to have stick. Still don't know if I'm a good enough man to raise a son. I didn't have a good father figure in my life, either."

"Leo was just confused. He didn't mean to call you Daddy."

"Baby, I liked it. I liked hearing him call me that. Just as much as I liked hearing you tell me you love me. Hearing that from both of you, it broke those chains inside of me. There will never be a day where I don't have panic attacks, where I forget being trapped and fear it might happen again. But having you and Leo in my life won't be the cause of it."

Her pulse began to pound in her temples. "What are you saying?"

"I want you and Leo in my life. I want you two to be a part of it. I could have lost both of you tonight and I won't risk that again. I swear I won't ever walk away again, Frankie. Work might take me away, but I'll always come home. And when I do, I want you to be there waiting. I want to help raise Leo, be there when he needs me. Be the man he needs in his life. Be his father."

"You hate this house."

"Yeah. You're with me. Gonna pack your shit up and you and Leo are coming back with me. Sell the house, quit your job. Your mom wants to be close, I'm okay with that, we can get that figured out. Slade wants his nephew nearby, wants Leo to grow up with his cousin. Family's important, Frankie, you know that. Here you got your mom. With me, you got a whole fucking network of people for support and to help out when needed. Family. Maybe not all blood, but family just the same."

"Are you asking me to move in with you? Because that doesn't sound like it."

"What's it sound like?"

"Well, first of all, it sounds like you're laying it all out and not leaving me a choice. Second of all, you mention home, but do you want to live together? I love you, Hunter, and it's clear Leo is attached to you."

"You were afraid of that."

"I was. We both fell for you hard. But how do you feel," she pressed her palm into his chest, "about us? You haven't said. Again, you're just making demands and expecting me to follow them like I'm that kind of woman."

"Know you're not, Frankie. I know what kind of woman you are. And I wouldn't have you any other way. But decisions need to be made and I can't wait around while you make them. So, I'm making them."

'Bout fuckin' time you listened.

"Baby, how do you feel about me?"

"I love you, but right now you're making me rethink that. And you made it clear many times that I should think before I act. However, you're pressuring me to act before I get a chance to give your demands some serious thought."

"You love me?"

"I just said I did."

"How much do you love me?"

"Enough I can resist kicking you in the balls right now for being so damn bossy."

His lips twitched and he dropped his forehead to hers.

"I'm so glad you think this is amusing. This whole night has been fucked up. I'm mentally and physically exhausted, Hunter. And now you're hitting me with this. And this is on top of whatever we're going to deal with tomorrow when it comes to Taz kidnapping Leo and those after effects."

"That shit won't stick to you. I'll make sure of it."

"By lying to the police and taking the blame." She didn't like any of the plan him and his crew had come up with. Lying to the police, pushing Taz's death on Hunter instead of her. More sacrifices he was making for her and Leo.

"It's self-defense, Frankie. He would've killed me and might have killed you and Leo. Cops will interview me tomorrow and pass that info on to the DA. If I gotta deal with it, I'll deal with it. Kiki will represent me if needed."

"Who's Kiki?"

"Club attorney."

"The MC has their own attorney?"

"Yeah. Like I said, it's a network, baby. But it's going to come to nothing in the end. They're not gonna arrest me for taking out a felon who kidnapped, gagged and tied up his three-year-old son. We made sure any evidence left behind was clean of your fingerprints. A couple annoying hiccups that will pass."

Hiccups.

Manipulating evidence and lying to law enforcement was more than a couple hiccups.

"You have to trust me, Frankie."

Frankie released a breath. "I do."

"Then we're good. Got a few days of dealing with the cops ahead of us, while I'm doing that, you pack the shit you want to keep. The rest is getting thrown in a dumpster. Moving you and Leo into my condo until we find something better. Slade's gonna want you and Leo living close in the compound. I won't argue with that. It's gated, secure and safe. Leo will be around a bunch of little kids because bikers like to fuck. Obviously, with fucking comes babies."

Obviously.

"I never want you to worry again. Not how you're gonna pay the utility bill, pay for Leo's clothes, pay for daycare. You wanna work, you work. You don't, I'm okay with that. You raise our boy, you grow a garden, you make me fat with your cooking. Whatever you want."

Frankie rolled her lips inward. "I don't want you fat."

Hunter smiled. "Then I'll bust my ass to make you happy."

It hit her then he'd said, "*You raise our boy.*"

"Are you sure about this? You said—"

"I know what I said. And it was true."

"What changed?"

"Tonight, I realized something…"

She waited.

He tangled his fingers into her hair, pressed a kiss against her lips but didn't take it deeper, instead he put his mouth to her ear and whispered, "I love you, too."

Her heart squeezed and then exploded in her chest.

"I thought my head was fucked before. But if something would've happened to you tonight, I never would've recovered. Leo is your everything, Frankie, but you're mine. You raised a boy I'd be proud to call my son. And you're a woman who I'd be proud to call my wife."

"Hunter, this is huge."

"Yeah."

"Not for me, but for you."

"Yeah."

"I'm going to ask again, are you sure about all this?"

"Never more sure of anything in my life."

"I don't know what to say…" she whispered.

"You can say yes, baby."

"Yes, baby."

Epilogue

IF IT WASN'T for Slade asking Diesel to find his brother, Hunter never would have met Frankie or Leo. He owed the man a beer. No, a case of beer. Hell, a whole fucking beer truck.

Hunter turned his head to watch Leo running around in circles being chased by a slower, stubby-legged Hudson in Slade and Diamond's front yard. Leo tripped, face-planted into the grass and none of the adults even blinked. A second later, Hudson tackled him, and the two boys rolled around on the ground screaming, laughing and wrestling.

Leo was tough and showed no lasting effects from the day he was kidnapped. Though, they were aware that issues could pop up later. Naturally, they'd keep a close eye on him and get Rissa involved, if necessary.

Slade was in his driveway, one eye on the boys, one on what he was doing, which was waxing his Jag Jamison custom Harley. He lifted his chin to Hunter, who returned it.

Hearing "How long are we going to stand here?" made him tip that chin down to look at the woman whose shoulder he had his arm draped around.

"As long as it takes to imagine what it's gonna look like when it's done."

Frankie released a long dramatic sigh since this wasn't the first time Hunter dragged her out to stare at the construction and they'd had this conversation before. But she just needed to deal with it.

"We know what it's going to look like, we designed it and have seen the plans."

He tugged at her long dark hair, then wrapped a lock of it in his fist. He loved pulling her hair, especially when he was making her come. "Let your man have his fantasy, will you?"

Frankie snorted and lifted her face to his, her grin wide. "You want a fantasy, I can whisper one in your ear, which would be better than picturing a house."

"First of all, it's not gonna be just any house, it's gonna be our home. And, secondly, I don't need that sort of fantasy, I have you."

"While that's sweet, it's bullshit. All men have fantasies," she told him.

That was true. But all of his involved Frankie. Admittedly, some were pretty fucking obscene. However, when he shared some of them, Frankie was always willing to try them.

He loved that his woman was sexually adventurous and sometimes came up with crazy ideas of her own. His *loquilla*.

"On the subject of fantasies, once we move in, one of the house rules is you don't mow the lawn in a bikini top, hear me?"

She raised one of her eyebrows. "It's humid in the summer."

He raised one of his. "We'll hire a lawn boy."

"If he's at least twenty-six and really hot, I'm okay with that."

"How about if he's thirty-seven and really hot and he

knows how to fuck you until your toes curl and you leave a massive wet spot on the sheets?"

She planted a hand on his chest and, even though he now had a firm grip on her hair, she turned into him. "Remind me to buy some more towels."

"They better be really thick."

"Are you complaining?"

"Fuck no. The wetter you get, the better, baby. That means I'm doing my job right. I just don't like sleeping in the wet spot."

"And that's why we need more towels, because somehow *you* never sleep in the wet spot, I do."

He grinned. "Are we fighting?"

"No."

"Damn. I like the rough, angry sex we have when you get pissed off."

She rolled her eyes and turned her head back to look at the concrete foundation where their future home was being built, two lots down from Slade and Diamond's house.

Slade was getting what he wanted.

Hunter was getting what he wanted.

Leo was getting a father, an aunt, an uncle and a cousin. Along with a whole bunch of other kids to play with.

Most importantly, Frankie was getting Hunter's dick every night when he was in town.

Life was perfect.

For the most part.

He had something else he'd been thinking about and needed to address with her.

With her being in a good mood, and no baseball bat in sight, now might be the perfect time to discuss it.

He had mentioned it a few months ago in Manning Grove. But with all the shit that had gone on since then with the investigation, moving Frankie and Leo, getting them settled in his condo, getting her introduced to the DAMC sisterhood, finding her a job within one of their businesses, then moving Diane down a month later, they hadn't discussed it again.

He expected her to bug him about it since it was usually more important to a woman than a man. However, she hadn't said a word, which made him believe she didn't think he'd been serious about it.

He was.

He never thought he would be. The thought of being tied to one woman for the rest of his life should put him in a tailspin. It didn't.

While he wasn't in a rush to put a ring on her finger, he also didn't want to wait too long. He was creeping up on thirty-eight and wouldn't mind giving Leo a sibling before he was forty.

That was if Frankie agreed. If she didn't want any more kids, he was fine with that, too. He planned on adopting Leo legally, so if Leo was all they had, he was good with it.

But if Frankie wanted him to plant his son or daughter in her belly, if she wanted to nurture their child inside of her and give him that gift of life, he'd accept it and cherish that decision.

But knocking Frankie up wasn't the discussion he wanted to have. They could have that one night while they were naked and she was at her most agreeable.

"What are you gonna do about your name?"

"You mean because I no longer have to avoid using my real name? I like Frankie, it's grown on me. And it's short for my middle name Frances anyway, so there's that."

Hunter fought the roll of his eyes. They'd been over this before. "Frankie, it's no shorter than—" She jammed a finger against his lips. He pulled his head away, grabbing her hand and planting it once again on his chest, this time directly over his dog tags.

He never wanted to hear the nickname Sussy again after

Taz used it, and there was no way he was calling her Sucely, so he was fine with her continuing to use Frankie. It fit her. "I meant your last name."

"What do you think we should do?"

His brows knitted together. "We?" Apparently, they weren't on the same page.

"Yes, Leo and I. If I change my name back then he also needs to."

"Well, there's nothing wrong with either Reyes or Hernandez, if that's what you want. I know which one I'd prefer, though."

"Which?"

"Delgado." When she didn't say anything and simply stared at him, her dark brown eyes becoming soft and warm, not typical Frankie, he continued, "You could always hyphenate. Sucely Frankie-short-for-Frances Reyes-Hernandez-Delgado."

"Jesus," she muttered.

Hunter shrugged. "Okay. Sucely Frankie-short-for-Frances Reyes-Hernandez-Delgado-*Jesús*. But that seems a bit too long, just saying."

Her lips twitched, but just barely. "Adding the *Jesús* is the tipping point?"

"Yeah. Easier just to pick Sucely Frances Delgado and Leonardo Francis Delgado. No one needs more than three names."

"Uh-huh. Just like Danny Just-Call-Me-Hunter Delgado, Jr."

"Forgot my middle name."

"Which is?"

Hunter grinned. "Diego."

Frankie covered her mouth and a muffled "noooooo" escaped. "Danny Diego Delgado, Jr.?"

He nodded, trying to keep his expression serious.

"That's what we're naming our second son." *Shit*, so much for waiting for the naked pillow talk.

"We are not naming him Diego!" She face-planted hard into his chest. Like mother, like son, apparently.

He wrapped his fingers around the back of her head. "It's a good, strong name."

"And you can keep it. We're having a girl anyway."

"It's my sperm that decides and I'm going to start coaching my balls to only shoot the male chromosome."

"Not sure your balls are going to listen."

"I'm sure they'll listen better than you do."

She lifted her head and set narrowed eyes on his face. "Are you trying to pick a fight?"

"I'm just trying to prove you don't listen."

"You're just trying to piss me off, so we go home and have rough, angry sex."

He grinned. "I was wrong. You do listen."

"There are other ways to have rough sex without being angry."

"Okay, now *I'm* listening."

Frankie smirked, her eyes sliding to the kids rough-housing in Slade's yard. "Think Slade could babysit for a bit?"

"If we return the favor later. I think they've been trying for number two, but number one keeps cock-blocking them."

"That sounds familiar."

"Which is why I think he won't have a problem with keeping Leo for a couple hours."

"You won't need a couple hours."

Smart ass. "I didn't say you were getting fucked for a couple hours. You're getting it for five minutes. The rest of the time I'm taking an uninterrupted nap."

Frankie slapped his chest. "Whatever." She sighed. "Though, that does sound good."

"Stick with me, baby. I've got good ideas... Like this one..." He grabbed her hand, dropped to his knee in the dirt and stared up at the woman he wanted to spend the rest of his life with. Even though he didn't have a ring, since he knew better than to pick one out without her approval first, he asked, "Sucely Frankie-short-for-Frances Reyes-Hernandez will you marry me?"

She tilted her head and pursed her lips. "Can I think about it?"

"Do you need to?"

"Well, how many times have you told me to think before I act?"

Hunter dropped his head and grumbled, "Fuck me."

She *hmm'd*. "I've thought about it and I'll say yes to both."

He lifted his head, his brows raised. "Both?"

She waved the hand he wasn't gripping around in the air. "Yes to the first thing you asked, whatever that was," she teased, "and also the second thing. But my only request is, can we do the second one first? A wedding takes a lot of planning. And I think all those biker chicks will want to help with that. The fucking only takes me and you. Well, and Leo's uncle babysitting."

Hunter shot to his feet. "I'll go talk to Slade."

"Make it quick."

He barked out a laugh.

"The talking, not the fucking," she added.

Before he released her hand and walked away, she gave it a sharp tug, pulling him into her. "Hunter," she whispered.

"Yeah?" he whispered back, her dark brown eyes could trap him forever. And he was fine with that.

"As your future wife, is it okay to call you Danny now?"

"Hell, I was hoping you'd start calling me Master."

Once again, she face-planted into his chest, her body shaking against his. And he loved it when she did it.

"Remind me to hijack a beer truck and park it in Slade's driveway as thanks."

"For babysitting Leo?"

"No, for putting me in your path."

"It wasn't for a great reason," she reminded him.

"The reason doesn't matter, the result does."

She blinked quickly a few times before urging, "Hurry up and go talk to Slade. I need to tell you how much I love you while we're naked."

He pulled the Range Rover keys out of his pocket and shoved them at her. "Go start the Rover, and start driving, I'll jump in while it's moving. We're wasting time." He took off at a run over the unfinished yard, hoping he didn't do a face-plant of his own.

"Tell him if he takes Leo for three hours, we'll keep Hudson overnight," he heard yelled from behind him.

"Deal!" Slade shouted from his driveway.

Hunter gave the man a thumbs up, changed directions and ran back to the Rover where Frankie was still climbing into the driver's side. He smacked her ass hard, grabbed her waist and put her back on the ground. "Passenger side," he ordered.

"Yes, Master," she teased.

Fuck, he loved her. And he didn't give a fuck what she called him. Danny, Hunter, Delgado, Master, or any other nickname she could come up with.

No matter what, he would always answer whenever and whatever she called him.

As long as in the end, she called him her husband, and Leo called him Daddy, he was good with it.

His shallow roots were now growing deep.

He was good with that, too.

**Turn the page to read a sneak peek of In the Shadows Security, book 4:
Guts & Glory: Walker**

Sign up for Jeanne's newsletter to keep up with book news and upcoming releases:

**https://www.jeannestjames.com/
newslettersignup**

Sneak peak of Guts & Glory: Walker

Chapter One

WALKER STOOD outside the door and heard it.

He hated that apartment complex because the walls were so fucking thin. Anybody and everybody could hear what was going on behind them.

Which made it clear.

The woman he was banging was banging someone else.

He dropped his fist, deciding there was no reason to knock and instead turned, leaned back against the wall next to the door, cocked his leg and planted his boot on that wall. Then he crossed his arms over his chest and settled in to wait.

The Harley parked out front of Building C wasn't his, but that was his normal parking spot. Whoever was riding that bike was also riding the woman inside the apartment.

He wondered how long he'd have to wait.

Not too long, luckily.

Sami's familiar cries began to crescendo, a good indication she was about to come.

Or about to fake it.

She'd been known to do that, too. In fact, the second was more likely.

Sami was easy and convenient for when he needed to bust a nut. And it wasn't like they were exclusive or serious. They weren't. Or even that they cared about each other. They didn't.

Hell, they barely liked each other.

He'd come over, occasionally she'd feed his ass, they'd bang one out and when he was in the shitter getting rid of the condom, she'd steal a twenty from his wallet. Sometimes more.

Whatever.

Having his wallet lightened by a twenty was still fucking cheaper than having a wife or a girlfriend. They could financially break a man. He'd witnessed it and it was something he wanted to avoid.

What he couldn't avoid was hearing Sami's last high-pitched scream, which meant she was definitely faking it.

Walker twisted his wrist enough to see his watch and time the inevitable. He watched each minute tick by. He'd give it ten since that's how long it normally took him to bust and roll.

Ten...

Low voices were heard, though he couldn't make out words.

Nine...

The pipes in the walls squealed with the flush of the toilet.

Eight...

More low voices. One female. One male.

Seven...

A fake giggle. Typical Sami.

Six...

Walker rolled his eyes when he heard nothing, which meant Sami's guest was probably giving her a parting kiss and ready to split.

Five...

Footsteps heading his direction. *Yep.*

Four...

The pace getting quicker. Whoever it was wanted out of there.

Three...

More voices. The man throwing a last quick thanks over his shoulder and Sami inviting him to a "next time."

Walker snorted and shook his head.

Two...

The deadbolt being thrown. The door flying open.

One...

Game time.

"First time?"

The blond-haired man froze in the doorway, his eyes widening as he spotted Walker perched against the wall. The way the man was dressed and because his bike was still stock meant he wasn't a true biker, just a wannabe. Some weekend rider who wore a helmet and worked a nine-to-five. Got a bike to snag pussy. But he was a sucker and an easy mark for Sami.

"Check your wallet," he advised the wannabe, jerking up his chin.

As the man stared at him, his mouth opened and closed a couple of times, then he dug for his wallet in his... *yeah...* khakis.

"Fuck," Wannabe grumbled as he peered into his empty wallet. Walker doubted it was empty before the man walked through Sami's door. "She lifted a fifty."

Walker's lips curled at the corners. "Yep. Was she worth it?"

Wannabe's brow dropped low. "No. Maybe ten."

"Then I'd go back in there and get your change."

Wannabe glanced back over his shoulder. "Really?"

"Yeah," Walker said with a single nod. "Or go back in and get your money's worth."

Wannabe's eyebrows knitted together. "Are you her pimp?"

"Nope. Just passing through."

Sami appeared behind Wannabe in the open doorway. She finished tying the belt around her robe, then smoothed her hair down with her hand. She had sex hair and unless the sex sucked, it normally wasn't tamable with just combing her fingers through it. No, he liked to leave a woman's hair in knots.

Sami was able to straighten her hair with a few passes of her fingers, so the sex must have sucked.

Like he suspected, all that caterwauling had been fake. A way to get it over and done with quickly so she could slide into his wallet and out before the bathroom door was even shut.

"What are you doing here, Walker? I wasn't expecting you."

"Apparently," he murmured, letting his gaze roam over her from top to toe. He pushed off the wall. "You owe him some change. Or a real orgasm."

"What are you talking about?" Sami didn't bother to hide her outrage, as she pulled her robe belt tighter around her too narrow of a waist.

Walker wondered why his attention ever landed on her. She wasn't even his type. But then, he wasn't looking to put a ring on it. She was good for taking off the edge when he was still amped up over a job. Like tonight.

Ah, that's right. She had walked up to him at the local VFW, grabbed his dick, squeezed and whispered in his ear, "Want to fuck me?"

He'd turned on his stool at the bar, since his attention had been pulled from the Steelers game he'd been watching, took one look at her, and with a shrug, said, "Why the fuck not."

They went back to her apartment that night and fucked like rabbits.

Then she became a habit.

Now he was kicking that habit cold turkey.

He stepped closer to Wannabe, slapped him hard on the chest, almost knocking the guy back a step, and murmured a "good luck" before giving Sami a look over Wannabe's shoulder. "It's been real, honey."

He turned on his boot heel and strode down the hall to Sami screaming, "Walker! Walker! This didn't mean anything!"

No shit.

He ignored her and at the end of the hall, loped down the steps to the front door of the building, slammed the exit push bar and headed out into the late summer night.

———

WALKER LEANED his weight into one palm which was planted against the shower wall. His head tipped forward, the water from the shower soaking his hair and sliding down his back and chest.

He went through his Rolodex of women he used for jack-off material in his mind. Problem was, he always kept going back to one. An old memory. One he'd never forget. Not because he didn't want to, but because he couldn't. No matter how many women he'd been with for the past nineteen years, none could knock her off the top of the list.

Not one.

His fist tightened around the root of his cock, squeezed

and he began to pump in earnest. Long steady strokes from root to tip.

The hot water continued to beat along his back, and he closed his eyes, his lips parting, inhaling the humid air from the shower, then releasing it.

He could've gone to the bar and found another woman to relieve his load since he wasn't in the mood for leftovers with Sami, but he didn't feel like making the effort of finding someone new.

The fake smiles, the fake laughs, the fake name and stories.

The questions. The made-up explanations.

Finding a woman to fuck for the night took work. He was tired, so his own hand would have to do.

He continued to stroke, closing his eyes, thinking back to soft thighs and soft sighs. A smile, a laugh. Green eyes sparkling. Auburn hair loose over the blanket he had spread out for them in the back of his truck.

Beautiful.

Nothing fake. All genuine.

What a lucky man he'd been.

His pace stuttered.

He hadn't been a man. He'd still been a boy.

Foolish.

But fucking in love.

Jesus fuck.

He needed to get out of the shower, find a porno with a little girl-on-girl action and just bang it out. This reliving history shit was fucking up his groove.

He shut the shower off with a curse and, balancing with one hand on the edge, leaned out of the stall to grab a towel. While he was wiping the water out of his eyes, he paused, tilted his head and listened.

His phone. Vibrating on the bathroom counter.

"Fuck," he muttered under his breath and wrapped the

towel around his waist. He hopped out of the shower and made his way to the counter.

The vibrating stopped.

He shifted closer to the sink and snagged it.

UNKNOWN CALLER.

It was almost ten p.m.

He saw he'd missed several calls, but no voicemails had been left.

The phone started vibrating in his hand. Once again, an unknown caller. Something he normally didn't answer.

But it was late. And he wouldn't put it past one of his fellow Shadows to call him from a burner phone.

He swiped the screen and barked, "Yeah," into the phone.

"Trace?"

That name brought a head jerk and a frown. He had no idea why someone would be looking for Trace. The hairs on the back of his neck prickled.

"Trace?" A female voice. Quiet, but thick with worry.

He had no fucking clue who it was. "Got the wrong number."

A pause. A shaky intake of breath.

His spine stiffened and every muscle locked.

"I'm looking for Trace."

No shit. "There's nobody here by that name."

"Please, Trace, don't shut me out."

He glanced up from where he'd been staring at the water dripping onto the floor. He caught his reflection in the mirror. Walker stared at the man staring back at him.

He hadn't seen Trace in a long fucking time.

He also had no idea why someone would be looking for him.

There was no reason. None what-so-fucking-ever.

"How'd you get this number?"

"Your sister."

His blood ran cold when it hit him. Who it was. Why she was asking for Trace.

Nineteen years instantly disappeared. The object of his masturbation fodder was talking into his ear.

"I'm sorry. You're probably not happy about me doing that. But I had no choice."

"We all have choices, Ellie. You made a choice years ago."

"You're right, I did. And I made another difficult choice by contacting your sister, begging her to give me your number. I made an even more difficult one by calling you. But I had no choice," she repeated more firmly. Whatever was in her voice was no longer trepidation, but determination and a touch of stubbornness.

"I'm assuming you're between a rock and a hard place right now and you need me to be the crowbar. But if it wasn't for whatever you're involved in, you wouldn't have ever reached out."

"With... With everything that happened.... I assumed you didn't want me to."

"I didn't. Still don't. I should hang the fuck up." He should, but he wouldn't. He couldn't wait to find out why Ellie Cooke was calling him.

No, that wasn't right. It was Ellie McMaster since she married one of the rich motherfucking McMasters. A man who could give her way more than Walker ever could.

"No! Please... don't hang up. Please." The determination was now gone, replaced with desperation.

He set his jaw. "Why the fuck are you calling me, Ellie?"

"I hear you do... jobs."

Jobs.

"Whatever the *job* is, Ellie, have your husband handle it."

"I... I don't have a husband."

Walker stilled. "You leave him, too?"

"In a way, he left me," she whispered.

"Hurt, did it?"

"I—"

"Bye, Ellie." He pulled the phone from his ear and swiped his finger across the screen, cutting off her plea.

Get Walker and Ellie's story here:
mybook.to/Shadows-Walker

If You Enjoyed This Book

Thank you for reading Guts & Glory: Hunter. If you enjoyed Hunter and Frankie's story, please consider leaving a review at your favorite retailer and/or Goodreads to let other readers know. Reviews are always appreciated and just a few words can help an independent author like me tremendously!

Want to read a sample of my work? Download a sampler book here: BookHip.com/MTQQKK

Also by Jeanne St. James

Find my complete reading order here:

https://www.jeannestjames.com/reading-order

* Available in Audiobook

Standalone Books:

Made Maleen: A Modern Twist on a Fairy Tale *

Damaged *

Rip Cord: The Complete Trilogy *

Everything About You (A Second Chance Gay Romance) *

Reigniting Chase (An M/M Standalone) *

Brothers in Blue Series:

Brothers in Blue: Max *

Brothers in Blue: Marc *

Brothers in Blue: Matt *

Teddy: A Brothers in Blue Novelette *

Brothers in Blue: A Bryson Family Christmas *

The Dare Ménage Series:

Double Dare *

Daring Proposal *

Dare to Be Three *

A Daring Desire *

Dare to Surrender *

A Daring Journey *

The Obsessed Novellas:

Forever Him *

Only Him *

Needing Him *

Loving Her *

Tempting Him *

Down & Dirty: Dirty Angels MC Series®:

Down & Dirty: Zak *

Down & Dirty: Jag *

Down & Dirty: Hawk *

Down & Dirty: Diesel *

Down & Dirty: Axel *

Down & Dirty: Slade *

Down & Dirty: Dawg *

Down & Dirty: Dex *

Down & Dirty: Linc *

Down & Dirty: Crow *

Crossing the Line (A DAMC/Blue Avengers MC Crossover) *

Magnum: A Dark Knights MC/Dirty Angels MC Crossover *

Crash: A Dirty Angels MC/Blood Fury MC Crossover *

In the Shadows Security Series:

Guts & Glory: Mercy *

Guts & Glory: Ryder *

Guts & Glory: Hunter *

Guts & Glory: Walker *

Guts & Glory: Steel *

Guts & Glory: Brick *

Blood & Bones: Blood Fury MC®:

Blood & Bones: Trip *

Blood & Bones: Sig *

Blood & Bones: Judge *

Blood & Bones: Deacon *

Blood & Bones: Cage *

Blood & Bones: Shade *

Blood & Bones: Rook *

Blood & Bones: Rev *

Blood & Bones: Ozzy

Blood & Bones: Dodge

Blood & Bones: Whip

Blood & Bones: Easy

Beyond the Badge: Blue Avengers MC™:

Beyond the Badge: Fletch

Beyond the Badge: Finn

Beyond the Badge: Decker

Beyond the Badge: Rez

Beyond the Badge: Crew

Beyond the Badge: Nox

COMING SOON!

Double D Ranch (An MMF Ménage Series)

Dirty Angels MC®: The Next Generation

WRITING AS J.J. MASTERS

The Royal Alpha Series:

(A gay mpreg shifter series)

The Selkie Prince's Fated Mate *

The Selkie Prince & His Omega Guard *

The Selkie Prince's Unexpected Omega *

The Selkie Prince's Forbidden Mate *

The Selkie Prince's Secret Baby *

About the Author

JEANNE ST. JAMES is a USA Today bestselling romance author who loves an alpha male (or two). She was only thirteen when she started writing and her first paid published piece was an erotic story in Playgirl magazine. Her first romance novel, Banged Up, was published in 2009. She is happily owned by farting French bulldogs. She writes M/F, M/M, and M/M/F ménages.

Want to read a sample of her work? Download a sampler book here: BookHip.com/MTQQKK

To keep up with her busy release schedule check her website at www.jeannestjames.com or sign up for her newsletter: http://www.jeannestjames.com/newslettersignup

www.jeannestjames.com
jeanne@jeannestjames.com

Newsletter: http://www.jeannestjames.com/newslettersignup
Jeanne's Down & Dirty Book Crew: https://www.facebook.com/groups/JeannesReviewCrew/
TikTok: https://www.tiktok.com/@jeannestjames

f facebook.com/JeanneStJamesAuthor

a amazon.com/author/jeannestjames

O instagram.com/JeanneStJames

BB bookbub.com/authors/jeanne-st-james

g goodreads.com/JeanneStJames

P pinterest.com/JeanneStJames

Get a FREE Romance Sampler Book

This book contains the first chapter of a variety of my books. This will give you a taste of the type of books I write and if you enjoy the first chapter, I hope you'll be interested in reading the rest of the book.

Each book I list in the sampler will include the description of the book, the genre, and the first chapter, along with links to find out more. I hope you find a book you will enjoy curling up with!

Get it here: BookHip.com/MTQQKK

Printed in Great Britain
by Amazon

17329334R00180